*Fallen Angels*

Dr. Bridget Maher is a doctor and medical writer/journalist and lives in County Cork, Ireland. She has written extensively for the medical and the lay press. She is editor of *Modern Medicine* (Ireland) and writes health articles for the VHI medical website. *Fallen Angels* is her first novel.

# Fallen Angels

*Bridget Maher*

**Blue Mango**

Fallen Angels

Published 2008 by Blue Mango

ISBN: 978-0-9558355-0-6

Printed in Ireland by Colourbooks.

First published (2007) in the U.S. by Lulu.

For Con, Helen, Joanne and David.

**Primum est nil nocere**

(The most important thing is not to cause harm)

From the Hippocratic Oath

# 1

Strong black coffee would be nice. So would a goat's cheese panini. And both, Charlie reckoned, should be here any moment now. A slow smile eased across his lips. God bless that student nurse from ICU with her earnest face and her country innocence.

He stretched and yawned; a long, measured, yawn. Charlie liked to yawn. It was a natural punctuation in the order of things, a way of slowing things down, his body reminding his brain to chill out.

Even as a child he yawned a lot. Edie said it was because he was lazy. Mother said he was anaemic. The poor woman had diligently laced his childhood with iron tonics, making his bowel motions dark and sinister. His first normal bowel motion had been at boarding school after Matron Hennessy had confiscated the big brown bottle of ferrous sulphate from his locker. He smiled at the memory. Thank you, Matron, wherever you are.

His eyes flicked to the screen in front of him. No shift in the NASDAQ; all quiet in good old U. S. of A. Time for shut down. Click. Click. The screen pinged black and the soft hum mumbled to an uneasy silence.

Instinctively, he looked around, checking the sudden stillness for God knows what. As usual, nothing; just him, alone, in the hospital library, all lights off apart from a solitary desk-lamp bathing his notes in a soft, opaque light. Grey shadows danced on the bookshelves and a myriad of lights blinked behind the desk, dancing in preparation for the following day.

He turned back to the desk. Right. Time to get stuck in. He'd been here for nearly two hours and apart from checking the NASDAQ, he'd been asleep for most of the time. Story of his life. He reached for an ECG tracing and held it up in front of him. Slow atrial fibrillation – this guy needed warfarin, maybe even pacing. Yep. That was the good thing about cardiology, it made sense. It gave answers. Like these cardiograph tracings, for example. No lies, no grey areas, no room for subjective interpretation. You're either in atrial fibrillation or you're not. And certainly no grey areas when it came to asystole; you were well and truly fucked when that thin black line appeared. Hearts, like he told Edie, were just like engines; they needed oil, they needed electrics. You saw the problem. Then you fixed it. Unlike psychiatry where you worked in the dark. And fixed nothing.

No, cardiology was the business all right. Cardiac failure, hypertension, raised cholesterol, atherosclerosis. All conditions with a sound mathematical explanation, solid diagnostic tools and effective, logical remedies. Just a few simple numbers. Keep blood pressure below 140/90, cholesterol less than five. Open up blocked coronary arteries. Replace leaky valves. Pig simple. Kind of like plumbing, really, only far better paid. Straightforward, logical, predictable. Everything mapped out, just as he liked it.

Suddenly he straightened. There it was again, that feeling, like a breeze on his face, like someone had opened a door. His eyes peeled the darkness. Nothing. No open windows, the door firmly closed. He often got that feeling; a strange sensation that he wasn't alone. Not that it freaked him or anything;

he didn't have any time for all that rubbish Edie was into - angels and stuff. Anyway, why should the library, of all places, have a ghost? It was probably the only place in the hospital where people didn't die. Libraries had good Karma, according to Edie. And he agreed with her; he liked this cosy little room, tucked low under the eaves of the roof; a warm cocoon of tranquillity in the madness of the crazy, crazy hospital that lay beneath.

His eyes travelled to the bookshelves, to the neat stacks of journals; the *BMJ, Lancet, JAMA, New England Journal of Medicine.* All in chronological order, of course, the most up-to-date edition out front. He'd always loved the touch and feel of a new journal; being the first to turn the cover, the crispness of the paper and the fresh inky smell of an unopened journal. He closed his eyes, gathering up the memories. Yep. He would miss this place; the smell of old volumes, the hushed tones, the occasional whirr of the fax, the changing seasons playing on the windows above.

He felt a familiar rawness grip his throat, the same strangling feeling that used to grip him on his way back to boarding school after the holidays or on sports days at school when he longed for a father to cheer him on. It wasn't just the library; he'd miss all the other stuff too; the crazy all-night parties, the on-call Chinese take-aways, the endless cups of coffee to keep you going, the running and racing, the feeling that you were living life on the edge, that you were right in there, right in the middle of it. Yep, he was going to miss St Anne's; he was going to miss Dublin. And, of course, he would miss Edie.

He reached into his pocket for the photograph, its edges curled with age. He looked at it for a moment and sighed. If only. Then he slipped it back into his pocket. Right. Snap out of it. Ashling (or was it Leslie?) would be here soon with his panini. Hope she remembered the pesto; the kid probably didn't even know what pesto was. He closed his eyes, sizzled dry from lack of sleep. At least he was off this weekend; two full days away from St

Anne's, just him and the remote. Maybe a little female company on Saturday night. No bleeps, no monitors, no mad dashes to cardiac arrests. Just him and the flatscreen. He'd probably spend Saturday morning in bed. Later, he'd watch some soccer, order a pizza, have a few beers. Then sleep some more. He could do with some proper sleep, real sleep, not broken hours punctuated by fitful dreams and other people's crises. The day's images flashed in front of him, unbidden. A nightmarish outpatients clinic that went on forever and not one, but two cardiac arrests. Just as well he was fit, the dash to ICU took three minutes at full sprint. He liked to be first on the scene. Get the best spot at the head of the bed, be the one to intubate. For all the good it did…

He opened his eyes and smiled; the footsteps in the corridor were getting closer. Great stuff. She was back, quicker than he had expected. Must make sure to get her name right.

'Good evening, Charlie.'

Instantly, Charlie snapped his feet off the desk. Clements! What was he doing here? Finding Clements in the hospital after dark was like finding Dracula sunbathing in Brittas.

'Stay where you are, Charlie boy!'

Charlie slipped back to sitting. He could smell the familiar sweet odour of spirits. Our man Clements liked his malt. Not that Charlie would ever dream of mentioning it. No sirree.

'Were you looking for me, John?'

From his first day in St Anne's, Clements had insisted that Charlie call him 'John' and not 'Dr Clements' like everyone else. Clements was big into the old school tie thing; he never missed a Clongowes match.

'I bumped into that intern with the red hair, he said I'd find you here.'

Charlie nodded. Clements always referred to interns by hair colour and body size rather than by name. Then Charlie noticed that Clements' shirt was

4

different to earlier; tonight's shirt had a thin red stripe matched by a plain ruby tie. With his sallow skin and shining shoes, Clements could be Italian; Sicilian perhaps, maybe even Calabrian …

'Nearly finished?'

Clements spoke in his usual way, filtering certain syllables through his nose and cocking his head sideways, like a gun dog on the scent of a rabbit. Initially, Charlie used to find his vocal mannerisms irritating; now he hardly noticed. Besides, it wasn't as if Clements' tone was an affectation or anything, it was just the way he was, the way he spoke. El Duce Siciliano. Pricko Italiano. Clements' brother in Johns Hopkins, the other Dr Clements, spoke exactly the same. So did Clements' children, God love them, who all sounded as if they needed their adenoids out.

'So, what are you doing?'

What was he doing? He could hardly say sleeping, Sudoko, and checking his shares, the three main reasons he came to the library. Thanks be to Jesus the computer was off.

'Just checking some Holters.'

Clements nodded.

'No hurry. They can wait until the ward round.'

Charlie could feel Clements' eyes pressing into him. If he wasn't one hundred per cent certain of Clements' unwavering heterosexuality, he might have felt a vague unease. He watched Clements pick up a pen. Click. Click. Clickety-click. Click-click. Jesus.

'Did you want me for something, John?'

The clicking stopped. Clements looked up.

'Bit of trouble, Charlie, I'm afraid.'

His voice was low, a man-to-man, between you and me, kind of tone. Charlie instantly straightened. What trouble? He had just come back from

ICU; the coast was clear, everything seemed fine. He reached for his bleep; maybe he had missed a call.

'Not here, Charlie, not St Anne's.'

Charlie swallowed. Shit. Not a cock-up at Johns Hopkins. Not six weeks before he was due to start there.

'Is it my rotation?' Might as well get straight to the point.

Clements' lips parted in a half-smile. He shook his head.

'No, Charlie, nothing to do with that.'

Charlie breathed a sigh of relief. That only left one thing; one of his boss's little flings come home to roost, perhaps. He watched Clements flick something off his jacket.

'Pills and potions world, Charlie, our good friend, big pharma.'

Charlie caught the glint of a white veneer. Everything about Clements was shiny: teeth, nails, shoes. Even his stethoscope seemed to sparkle, like as if he had just polished it.

'I've just had a phone call from WorldPharma.'

A short pause.

'Cardelia.'

Charlie frowned. Cardelia? Cardelia was their number one blood pressure drug. First choice for all newly diagnosed hypertensives. All patients with uncontrolled hypertension were started on Cardelia. 'The cardiologist's little helper' was what Clements called it. Next best thing to aspirin.

'What about Cardelia?'

'That goddam Swedish trial showed a problem.'

Charlie swallowed. The results of the multi-centre Swedish trial weren't due for another six months, maybe a year. The trial must have been stopped prematurely. This didn't sound good.

'What kind of problem?'

6

'Oh nothing too serious… just a few unexpected KTBs.'

Charlie stared. KTB. Kick the bucket. Clements had his own medical abbreviations, thought they were hilarious.

'A number of sudden deaths, I'm afraid.'

Clements' lips curled around the words. Charlie met his gaze.

'Statistically significant?'

'A thirty per cent increased risk of sudden death compared to placebo, statistically significant in anyone's language, I should say.'

A low chuckle, then Clements' smile faded.

'Cardelia's finished, Charlie.'

Charlie blinked. Christ. Half the bloody hospital was on Cardelia. The Swedish trial was supposed to prove that everyone, even patients with mild hypertension, would benefit from the drug. There hadn't been a whisper of a problem before now.

'Do they know what caused the sudden deaths?'

A slow nod.

'Arrhythmias, possibly SVTs.'

Charlie felt a sudden niggle deep in the pit of his stomach. SVT or supra-ventricular tachycardia, was a dangerously fast heart rhythm that sometimes progressed into ventricular fibrillation. Both patients who had arrested today had been on Cardelia. Had they developed an SVT? Did that SVT develop into a fatal ventricular fibrillation? Was that what had killed them? He jumped to his feet.

'Take it easy, Charlie, boy, it can wait until morning; another few tablets won't kill them.'

He could feel Clements' hand on his shoulder, pushing him back into his seat.

'Hopefully….'

Clements' laugh reverberated through the empty library, bouncing off the bookcases. Charlie made a quick calculation. They had at least fifty patients on Cardelia, more if you counted the surgical wards.

'Terrible news, really bloody awful.'

Charlie was silent. Why was Clements so pissed about this? OK, it was curtains for Cardelia but there were plenty of other blood pressure drugs that patients could be changed to. Apart from crossing Cardelia off and writing in another drug, there wasn't much else they could do, apart from contacting GPs and the pharmaceutical company would probably do that.

'We've got to help, Charlie.'

Charlie reached for his white coat.

'I'll check all the drug charts.'

'I mean WorldPharma, Charlie.'

Charlie blinked. WorldPharma? WorldPharma was the company that made Cardelia. It was also one of the biggest multi-national pharmaceutical companies in the world. Last year it merged with another big cardiology company and doubled its product portfolio. Its profits were steady and solid, its NASDAQ rating climbing. It was a big player, maybe the biggest.

'I'm kind of lost here, John. Cardelia's a goner, you said so yourself, they'll have to withdraw it.'

Clements' eyes were granite.

'WorldPharma's in deep shit, Charlie. GoldMed want to talk to us.'

Aah! Charlie felt a tiny trickle of comprehension. GoldMed was the PR company that handled WorldPharma products; press releases, product launches, marketing surveys and anything to do with the media. Recently they had branched out into medical education and were involved in setting up some high-profile advisory boards, including a new hypertension one that Charlie had been invited to join; an independent board, apart, of course, from the little matter of being funded by WorldPharma. According to Clements, advisory boards were part and parcel of medicine, money for jam.

'Throw a few ideas around, don't lash their product and everyone's happy.'

Not too happy tonight, though, thought Charlie.

'Marianne wants to meet us at eight tomorrow.'

Charlie nodded. He'd be happy to meet Marianne any time she wanted.

'Both of us?'

'Well, me, really, Charlie, no offence. But you're on the advisory board too so they'd like to brief you as well.'

Charlie raised an eyebrow. What was with this 'brief' business? Then, as if he could read Charlie's thoughts, Clements smiled.

'Why do they want to meet us? Damage limitation, Charlie, that's why. I'm the public face of Cardelia, our department is the biggest prescriber of Cardelia in the country, the media is going to be on my door first thing tomorrow, I need to know what to say.'

Charlie's mouth opened. Know what to say? Clements always knew what to say. He was as smooth as hot fudge sauce.

'But what is there to say? Cardelia's dangerous, it's being taken off the market.'

Clements threw back his head and laughed as if Charlie had just said something hilarious.

'Charlie, Charlie, Charlie! I'm going to have to knock a few more corners off you before I let you loose on my brother!'

He moved closer and his voice lowered.

'WorldPharma has been very good to this department.'

Charlie nodded. WorldPharma funded most of the cardio research at St Anne's. The company sponsored the last two cardiology conferences that

Charlie had attended; flights, hotel, everything. There was no doubt that WorldPharma was a very generous benefactor. And, of course, they were the ones sponsoring Charlie's cardiology scholarship to the States. Oops. Now he understood. Payback time already and he hadn't even left the country.

'Like I said, Charlie, the minute word gets out, I'll have medical reporters swarming me in the car park. The bloody HSE and the Minister will probably want a statement. I need to know exactly what to say and how to say it. There's no point in causing hysteria.'

Charlie raised an eyebrow. Giving sound bytes to reporters and statements to the Government was right up Clements' alley. He could do it in his sleep. So why all the fuss? Surely a big shot medical communications company could handle a simple product withdrawal press release?

'We need to do this the right way, Charlie.'

Charlie nodded. Was there a wrong way?

'Eight o'clock, so, Charlie. You won't forget?'

Charlie shook his head.

'I'll be there.'

So much for heading home early tomorrow. They'd be hours behind with the ward round which meant that the clinic would run late too. The domino effect was very apparent in hospitals.

'Oh, thanks for taking over today, Charlie, the bloody rooms were crazy. Cardioversion go OK?'

'Fine, back to sinus, I'll keep him on the monitor overnight.'

'Better than the other two anyway.'

Clements pointed up and smiled. Charlie swallowed. Did Clements mean upstairs Intensive Care or upstairs, upstairs?

'We tried our best.'

Clements' laugh was tinny.

'Sure you did, Charlie. These things happen. They were goners anyway; the old guy shouldn't even have been resuscitated. Should have been an LHD'.

Charlie turned his face into the darkness. LHD meant 'leave him die'. But that 'old guy' was somebody's father. Somebody's father on Cardelia.

He waited until Clements' footsteps faded, then swung his legs back on top of the desk. OK, here's the deal. Cardelia is being withdrawn. GoldMed wants Clements to handle the media. Clements wants him along for support, maybe throw in the odd comment. So what's the problem? State the facts, keep it short, end of story. So why did he have that niggle deep in his gut, the kind of niggle you got when you ate chocolate during Lent or you slept with your best friend's girl? Conscience? Surely not; conscience was a negative little voice that stopped you enjoying yourself. Edie always said that he had no conscience, never had and never would.

Suddenly, a gentle knock, the door opening. He looked up and smiled. Panini time. The young girl's jacket was dark with rain and moist strands of hair snaked across her forehead. She hurried towards him and held out a foil-wrapped package. Her hands were blue-red, like bruised raspberries.

'Thanks a mill.'

He reached for his white coat and saw her smile collapse. Shit.

'I have to go to ICU. I'll catch you next time, OK?'

At the mention of next time, her smile returned. Silly girl. She reminded him of Edie, so trusting, so open, so bloody vulnerable. When the door closed, he sat back down again and opened the foil. Good. Lettuce all squashy and wilted, molten cheese oozing around the edges and the top striped charcoal just the way he liked it. And she even remembered the pesto! Maybe he should have let her stay for a few minutes, asked for her mobile number. She was pretty in an old-fashioned kind of way and had small gold glasses like Edie's.

At the thought of Edie, he began to smile. No prizes for guessing what she'd have to say about this! She hated the pharmaceutical industry, said it was responsible for most of the world's problems; health and economic. There was no stopping her when she started on about antibiotics and superbugs and faulty clinical trials. God knows where she got her facts from; probably some left wing loony alternative group hell-bent on turning back the clock on every therapeutic advance. He shook his head. Poor Edie, she hadn't a clue, God bless her. Not a clue.

He crushed the foil into a compact little ball and aimed. Bingo. It glided into the bin with a satisfying little thud. Who'd believe it, Cardelia, of all drugs! The wonder drug of cardiology! And not a hint of any problem before now, no changes in the QTc interval, no effect on electrolytes, nothing.

This was news, big news, maybe as big as that HRT Women's Health Study that linked HRT with stroke and heart disease. It would cause panic in the medical community. This very minute, the Irish Medicines Board was probably sending out email alerts. Every GP in the country prescribed Cardelia, which wasn't very surprising since all the cardiologists used the drug, especially numero uno himself, John Clements, El Duce. He shrugged and picked up his bleep. Not his problem.

He reached into his pocket for Edie's bar of organic chocolate. Seventy per cent cocoa solids, according to the recycled wrapper. And shag all sugar, probably. Still, it was better than nothing. He popped two squares into his mouth and reached for the journal in front of him; *Doctor Now*, last week's copy. The header read *'Ask the experts - managing hypertension'*. His article. Star billing. But, in the light of tonight's revelations, all bullshit. It had been

Clements' idea that he write some articles for the medical mags. 'It'll get you out there, Charlie boy, get your name known.'

Yeah. Right. The treatment of choice for hypertension? Cardelia of course! What was that song again? What a difference a day makes… You bet. But WorldPharma was a big boy. And from the looks of things, they were up and kicking already.

He snapped off another two squares of chocolate. Not bad for organic. Soon he could feel the direct hit of neat cocoa. The endorphins were doing their job. As the sugar surge washed over him (so there was sugar in organic chocolate after all), he began to feel better. Hey, drugs were withdrawn every day of the week. It wasn't his problem that some company got their cocktail wrong. He grabbed his stethoscope. Time to shift his butt and find a red biro. As they say in the Westerns, hasta la vista, Cardelia.

# 2

Edie plopped her keys on top of the hallstand and dropped her bag on the floor. A book slipped out and skimmed across the polished parquet. *Write this Way 4.* She watched it hit the coir mat and come to a sudden stop, its dash for freedom halted as abruptly as it had begun. Poor book. She knew exactly how it felt.

'Is that you, Edie?'

Edie closed her eyes. No, it's Jack the fuckin' ripper, Mother. I mean, who the hell else, apart from Charlie, let themselves in with a key? At three-thirty in the afternoon? And, in the highly unlikely event of an armed robber/rapist/escaped convict standing in the hall, surely Lucy would have barked? Wouldn't you, Lucy? She bent down and stroked the Labrador at her feet.

'Good Lucy.' Good, silent, undemanding, all-forgiving Lucy.

'Edie?'

This time, a note of irritation, a slight raising of pitch. Best say something.

'Yes, Mother! It's me, I'm home.'

Same words, most days, every day, all part of the unwavering constancy that was her life. Even her periods were regular. Like clockwork. Not a day late. Not even one blasted day.

Her eyes turned to the hallstand, to the nut-brown sheen of the burnished mahogany. She could smell sandalwood. Must be Thursday, polishing day. Monday was laundry, Tuesday ironing, Wednesday floors, and Friday, well Friday was usually a bit of everything, especially if Charlie was coming home. The smell of furniture polish, undeniably and irreversibly, also meant bacon and cabbage for dinner. Mother rarely varied from the weekly menu plan. For as long as she could remember, Edie associated certain domestic smells with particular foods. Domestos meant beef stew. The sweet fragrance of fabric conditioner was inexorably linked with roast chicken. And sandalwood, tragically, meant bacon. Yuck!

She slipped off her jacket and placed it on the second hook from the top, just below her mother's coat, the one assigned to her since she had been tall enough to reach it. Her reflection stared back at her from the yellow mottled mirror. She looked like Charlie after a weekend on call. Her skin was dusky lemon after a long winter indoors and her hair needed a good cut; it was too long, too tangled, like Mrs Sampson's knitting bag at school. Mother, as usual, had been nagging her this morning to tie it back. And, as usual, she hadn't. There are worse things than wild hair as Mother should well know; like a wild tongue and wild eyes. She closed her eyes for a moment, then took a deep breath. Best go in.

A blanket of warm air wrapped around her the moment she opened the kitchen door, as if the room was hugging her. This was always her favourite room; maybe it was the bright yellow walls or the old pine table with its heavy indents of life's graffiti. Or maybe it was because the kitchen was the only room in the Lodge that wasn't like an icebox. She glanced around. The lids of the Aga were up, pots simmering quietly, obediently, never daring to boil over or splutter. Things were under control in this kitchen. Over the Aga, stacked neatly on the airing rack, were two piles of shirts, freshly ironed and airing. All Charlie's, of course.

Her mother was sitting at the table, a large green kitchen scissors in her hand. Brightly coloured cards splattered across the table. Edie moved closer to investigate. Christmas cards! Somehow it seemed rather strange, almost sacrilegious, to see images of the Baby Jesus scattered among the robins, laughing Santas and snow-covered mountains.

'Any news?'

Her mother's reading glasses sat perched at the end of her nose and her ash-blonde hair was tucked behind her ears. Their eyes met above the glasses.

'What are you doing with those cards?'

'Shame to waste all those nice pictures, they'll be very handy for school, the children could trace them for their own cards next year. You can have some too, I'll get -'

'- I don't want any.'

The scissors stopped mid-air. Wrong answer.

'And what, might I ask, are you going to use for inspiration when you do Christmas cards in school next year?'

Edie blinked. It's only paper. Take the damn cards.

'I'll take some, so.'

The scissors swung back into action. Eddie could see its glint, silver and swift, big jawed and powerful, a super-scissors. She wondered where Mother kept it. It looked too big for the cutlery drawer.

'Well?'

The scissors swooped and dived. Edie looked up.

'Well what?'

Blue eyes, her own eyes, met hers.

'Like I said, any news?'

'No.'

No news for Mother, never any news for Mother. Never had, never would have. Even if the school had been burned to the ground. Then she smiled her secret inside smile. She had news, good news, but not for Mother's ears. She could hear her mother take a deep breath.

'Surely, Edie,' pause for a medium length sigh, 'surely to God something happened in school today to relate to your inquisitive mother? Is your school so different from mine? No cranky parents? No bad language in the yard? No ball kicked over the wall?'

Edie shook her head. Maybe she should make something up. What would you like to hear, Mother? How does an attempted abduction sound? Or what about 'the Principal and the special needs assistant were caught shagging in the office'. Or maybe not.

'How was your day, Mother?'

Edie slipped to sitting. This could take a while. She listened quietly, zooming in and out as her concentration allowed. Key words, Edie, get the key words. Just in case she checks to see if you've been listening.

'So I told her that she couldn't blame ADHD for everything, that maybe she should look at her parenting skills.'

A short silence. Edie knew it was her cue to agree but she remained silent.

'What do you think, Edie?'

'You were right, Mother, absolutely right.'

This was usually a fairly safe reply. Her mother smiled a hint of a smile and looked at the clock.

'Dinner will be ready at five, Edie.'

Edie nodded. It was Mother's way of saying she was free to go. She stood up. Dinner had been at five on weekdays for as long as she could remember,

17

always signalled by Mother ringing an old school bell, even if Edie was right next door in the sitting-room. Mother said five o'clock was a good time for dinner; it gave your digestion plenty of time to work before you went to bed. And everyone knows that your digestive system needs all the help it can get.

'If you're hungry, there are some probiotic yoghurts in the fridge.'

Edie nodded. Mother had an obsession with 'inner cleanliness' (poor Charlie used to have terrible constipation). In the past, it was Epsom salts, prunes and liquid paraffin, now it was probiotics, linseed and functional foods. Supplements were her other thing. Charlie joked that Mother should change her name to Primrose on account of all the evening primrose oil she bought. She was the diva of multi-vitamins; zinc, selenium, omega three fatty acids, you name it. But at least it was one thing they agreed on. Only last week she'd bought Mother some new herbal thing that was supposed to be good for the menopause. Not that Mother would ever admit to being anywhere near the menopause, which in Edie's reckoning, must make Mother the oldest pre-menopausal woman in the country.

Charlie, of course, had no time for this gobbledygook as he called it. But that was hardly surprising, was it? It probably pissed him off that they were buying stuff in a health store rather than a pharmacy. After all, doctors and pharmacists were all part of the same cosy cartel. Fraudsters, the lot of them. OK, Charlie probably meant well, but he was a doctor, and all doctors see are drugs. And well did she know. They pumped her with enough of them.

'Any word from Charlie?'

Edie looked away. Charlie had mentioned that he might not be home that weekend. But best say nothing yet. Charlie often changed his mind.

'I'll text him.'

A short silence, a slowing of the scissors.

'Five weeks, imagine.'

18

Her mother's voice was barely audible, as if she was talking to herself. Edie watched her eyes stray to the calendar on the wall beside the dresser; the days marked off with a black felt pen, dark and sombre like a death knell. They often referred to the 15$^{th}$ of March in a matter of fact, 'we'll take one of our course days' kind of way but neither ever discussed it further than that. Neither of them wanted to acknowledge what was happening on the third week in March. Edie felt a sudden flash of anger. For a fleeting second, she felt like grabbing the scissors and pinning her mother to the wall. She could just imagine the feel of the scissors between her fingers. It was all Mother's fault. She was the one who wanted Charlie to go to the States. The same way she made them do everything. It was fine for her, of course. All she ever wanted was to be stuck here in this big draughty house making marmalade and chutneys and cutting out pictures from stupid Christmas cards.

But what about her? What was she going to do without Charlie? All week she looked forward to him coming home on Friday night; the way Lucy would bark like crazy and the paint in the kitchen would brighten the minute he walked in the door, swinging his bag full of dirty laundry on top of the washing machine and grabbing each of them in turn and swirling them around until they begged him to stop. Oh, Charlie.

The scissors clattered on the floor and Edie jumped. She watched her mother bend to pick it up. There was something slow and laboured about her mother's movements that Edie hadn't noticed before. She swallowed; Mother was getting old.

'Oh Edie, I forgot to tell you, there's a letter for you on the dresser, an American postmark.'

Edie's heart skipped a beat.

'It's probably the Pilates brochure I sent away for.'

19

Damn. Why had she said that? Maybe Mother would want to see it. Quickly, she grabbed the letter and stuffed it in her pocket.

'I'll change my clothes.'

'I'll call you when it's ready. It's bacon and cabbage.'

'I know.'

I know. I know. I fuckin' well know.


Edie closed the bedroom door and sat down on the edge of the bed. For a moment she hugged the envelope against her chest. Then, slowly, carefully, she opened it. Her eyes skimmed down the page. Yes! They had received her application and her booking was confirmed! The bank draft had arrived safely - she was going to the States! A stray strand of chestnut hair fell across her brow, fissuring her line of vision. She pushed it away and noticed the fine tremor that wired her fingers. Calm down, Edie.

She looked at the envelope again and felt a twist of happiness; in two weeks' time, she would be in San Francisco, riding on a tram, perhaps, or sipping café latte someplace famous like Fisherman's Wharf. Suddenly, she felt a familiar flash of panic. Maybe no-one drank café latte on the West Coast anymore, maybe it was only in *Frazier* that people said 'latte - to go.' She must remember to watch what people ordered before she ordered anything. That way, she'd get it right. Not make an eejit of herself.

She read the letter again. The course was very intensive; workshops, morning lectures, lots of group work. Personalised sessions cost ten thousand euro and had to be pre-booked and paid for on the day of arrival. Another ten grand! She'd already paid twenty thousand euro. It was a lot of money; all her money, in fact; every single euro. She'd had to get a bank draft, as thanks to Mother, her credit card limit wasn't high enough. But it would be worth every cent. This course was going to change her life. Besides, like they said, it would come back to her hundreds of times over.

She ticked 'Yes' to the personal session box and reached into the locker for an envelope. Then, very carefully, she began to write the address. She checked the numbers of the postal code a second time. You had to be careful with postal codes, especially when you weren't used to them. Her writing was the nearest to block capitals her spidery scrawl would allow. Oops. She'd almost forgotten to write 'USA'. Presumably the postman would know that California was in America but you never knew these days. Only last week on the radio someone didn't know where Fermoy was.

She licked the envelope, slowly, carefully, savouring the nutty flavour of the glue. Then she reached for the little booklet of stamps that she had taken from the dresser, after Mother had gone to bed. Mother kept a miscellany of supplies in the drawers of the dresser; mass cards, batteries, parking tickets for Dublin, Cork and Limerick, and, of course, stamps. How many stamps? Three euro? Four? Better to be safe than sorry.

A soft smile crossed her lips. Mother would go ape-shit if she knew. No way would she have allowed her pay that amount of money for anything, especially after what happened before. But Mother didn't know, and she wasn't going to tell her, not now, anyway. As Mother herself always said, there are some things best left unsaid.

# 3

Charlie picked up a tray and looked around. The canteen was empty apart from two med students holding hands in the corner. Suckers. Charlie made a mental note to sit well away from them. The only people here this time of night were the perpetually hungry. Like himself. The room was in darkness apart from the small serving area at the top. It reminded him of a bar serving out of hours drink. Pity he'd had that ciabatta earlier on, but of course he didn't know then that he'd still be here at this hour. He picked up a plate. Might as well have something to eat, a scone perhaps, or maybe a Twix.

He began to hum along to the Abba song playing in the background. It had been a good night's work; he had crossed out Cardelia from all the drug charts on the medical side. It hadn't taken that long, really; first he'd sent a nurse around to collect all the charts, then he'd gone through them one by one, crossing out Cardelia and replacing it with another anti-hypertensive. The difficult bit was checking the patient's medical history to decide on the most appropriate replacement drug. You didn't, for example, want to start someone with gout on a thiazide diuretic or someone in renal failure on an ACE inhibitor. By the time he returned the charts, most of the patients were asleep. Asleep was good. It meant that patients didn't start telling you about their bowel motions or their dirty phlegm. Maybe he should suggest doing ward rounds at night.

Suddenly a smiley face popped up behind the counter.

'How's it goin', Charlie? The dinners will be ready in about ten minutes.'

'Think I'll pass on dinner tonight, Mary, maybe something small.'

He reached for a scone.

'Take two, pet, on the house; we'll be dumping them later anyway. Want me to heat them up?'

Charlie smiled. What was it about older women that they always felt the need to feed him? Edie said it was his scrawny, half-starved look.

'Thanks, Mary. You're a star, sent down from heaven to take care of me.'

A girlish giggle.

'Milky coffee as usual, luv?'

'On the ball, Mary. Thanks.'

He reached for a Twix. Might as well.

He stopped at a table facing the door, well away from the lovebirds, and put his tray down. A bunch of student nurses burst in, all loud voices and laughter. As they came closer, one of them said something and they began to giggle. Charlie looked away. There was a disturbing familiarity about the blonde one. Shit. Then his mobile started to ring. He glanced at the number and smiled. Good timing, hon. Edie often phoned him around now, before she went to bed. He could just imagine her; perched lotus-style on her purple yoga mat in front of the fire, watching *Scrubs* or *Green Wing*.

'Yoah! How's it goin', kid?'

'Hiya, Charlie, before I forget, Mother said to tell you that cousin Alice is in the Mater.'

Charlie closed his eyes. The Mater was the other side of town, not even on the Luas.

'Suppose she wants me to visit her?'

'No, she's only a second cousin, and she wouldn't know you anyway. She's gone a bit dotty. Mother said to let you know in case she dies and you'd say you never even knew she was sick.'

Charlie smiled. Good old Mother, she never lost it. There was logic in there, somewhere. One of these days he was sure he'd find it. He reached for his scone.

'You still at work?'

Edie sounded as if she was eating something. Something crunchy and sticky. Probably one of those disgusting muesli bars herself and Mother seemed to like.

'Yep, still here, one of our blood pressure drugs was withdrawn so I needed to change all the treatment charts.'

He smiled, waiting for what he knew was coming. She'd get good mileage out of this.

'Typical! Legalised poisoning, that's what those multi-nationals and trans-nationals do! And doctors are just as bad, allowing themselves to be bribed into prescribing every drug that hits the market.'

A short pause while she took another bite. Something crunchy. Maybe Ryvita with sesame seeds. Charlie smiled. Edie sounded exactly like Mother. Not that he'd dare to ever mention the fact, of course.

'Why shouldn't drug companies make profits, Edie? It's a business like any other business. The pharmaceutical industry spends a fortune on research and development. Your yoga isn't free, is it? And you and Mother leave a small fortune in the health store every week. And what about your Reiki and

Indian head massage, not to mention that hot stone thing, how much does that cost you every month?'

'C'mon, Charlie, that's totally different! You hardly think my Reiki therapist is going to spend an hour releasing my toxins for nothing! She's got to eat too.'

Charlie smiled. Good, she had walked straight into that one. A short pause. When she spoke again, her voice was soft.

'Have you eaten, Charlie?'

Charlie smiled. Edie had a habit of changing the subject when she knew she was beaten.

'There's a scone in my hand this very minute. And I had a very nice goat's cheese panini earlier on.'

'Bet you sweet-talked some poor student nurse into going out in the rain to get it for you.'

Charlie smiled. Edie was just like Mother. Genetic telepathy.

'She was getting one for herself anyway.'

'Yeah, sure!'

He could hear Edie's bubbly laugh. He loved that laugh; he could listen to it all night.

'Do they still heat the scones for you?'

'Yep.'

Another laugh.

'Lick-arse.'

'Cry-baby.'

'Small wonder I was always crying; I was the one who always got the blame, even the time you were caught smoking. It was my fault for getting you the matches. You were such a bloody lick-arse.'

Suppose if it meant doing and saying the right things, then he was a lick-arse.

'Your mistake, Edie, was owning up, even before she knew you'd done something wrong.'

Edie laughed.

'I knew I'd get the blame anyway.

Charlie reached for the milk. Edie was right. Mother was tougher on Edie, always had been. It was as if she wanted to prove that it didn't matter, the fact that he wasn't flesh and blood. She wanted to treat both children the same. Except, of course, that she hadn't.

'How is she?'

'Fine. Cutting up Christmas cards.'

'What?'

'Don't ask. She did some gardening yesterday. Bulbs and stuff.'

'She should mind her back.'

Mother tore into everything full steam ahead, rooting and digging for hours at the first hint of spring. There was a short silence.

'She wanted to know if you were coming home this weekend.'

Charlie bit his lip. He'd been planning to stay in Dublin.

'It's only five weeks tomorrow.'

Her voice was crackly, like a bad connection. Poor Edie. It hadn't been easy for her. And it certainly couldn't be a bed of roses being stuck at home with Mother all week.

'I'll be down Saturday night.'

'Brilliant!'

He could hear the smile in her voice.

'I've something to tell you, Charlie.'

Instantly, he straightened. He didn't like surprises, especially where Edie was concerned.

'Is something wrong, Edie, are you OK?'

'I'm fine! It's good news, I'll tell you on Saturday.'

'Give me a hint.'

By Saturday she could have eloped with some Polish guy she'd met in Lidl or ran off to join Greenpeace.

'I'll tell you Saturday. What time will you be down?'

'Seven'ish, depends on the traffic.'

'Great. We'll have dinner ready.'

And ready it would be. Mother would spend all day chopping and peeling, making roux, experimenting with complicated desserts that never seemed to work out. There would be a roast, of course. Maybe striploin of beef or lamb. Mother fussing over gravy.

'Edie, c'mon, hon, tell me.'

'No. I'll tell you on Saturday.'

He sighed. There was no point. Edie could be as stubborn as a mule.

'See you, Saturday, so, kid. Tape *Scrubs* for me, OK?'


For a moment he held the phone in his hand, fingers pressing into plastic, probing, searching, as if somehow it could tell him what he wanted to know, the bits Edie had neglected to tell him. What was her news? A new boyfriend? Hardly, unless it was her yoga teacher or one of the parents at school. Jesus. Now that would be some mess. He put down the phone and sighed. Stop worrying, for God's sake! Edie sounded fine, she sounded perfectly normal. Yet… he couldn't help it. There was always that worry in the back of his mind that it would happen again; that one day she'd wake up, eyes wild and staring, words tumbling and jumbling out her mouth. And this time, he wouldn't be there.

Suddenly he heard someone call his name and looked up. Tommy, rolling towards him like the King of Tonga. Charlie smiled.

'On the doss again, Tommy?'

'I beg your pardon!'

27

Tommy placed his hands on his hips.

'I'll have you know, young man, that as head porter I have responsibility for thirty-five porters. If it wasn't for me, this hospital would ground to a halt. Who gets things moving around here, boy! The porters, that's who!'

'When they're not on strike.'

Tommy folded his arms across his chest.

'The only reason they're not on strike, is that I keeps 'em happy!'

Charlie laughed. Tommy Hill, or Tommy Porter as he was more often called, due partly to his job and partly because of his fondness for Guinness, knew everything that needed to be known about St Anne's.

'Remember your first day here, Charlie?'

He pulled out a chair.

Charlie nodded. It seemed just like yesterday. There he was, just started third med, first day on the wards, all eager and keen, ready to start saving the world. He was standing beside a bed, proud as punch, taking a history from a patient, hands deep in the pockets of his new white coat. Suddenly, this small man wearing a blue hospital coat appeared beside him, his face creased in disapproval. Charlie could still remember his words: 'A bit of advice, son. First, take your hands out of your pockets when you're talking to a patient. Secondly, don't call elderly folks by their first name, they don't like it. And when the Prof. asks you the name of that pot plant on the window there, it's a geranium, OK?'

The man, who barely came up to Charlie's shoulder, had a palpable air of authority about him. Charlie had immediately taken his hands out of his pockets and apologised.

'That's OK, son. Hey, is that a Tipp accent I hear?'

'I'm from Clonmel.'

Charlie could still remember the big smile that followed. It seemed to light up the man's face, to go on forever.

'Us Tipp men must stick together.'

And that was the beginning of it. First it was pints after work, then poker games and trips to the races and now a joint share portfolio.

'So, Charlie, what's the crack with Cardelia?'

Charlie had already told Tommy about the drug being withdrawn.

'Cardiac arrhythmias. Best drug we had. Just goes to show.'

'Hmm. Bastards. Think it might have caused some of our arrests?'

Charlie shrugged. The same thought had crossed his mind.

'Maybe. You been at any resuscitation lately?'

Tommy's CPR skills were legendary. He often helped at cardiac arrests especially when interns were slow getting out of bed and had been known to squeeze bags of blood into patients after road traffic accidents. He was as good as any intern. Kept his eyes and ears open.

'Can't get there fast enough anymore, can't run as quick as them young interns.'

Charlie smiled. Tommy barely did walking, let alone running.

'What about theatre, any action there?'

Tommy shook his head. 'Nope, this keyhole surgery has it all shagged up. I'll have to learn all over again.'

Tommy knew the name of almost every surgical instrument. Some of the older surgeons used to even let Tommy scrub up and assist; mainly minor ops like appendectomies, hernias and varicose veins.

'You'd have been a good surgeon, Tommy.'

A quick smile.

'If I hadn't left school at thirteen. But thanks for the vote of confidence, lad. Us Tipp men must stick together. Speaking of Tipp, how's your mother and Edie?'

'I was just talking to Edie.'

Tommy looked up.

'Is something wrong?'

Charlie sighed.

'She's got something to tell me, I wish I knew what it was.'

Tommy shook his head.

'Poor girl. You'd think those clowns in Trinity would have spotted her earlier.'

Charlie shrugged.

'None of us spotted it.'

There was a short silence.

'Look, Charlie, I've said it before and I'm saying it again. I'll keep an eye on Edie when you're away. I'll be down in Tipp to see the nephews anyway.'

Charlie nodded and touched Tommy's arm.

'Thanks, Tommy.'

He knew he could rely on Tommy. The man might be twice his age and spend half his wages on horses, yet, Tommy Porter was probably the only friend he could really trust. He was the kind of friend you could sit beside for ages without saying anything, the kind of friend you could cry in front of, that is, of course, if you were able to cry. A familiar tightness grabbed his throat; Tommy couldn't fix everything; he couldn't take away the emptiness, he couldn't take away the pain. Nobody, anywhere, could fix that.

# 4

Grey. Everything so damned grey, thought Charlie, watching the February morning unfold. Grey buildings, grey sky, grey faces. No wonder people got seasonal affective disorder; winter just seemed to go on and on. Baltimore would be cold too, of course, but there would be more light, more open sky, not this suffocating blanket of greyness.

He pushed through the revolving door. At least it was nice and warm in here, despite the bareness of the foyer. The GoldMed office was one of those modern minimalist buildings where glass meets chrome meets pale wood. He glanced around. No shortage of money, no sirree. Then he noticed a figure on the steps outside. Clements. Eight o'clock on the button, not a second late, always bang on time. Charlie watched him through the smoked glass windows. The man moved quickly and lightly, almost furtively, feet barely tipping the ground, skipping up the steps, gliding through the door, silent and sure like an owl sweeping home.

'Morning, John.'

Today's suit was a wide navy pinstripe that would look pimpish on anyone else but looked great on Clements. Mind you, anything would look good on Clements; he had the perfect posture of a former show-jumper.

'Morning, Charlie, awful traffic.' Charlie nodded.

'I took the Luas.'

'Great stuff. Should have done the same. The Merc is a bitch when it's busy.'

Charlie nodded. He supposed it was.


The girl at the desk looked up and smiled. Charlie smiled back. Another GoldMed stunner, probably a part-time model. Wonder where they got them.

'Good morning, Dr Clements, Dr Darmody! Please sit down, Marianne will be with you in a moment. Coffee? Tea? Iced water?'

Charlie raised an eyebrow. Iced water? It was the middle of winter, for feck's sake. Clements flashed a smile.

'Coffee, black, no sugar, please. What about you, Charlie?'

'Milk, two sugar, please.'

Somehow 'two sugar' didn't have the same ring about it as 'no sugar', in the same way whiskey and soda wasn't the same as 'whiskey, and leave the bottle' or 'Martini and ice, shaken, not stirred.' Maybe it was time he gave up sugar. Sugar was probably a bad word in America. Like nicotine. And carbohydrates. Hey, maybe doctors didn't even drink coffee anymore in the States. Maybe it was all those disgusting herbal drinks.

'Thank you very much, Simone.'

Clements' words had the desired effect. Simone beamed and sprung from her seat. Charlie smiled. It was one of Clements' special qualities, the way he remembered names. Well, everyone's names except interns, that is. Clements also had the knack of noticing things; little things that passed everyone else by, like being the first to spot the ring on Dr Dennehy's finger when she got engaged or the new blinds in the canteen. Yep, you could certainly learn a thing or two from John Clements. He was the main man, no doubt about it.

Suddenly, there was a gust of perfume and colour. Marianne. Charlie watched Clements bend to kiss her, one, two, three. Should he do the same? What if he started on the wrong side? Ah hell, he could always go for the lips… No, it's OK, looked like he wasn't going to get to kiss Queen Marianne after all, not today, anyway.

She was holding out her hand, stretching her fingers towards him. Long, cool fingers that lingered. He was conscious of his own hands, hot and moist, wet with the coffee that had spilled when he had put his cup down too quickly. Her eyes locked his; dark, wonderful eyes; you could lose yourself in those eyes.

Boy, did she look good today; tight black top hinting at brown cleavage, fishnet stockings peeping above high leather boots, coltish legs folding and unfolding. She turned to speak to Clements and it was like somebody had turned off a light.

'So you made the exhibition after all, John. What did you think? Wasn't it wonderful?'

'Outstanding. Picked up two pieces, actually.'

Charlie could see an eyebrow arch.

'Did you really! Super!'

Suddenly she turned towards him.

'Are you interested in art, Charlie?'

Christ. Was he? He knew shag all about art. Crashed the odd opening as a student for the free wine. Never actually looked at any paintings, though. But no point in trying to fudge this.

'I don't know much about art, I'm afraid.'

She smiled and her hand touched his arm.

'You can't have time for everything.'

She moved her hand away and took a step backwards. He could feel a faint tingling where her fingers had rested.

'Shall we go? Joe Fleming and the team are in the boardroom.'

Charlie felt a twinge of sympathy. Wonder how poor old Joe was feeling this morning. Poor fucker. It wasn't a good day to be product manager of Cardelia, no indeed. He liked Joe Fleming; smiley, friendly kind of guy. Good golfer, apparently. At least he hadn't topped himself last night. Not that Charlie would have expected him to – those product managers were as tough as nails. Shoot their own granny if it boosted sales.


Charlie closed the door and looked around. Strange how alike all the WorldPharma guys were; dark suits, white shirts and that clean-shaven look of Mormons on circuit. *Medicus repus urbanicus*. Stepford husbands of the pharmaceutical industry. Even their haircuts were similar. The only odd one out was Colin, Marianne's sidekick, who was more into the gay creative look, with his gelled up hair and his brightly patterned shirts.

'Morning, Joe.'

For a moment, he felt the urge to shake the man's hand, like at a funeral, 'Sorry for your trouble' kind of thing. After all, this was a bereavement of sorts. Cardelia was dead. And Joe Fleming was the closest surviving relative.

'Sorry about Cardelia, Joe.'

'These things happen, Charlie. We'll survive.'

Charlie nodded.

'Sure.'

Charlie reached for the bottle of water in front of him. San Pellegrino. Class. Nice table, too. Pale, bleached wood. Beech or ash, perhaps. Same colour as Clements' kitchen. Totally different to Mother's pitted and marked pine. The chairs were beech too, Shaker style, with high straight backs. A

34

huge glass bowl sat in the middle of the table containing what looked like two river pebbles, one white, one black. Charlie smiled. Hmm. Definitely symbolic. Wonder what it meant.

Marianne lifted a hand and instantly the room fell silent. Charlie smiled. Marianne always had that kind of effect.

'OK, guys. First an update on what's happening in the States. It's now been confirmed that Cardelia or Carrdana as it's called over there, has been withdrawn as of today by the FDA. The news is splashed all across the FDA website.'

There was a low mumble from around the table.

'That probably gives us about three days before the Irish Medicines Board officially pulls Cardelia from the Irish market. Not a lot of time, but enough to pre-empt competitor activity and prepare our response.'

Charlie smiled. These PR people were all the same; all cool phrases and fancy terminology.

'You've been a busy lady.'

Clements' voice was velvet.

'Part of the course.'

A flash of white teeth. Large, round pupils. Probably on something. A lot of media types were.

'OK...'

Marianne's eyes fell on every listener in turn.

'Cardelia was the number one anti-hypertensive in Europe and the States over the last twelve months. As of today, it's gone. Nada. Rien.'

Charlie wondered if she was going to call for a minute's silence.

'What we have to do now is to quickly, and quietly, put Cardelia to bed and look to the future.'

Charlie looked at the screen and blinked. Was this some kind of joke? The image on the screen was of a rising sun with the word 'Diastora' written in red among the rays. He looked around. Nothing, not even a flicker of a smile on any of the faces. He glanced at Clements - still that same impenetrable, unwavering smile. As for Joe Fleming, it was kind of scary. The man was nodding vigorously, like a born-again Christian at a Bible session or one of those toy dogs people hang in their cars, the ones whose heads keep nodding up and down. He looked like he might break into clapping at any moment, or God forbid, start hugging people.

The rest of the WorldPharma team sat perfectly still, rigid and stiff in their corporate suits, precision haircuts and good, clear skin. What was it about pharmaceutical guys that they all had good skin? Was there a secret understanding that you didn't employ reps with acne?

Charlie looked back at the screen and winced as his knee banged off the table. Good, no more graphics; just bullet points. Now they were down to business.

'First, media link-ups. I've been on to *Morning Ireland,* we have four minutes at eight tomorrow.'

Marianne turned to Clements and raised an eyebrow. Funny, there didn't seem to be any wrinkles on her forehead. Botox, probably.

'Is tomorrow morning good for you, John?'

A quick nod. Clements liked media interviews; especially live radio at peak listening time. He was the master of snappy medical sound-bytes.

'Who's it with?'

'Áine Lawlor.'

'Perfect.'

'The main thing is to reassure the public and let them know that there's no cause for panic, no harm done, that the change of medication is just a safety precaution.'

Charlie smiled. Yes, indeed. No harm done. Marianne made it all sound so simple.

'OK, next, the withdrawal press release. There's a copy for everyone in the folder in front of you. The important thing, of course, is to highlight that WorldPharma has voluntarily withdrawn Cardelia in advance of any IMB recommendations.'

Charlie smiled. Nice one, Marianne. Jump before you're pushed. Always the caring face of the pharmaceutical industry.

'Next - the Communications Strategy for Diastora.'

Charlie smiled again. You had to hand it to them. This meeting wasn't as much about Cardelia fucking up as much as paving the way for Diastora, a new WorldPharma drug, which, if Charlie remembered correctly, had only received a product licence last week. Fortunate timing, amazingly fortunate timing! Well done, Marianne.

He skimmed down the screen. A dosage algorithm, a patient leaflet on preventing cardiac disease and a clinical supplement, lead article titled *'New choices in anti-hypertensive treatment'*. Marianne's eyes met his. Guess who'd be writing that one.

'We'll do the first draft of the articles. It will speed things up.'

Yep. Charlie could feel his left knee tapping rhythmically under the table, in time to Fleming's head nod. First draft my backside. First draft meant one thing and one thing only - writing the entire article. In the business, they called it ghostwriting. Initially he used to find it strange to see somebody else's name at the end of an article he'd written, but now it didn't bother him. After all, he got well paid for it. And it probably was a better article than the 'author' would have written anyway. And faster for all concerned. Besides, the authors always checked the final articles. Most times they made no changes at all. And the ghostwriters, often scientific writers with no medical qualifications apart from good research and writing skills, got their cheque. Everybody was happy.

'I know how busy you are, Charlie, but we were hoping that you might be able to pen the first drafts for us, especially since this is all so time sensitive. It would speed things up enormously.'

Fuck. Four articles to write. As if he wasn't busy enough already.

'Have the authors agreed?'

Marianne's eyes narrowed ever so slightly.

'We've had medical students write articles, Charlie, they're delighted with a cardiology senior reg.'

Charlie smiled. Nice one, Marianne.

'Most of these projects will come under the activities of the Hypertension Ireland Advisory Board.'

How convenient. Smooth movers, you had to hand it to them.

'The first meeting is next week. I'll email everyone with provisional days and times.'

A collective nod. If she had said the meeting was going to be on Mars, they'd probably have agreed.

Light flooded the room and Charlie blinked. He always felt a little disorientated after watching Marianne; it was like going out into the daylight after being at the movies. He glanced at his watch. Eight-thirty. Way to go, Marianne. That girl sure got things moving. Behind that smile, those fawn-like legs, those jangling bracelets, she was sure able to make things hum.

The girl could soft-talk the producers of *Morning Ireland* into giving her five minutes air even when their schedule was full. She seemed to be able to place articles where she wanted, when she wanted. She was on first name terms with everyone in the medical publishing world and a growing number of Government officials. As for the pharmaceutical industry, she was the Diva, their saviour, the putter righter when people misunderstood them and said nasty things about them. When the shit hits the fan, just leave it to Marianne.

He was almost at the door when he heard someone call his name. He swung around. Click. Click. Clickety-click. What high heels you have, Marianne. Soon she was beside him, dangerously close. He could smell her perfume, strong and musky and very Marianne. Her eyes were large and shining, challenging. Then, slowly, ever so slowly, she blinked. It was a practised, slow motion movement where for a nano-second, she looked at you from half-closed eyes. Like Marilyn Monroe. He had read somewhere that Nureyev used to clench his buttock muscles at the highest point of a leap, giving the illusion that he was going higher still, almost flying. Well, Marianne did the same kind of thing with her eyes.

'Thanks for coming, Charlie. I'll call you later.'

He could see a small brown freckle just above her left breast. Could be a melanoma, maybe he should suggest that she have it checked out. Then again, knowing Marianne, it could be eyeliner. It was a while before she looked away. He smiled and skipped down the steps. Maybe, just maybe.

Charlie edged his way through the crowded tram and grabbed a rail. He hated the Luas at this hour. It wasn't so much the standing, or the crush of bodies and the smells, it was more the diffuse hostility that emanated from the morning commuters, their faces blank with resigned detachment. All on their way to someplace they didn't want to be.

A few feet away, an elderly woman squeezed the rail with both hands, her knuckles white with concentration. Every time the tram stopped, she lurched dangerously. No-one seemed to notice her. No-one seemed to care.

He glanced around; tired, unseeing eyes fixed his without recognition or warmth. Mother was right; Irish people had changed in lots of ways. Like instantly adopting foreign tube behaviour the minute the Luas and the Dart arrived. Strange, really. You could still take the train to Cork and be best friends with the person beside you by the time you got to Limerick Junction. But the Dart and the Luas were different; foreign modes of transport, alien beings, cold, impersonal and unfriendly. Somehow, people seemed to behave like Londoners or Parisians the minute they stepped on board, as if that was how you should behave.

A few seats away, an elderly man struggled to his feet, his wheezes rough and rasping, becoming louder with every exhalation. The man's lips were that unhealthy blue Charlie was only too familiar with. Charlie's eyes met his. Maybe he should say something, make sure the man got medical help. Or maybe not. He looked away. You can't fix everything; he should know that by now. You can't keep jumping into other people's problems, like some perennial Good Samaritan always on the lookout for someone to help. You had to toughen up, to protect yourself. Otherwise, you just couldn't do it. His eyes moved to a girl standing near the door. At least she looked healthy enough.

He bent down and picked up his bag. Here we go. Next stop; St Anne's University Hospital. From where he stood, he could see the curved zinc roof of the new Casualty department. He always liked that roof; there was something cosmopolitan about it; it reminded him of the Sydney Opera House.

The tram slowed to a stop and there was a sudden surge of movement. A woman pushed past him, clipping his heel with her wheelie-bag. He stepped back, away from the body current. No point in rushing; he'd be in there long enough. He reached for the newspaper on the seat beside him and flicked to the financial section. NASDAQ up but rocky. Then he saw the headline and smiled.

'*WorldPharma drops 30% - Wonder Drug withdrawn in America.*' He felt a surge of adrenaline. It was time to buy.

A moment later, he joined the crowd surging through the hospital gates, some to heal, others to be healed. Good, the wheezy man with the blue lips was walking towards Outpatients. And, surprise, surprise, the sun was out.

# 5

Edie took a deep breath and pushed through the gates, lifting her basket high to clear the turnstile.

'Morning, Miss!'

The boys' coats were at half-mast, slipping off their shoulders, the way nine year old boys wear coats. She glanced at the open lunch boxes in their hands and raised an eyebrow.

'No time for lunch later, Miss. Soccer.'

Edie smiled. Charlie had been the same at that age; football, football, football. Hurling was his favourite but he liked Gaelic football and soccer too. The only thing he wasn't too keen on was rugby and she couldn't say she blamed him. Thick men with thick necks playing a thick game...

Edie's smile faded when she saw the woman standing outside the classroom door - Mrs Murphy, with a face that would culture yoghurt, arms folded across her chest. Folded arms were never a good sign.

'Ms Darmody. Finally.'

Edie noted the emphasis on the 'Ms' and how the woman's lips curled around the word 'finally'. Something about the way the woman's jaw jutted out made Edie watchful. Years of teaching had made Edie an expert. Folded arms, chin out and tight lips were always trouble.

'Billy said you put him sitting on his own yesterday.'

No grenades, straight for the scud missiles, Atta' girl, Mrs Murphy. Edie nodded.

'Yes, I did.'

Hands on hips now. Counter-attack. One. Two. Three. Fire...

'His counsellor says he shouldn't be excluded.'

Deep breath, Edie. Remember; don't attack emotion with emotion.

'I wasn't excluding him, Mrs Murphy, at least that wasn't my intention.'

'And you don't think being made sit on your own isn't being excluded?'

Arms swinging dangerously free now. Edie met her hot stare.

'Billy, why don't you tell your mother what you did to Melissa?'

Billy's eyes darted nervously.

'It's OK, Billy, go on.'

'I sprayed orange juice over her books.'

Edie could hear the sharp intake of breath.

'Want to go back to your own desk today?'

'Yes, Miss.'

'Off you go so, Billy.'

Edie looked up.

'Billy understands why he was punished, Mrs Murphy. He's a good kid.'

Without saying a word, the woman turned and began to walk away. No 'Thank you', no 'Sorry for delaying you'. Edie shook her head. Typical.

A moment later, Edie pulled out her chair and smiled. Third class was a grand old class really. Communion over, so no hassle with prayers. They were good little readers, and were flying through the library books. They had a handle on multiplication and had moved on to division and decimals. Irish was the only problem; poor little mites, she could see the look on their faces when she asked them to take out their readers. God love them when they got to fifth and sixth classes; the principal, Mr Sampson, was nuts on the Gaeilge. Mind you, it wasn't his fault he was born in Ballyferriter. And he was a nice man, harmless and sweet, just like his wife, Beth, who taught first and second classes. The Sampsons had five grown up children. Which meant that they obviously had sex. Five times. Amazing. Edie couldn't imagine anyone in the school having sex. Especially Mrs Dunne, with her laced-up orthotic shoes and her polyester floral blouses that, amazingly, were back in fashion. Retro wasn't the word for it. Mrs Dunne was fuckin' feudal.

As usual, the morning flew and Edie was surprised when she heard the bell for lunch. She took her time tidying away her books. Funny, really, how teachers all over the country were this very minute rushing for their dash of freedom when it was the part of the day she dreaded most. At least with the children, there was always the possibility that someone might say or do something different. But lunchtime conversations were standardised and predictable; Super Valu hotel breaks, funeral times and people riddled with cancer that had only been sick for a week.

She opened the door of the classroom and smiled. The others were here before her, as usual. The room smelled of chalk and damp and old copies; a wet day school smell mingled with Mrs Dunne's mothball eau de cologne smell. She sat down in her usual place and placed her lunch box on the table. Mrs Sampson's head was in her knitting bag, searching. Edie smiled. It was the same story every day; Beth could never find the lunch-boxes.

'Just a second, Dad!'

Imagine, calling your husband 'Dad'! She'd never call the father of her children 'Dad', that is, of course, in the extremely unlikely event that she ever had children. Or a husband.

'Here we go. Ham with mustard.'

44

Edie watched the foil wrapped package change hands. Always ham sandwiches for Mr Sampson. And always mustard. She waited, she longed for the day when Mr Sampson would say 'I hate fuckin' ham, I want tuna on rye with rocket.' But, of course, he never did.

'Some spotted dick, Edie?'

'No thank you, Mrs Dunne.'

'Edie, love, fancy a Ryvita?'

'No thank you, Beth.'

Edie didn't like Ryvita, neither apparently did Mrs Sampson, even though she brought it to school every day. She never ate any, opting instead for two slices of Mrs Dunne's spotted dick, three on a Friday.

Now it was Edie's turn. She opened her lunch-box and held it up so that the others could see; it was always good manners to let the others know what you were eating.

'Couscous, left over from last night.'

Mrs Sampson nodded approvingly.

'Organic, I suppose?'

Edie nodded. Beth liked strange foods to be organic. It excused their strangeness, made them more acceptable. Edie made a point of bringing a different lunch to school every day. It was her little way of revolting against the sameness of the other lunches. I mean, if she brought the same lunch to school every day like the others did, it would be like saying that she too was on the same road to sameness, to conformity, to waiting for the pension, with nothing to look forward to but the first flushes of an early menopause and sure and certain death. Pity. She actually liked ham sandwiches.

'How's the South Beach diet going, Beth?'

Mrs Sampson shook her head.

'I can manage perfectly fine without the carbs, Edie, it's the sweet stuff I can't resist. Can't do without my few slices of apple tart. Haven't had bread for two years, though.'

Edie smiled. Wonder what food category Beth thought spotted dick was in. Beth reminded Edie of Mother. Taking bits and pieces of information that suited her, ignoring stuff that didn't. Maybe women of that age all became like that, à la carte digesters of information. Maybe she would too.

'I suppose your poor mother is looking forward to the mid-term break like the rest of us, Edie.'

Edie nodded.

'She's a great woman, your mother.'

Edie looked away. Sometimes you'd think Mother was the only widow in the country the way people went on.

'How's Charlie?'

Edie put down her fork.

'Grand, thanks.'

'Any girlfriend?'

Edie shrugged. 'I don't know.'

'No shortage of girls after Charlie, I'd say. He reminds me of that actor from Cork, what's his name, Jonathan Ross.'

'Jonathan Rhys-Myers.'

Edie smiled. Charlie did look a bit like Jonathan Rhys-Myers.

'When is he heading off to the States?'

'Five weeks.'

Four weeks and six days to be precise.

'Imagine, Johns Hopkins! Of course he was always very bright. My neighbour's cousin's son was in Clongowes with him and he used say that Charlie was top of the class in everything. All the first years were mad about him, he was always nice to them, especially the little ones when they were home-sick.'

That would be Charlie, thought Edie. Man of the match, man of the school. Cheerer-upper of women and children.

'Your mother must be very proud of him.'

Edie felt a warmth creep across her cheeks. It must be the hundredth time that Mrs Dunne had said those words.

'Of course she's proud of him. She's spent her entire life being proud of him. She's been proud of him since the day he took his first steps, three months before I did. She was proud of him the day he was toilet-trained, six months before me. She was proud of him the day he was made captain of the under 12 hurling team. And I would imagine she was proud of him the day he was made head prefect.'

Mrs Dunne's mouth opened and closed, like a goldfish. Hold on, Mrs Dunne, I'm not finished.

'She was proud of him the day he got the same number of points as me in the leaving cert, she was proud of him the day he graduated with first class honours, she was proud of him the day he won the Lordan-Barry medal in Medicine. Is that enough 'being proud of' for you? In fact, Mother is so busy being proud of Charlie, it's amazing she's able to go out to work. If pride were a disease, it would have killed her years ago.'

Edie could feel a hand touch her arm. Beth.

'It's OK, Edie, love. Your mother will miss him too, you know.'

Edie reached for an apple.

'Charlie hasn't lived at home since he was eleven.'

'Imagine, the two of you were only eleven, God love you! Mind you, sixth class in Ring is great for the Gaeilge. And at least you were together, you had each other.'

47

Yes, they had. Edie had loved that year in Ring, even though they were only allowed home once a month. Charlie was the most popular boy in the school. And she was his almost twin sister.

'She's a great teacher, your Mother, topper of a Principal.'

True.

'She's in a tough school and not a bother on her.'

True again. Edie tightened the lid of her lunch box. No, never a bother on Mother. Mother was one of those people who could leave parents wilting in her gaze and reduce big stropping sixth class boys to tears. Mrs Darmody was always right. Always.

'Got your angel cards, love?'

Good, subject changed. Edie smiled and reached for her bag. Out of the corner of her eye she could see Mrs Dunne blessing herself.

'It's OK, Mrs Dunne, they're good angels. We all have them.'

Mrs Dunne shook her head.

'I don't.'

'Of course you do, Mrs Dunne. You've just lost contact with yours.'

Mrs Dunne's eyes darted nervously around the room and Edie smiled. Then, slowly, carefully, she began to shuffle the cards. Her fingers felt light and alive. Suddenly she stopped. Funny, she always knew exactly when to stop shuffling. She laid out the top three cards and picked up the first one.

*He who loves you so completely cannot understand what makes you worry about your goodness. You are always lovely in His sight.'*

Mrs Sampson smiled and nodded. Edie picked up the next card.

*'Do not seek for what you can have, but seek only for what you can give. And, in this way, you can have everything and more'.*

'Isn't that beautiful? Read me another one, Edie, quick, before the bell goes.'

*'Your flesh and blood that nurtured you continues to nurture you. You are always safe while she watches over you.'*

Edie could see Beth's eyes begin to glisten. Beth's mother had died just before Christmas.

'Oh God, Beth. I'm sorry.'

'No, it's fine, Edie. What a lovely message! I was just thinking of Mam this morning.'

Edie began to gather up the cards. The same thing often happened to her, reading something in a card that she had just been thinking about.

'Which one is Michael, again, Edie? I'm always mixing them up.'

'Michael is the defender of light and goodness, the patron saint of police officers and soldiers.'

A slow nod.

'Gabriel is God's messenger.'

'Behold I bring you good tidings of great joy.'

Beth stretched her hands up in the air and Edie smiled.

'The very man, Beth. Gabriel is the herald of change in our lives. He helps with creative ideas and new opportunities.'

'A handy little man to know.'

'Uriel, the light of God, heals our painful memories. He helps us see the good in people and brings us peace of mind. He helps us fulfil our dreams and our goals. He's my favourite.'

'I can see why, love. You see good in everyone.'

'The last archangel is Raphael, the healer. Raphael intervenes in medical crises and helps people recover miraculously.'

'Except of course where a person's illness is part of their overall divine plan.'

'Of course, Beth.'

49

Edie smiled. Like all good angels, Raphael knew his limitations.

'Raphael may not heal you directly but he will lead you to the person who will heal you. Raphael is associated with an emerald green light, the colour of healing and of the heart charka's love energy.'

'Maybe that's why surgical gowns are green Edie, what do you think?'

Edie smiled. Beth adored medical soaps, everything from *ER* to *Scrubs*.

Just then, Mr Sampson's head appeared around the door, his curly Gaeltacht hair tossed wild from the wind. Edie took a deep breath. Here it comes, as predictable as night follows day.

'Shall we hit the decks, ladies? Ar aghaidh linn!'

Don't Edie, don't. But she couldn't help it. It was like shaking hands at mass, you just couldn't stand there and not do it. Her lips began to move.

'Ar aghaidh linn.'

For a moment, she lingered, watching them, three middle-aged people, doing what they did at this time every day, what they had done for the past thirty odd years, tidying away their lunch-boxes, standing up together as if on a silent count of three. They even fell into step together; Mr Sampson leading his troops, whistling some vaguely familiar traditional tune. He was probably about the same age her father would have been if he had lived, somewhere in his mid fifties. Again, that familiar longing draped her, smothering her with its intensity. Imagine if Dad was still here. Imagine what it would be like; having someone tell you that you looked pretty even if you didn't, someone who would make sure that your car was always filled with petrol and who would buy you little bars of chocolate like Mother did for Charlie. Someone whose eyes would glisten on your Debs night. Just imagine.

She began to wipe the stray crumbs of couscous into her hand. Best not attract mice. Then she reached for her bag and stumbled to her feet. She could see them, all blurry, standing in the corridor, waiting.

The bell rang and Edie breathed a sigh of relief. Another day over. And judging by the rain lashing on the windows, she'd be home early today. That was the good thing about wet days; no parents waiting to hijack you in the car park.

A few minutes later, she slowed down and stopped at the traffic lights. She glanced out the window. The sale was still on in that naff boutique Mother liked. Must remember to tell her. Then she noticed the 'For Sale' sign next door. Strange how she'd never noticed that shop before; with its old-fashioned windowpanes and brass bars across the middle; the shop that time forgot. She felt her heart skip a beat.

Suddenly there was a loud beeping behind her and she jumped. Shit. The lights were green. She glanced in the mirror and gave an apologetic little wave. The man's face was marble. Oh well. Maybe his dog had just died. Or his wife. Or his goldfish. You just never knew what was going on in other people's lives.

A few minutes later, she was home. Home. The word pressed down on her like a tombstone. Even the gates were depressing; tired, sad lumps of iron, chipped and rusty after the winter, the hinges creaky and arthritic with age. The further up the avenue she drove, the more the house seemed to loom in front of her, threatening her, dominating her, controlling her. She wished she could live somewhere else. But Mother wouldn't dream of it; no matter how much the developers offered. She liked being Lady of the Manor, with its high ceilings, polished floorboards and marble fireplaces. And the gardens with that creepy grove of Scots pines that tripped you with their branches. Edie didn't like that grove. Neither did Lucy, who slunk past it with her head down and her tail low.

She glanced at the roof. More loose slates over the porch. She sighed and shook her head. A house like this needed money to keep it maintained, lots of money, money that wasn't there. Money that was never there. For a moment, she sat in the car, staring at the house that she had been her home for almost thirty years. Her home, her prison. A place of shadows and secrets and tall angular windows that rattled even when there was no wind. She had tried to open her heart to it, to feel something, some shred of warmth, a small thread of affection for the place she had grown up in but there was nothing. Nothing but the desire to escape. Then again, she hadn't really grown up there, had she? Neither of them had.

Inside, the silence wrapped around her. Strange. There was no sign of Mother; the kitchen was empty. Both the Aga lids were down. No sign of dinner. She felt a wave of panic. Maybe they had been robbed and Mother was lying somewhere in a pool of blood. Dead. Then she took a deep breath. Oh for God's sake, Edie, cop yourself on!

'Mother!'

A few seconds later she heard her mother's voice.

'I'm up here.'

Her mother's door was open a tiny fraction. Edie knocked, two sharp little knocks, her usual knock. Charlie always knocked three times.

'Are you OK?'

It was strange to see her mother in bed.

'Of course I'm OK! I had a hectic day at school, thought I'd lie down for a little while. I must have nodded off.'

Edie stared. In all her mother's thirty years of teaching, the woman had never once gone to bed after school. Never. And Mother never 'nodded off'.

'You look a bit flushed, maybe you're coming down with something.'

'I'm fine, Edie! Stop fussing!'

'I'll do dinner.'

'The lasagne's on the drainer; it should be defrosted by now.'

Of course. Mother always defrosted something the day before Charlie came home, saving her energy for the following day's culinary extravaganza.

'Have you had your blood pressure checked lately?'

'It was fine last time. I'll ask Charlie to check it when he's down.'

'Maybe you should get Dr Browne to check it. It's not really fair asking Charlie…'

Her mother waved a hand.

'Charlie doesn't mind. Anyway, I've an appointment with Dr Browne on Saturday morning.'

Edie bit her lip. Mother wouldn't have made an appointment unless something was wrong. Had to be blood pressure. Mother's cheeks were ruby red, just like the Christmas poinsettia wilting on the kitchen window.

Downstairs, Edie slipped the lasagne into the top oven and cut two thick slices of bread for toasting on the Aga. When the toast was done, she was going to drizzle it with a quiver of that good olive oil Charlie had brought back from the Dordogne and dash the top with a clove of garlic. Easy peasy. Garlic bread, Edie style. Perfecto.

Twenty minutes later, she turned to inspect the table. Gently, she lifted the vase containing the solitary daffodil and moved it to the middle of the table (hopefully Mother wouldn't mind her picking the only daffodil in the garden). She looked at her watch. Five o'clock. She hesitated a moment. Should she, as Mother always did, ring the bell for dinner? Or was it only Mother who rang the bell? She certainly couldn't ever remember doing it. For a moment she looked at the dinner bell sitting on the second shelf of the dresser, between the brown Stephen Pearce bowl and the Oxford dictionary, mocking her. Then she hurried into the hall.

Edie gathered up the plates and put them in the sink. Her mother had eaten nearly everything apart from the garlic bread. She found it too garlicky. And too olive oily. Jesus. Not that this surprised Edie; there was bound to be something wrong; too garlicky, too hard, too soft, too hot, too cold...

She wiped her hands and took a deep breath. OK, here goes. Now was as good a time as any.

'Mother?'

'Yes?

'Did you ever think of taking a year off?'

Her mother put down her cup.

'Now why would I do that?

Edie's eyes remained fixed on her mug. Three tea-leaves floated on top in a perfect triangle. Wonder what it meant.

'You know, a break, a change.'

A short silence. She dare not look up. She could feel her mother's eyes sear her forehead.

'A break from what, Edie? I'm a teacher; it's what I do. Besides, I had to work. When your father died, I had no option, I had to teach.'

Edie bit her lip. We'd have kept you busy, if you hadn't packed us off to boarding school.

'But later on, when we... when we were grown up, you could have taken some time off, gone on a long trip, a cruise, maybe.'

'A cruise?'

It was like she had suggested a nudist holiday.

'You know, a ship...'

'I know what a cruise is, Edie! Look Edie, what's all this about? Are you planning a cruise? Surely you're not thinking of taking a year off, upsetting all those additional voluntary contributions I set up for you?'

Jesus Christ. Not that bloody pension again.

'I was just thinking, maybe...'

'You're fine here, Edie, you're fine now, hear me? Look what happened with that tsunami, or New Orleans, God love them. No, you're fine here, you're in a lovely school, and you might even get vice-principal when Luidín Mac Lu retires. An extra six grand a year, money for jam.'

Edie pushed her plate away.

'You're off to Paris for midterm and Easter is only five weeks after that. Before you know it, it'll be summer and time to visit Charlie.'

Charlie. Charlie in America. Oh God. She felt a wave of sadness. Soon there would be just herself and Mother, and one-way conversations about the stupid vice-principal's bonus and her pension AVCs. Then she remembered the course and felt her anger slip away. Let Mother say what she wanted. Things would soon be different. Soon she would know exactly what to do. And she would do it, no matter what Mother said.

# 6

Charlie opened the door and smiled. There they were, all his ladies, sitting up in front of their breakfast trays, in their beds, just where he wanted them. The smell of buttery toast reminded him that Sister had said something about a breakfast. The thought that a spare breakfast meant that somebody had died during the night didn't bother him. I mean, it wasn't as if the patient had touched the food or anything.

He liked this time of morning; the lull between the work of the day and the madness of the night, a brief interlude from the chaos that lay ahead. The wheelchair runs to X-ray hadn't yet started and the nurses were still at report. No visitors, no trolleys, no whirring floor cleaners. Just him and the patients. Suddenly he heard a familiar voice.

'Quick, Charlie! Head honcho's on the radio!'

He followed Tommy down the corridor to Clements' office. Just as well he'd mentioned the '*Morning Ireland*' interview to Tommy, otherwise he'd have missed it. One advantage of being head porter was that Tommy had keys for every door in the hospital, including the kitchens. Very handy for a bowl of cornflakes at six am. And for sneaking into the boss's office when he wasn't around...

'You take the boss's chair.'

It was an order, not a request. Charlie slipped into the chair and twirled around. He could get used to chairs like this. He liked the way the leather pressed into his lower back and the way you could adjust everything. Must be one of those orthopaedic chairs.

'So there's nothing to be worried about, you tell us.'

'No, not at all, your GP will switch you to another blood pressure tablet.'

Clements' voice was clear and measured. Total control.

'And this tablet that's being withdrawn, Cardelia, won't cause any long-term problems?'

'Absolutely not. In any event, it was only a very small number of elderly patients with other illnesses who were susceptible to these rare cardiac rhythm problems. However, in the interest of public safety, the company that makes the drug has decided to withdraw the product.'

'Good. And I take it, doctor, that there are other drugs available that can be used instead?'

'Yes, indeed. There are a number of highly effective anti-hypertensive drugs with excellent safety profiles available, for example, Diastora, a new type of calcium blocker.'

'And it doesn't cause heart rhythm problems?'

'Absolutely not. In fact Diastora has anti-arrhythmic properties which make it the ideal anti-hypertensive for any patient prone to a cardiac rhythm disorder.'

A short pause.

'So all these front-page headlines are just scare-scaremongering? There's no cause for panic?'

'None at all. Just make an appointment to see your doctor. I'd also like to take this opportunity to remind anyone over forty that they should have their blood pressure checked regularly.'

'Reassuring advice there from one of our best known cardiologists. That was Doctor John Clements, Consultant Cardiologist at St Anne's University Hospital, Dublin. Thank you, Dr Clements, it's nice to know we're in good hands.'

Charlie smiled. Tommy's face was thunder.

'He's one smooth bastard, no doubt about it. Smooth as runny honey and just as sweet. And too much honey ain't good for you, Charlie, we all know that.'

Charlie shrugged.

'He's good, you have to admit it, Tommy.'

A low grunt.

'Talk, that's all he does.'

Talk and lots of other stuff, thought Charlie. Clements made it all seem easy. He had that relaxed confidence of someone who knew what they wanted and how to get it. You could see it in his smile, in his slow, even stride, in the comfortable clack his shoes made on the hospital tiles. You could even hear it in his nasal intonation.

'Guys like him, you never really know what's going on in their heads.'

Charlie looked up. Maybe Tommy had a point. There was something about Clements, a kind of distance or something; it was hard to know what he was thinking, it was even hard to tell whether he liked you or not. You looked into his eyes and saw nothing. Impenetrable, emotionless, dangerous eyes. Kind of like George Bush, really. Only brighter, far brighter.

'RTÉ wants him as advisor to that new medical drama series.'

This would surely drive Tommy mad.

'I'm surprised he doesn't want a part, playing himself, of course.'

Charlie laughed. What was Clements' secret? Was it simply hard work, ambition, making the right moves? Hardly, lots of people worked equally hard and were just as ambitious. Confidence, perhaps? Knowing the right people? Or was it something else, like the ability to change, to keep one step ahead? Just when you thought that Clements had reached saturation point, that no way could he take anything else on, along came something new, like those new health podcasts he was involved in. Yep. Clements had his finger on the collective pulse of his profession. He didn't just adapt to change, he drove it.

'When he first came, everyone thought Clements was the bees knees, salt of the earth kind of fellow, all that smiling and slapping you on the shoulder and stuff. But he ain't no softie, far from it, he'd cut your throat with cotton wool, so he would.'

Charlie smiled at the image of a pack of hospital cotton wool being used as a murder weapon.

'He's a damn good cardiologist, Tommy. And he gives a load of money away to charity; I've seen him write a cheque for ten grand to Concern.'

Somehow Charlie felt it necessary to defend his boss; it didn't seem right to trash your colleagues, even to Tommy, and besides, he owed Clements, he owed him big-time. Without John Clements he wouldn't be going to Johns Hopkins.

'He can afford ten grand, for God's sake, loose change out of what he's earning. Notice how he always makes sure to pick a good team so that he can feck off to his rooms? You did that cardioversion for him yesterday, didn't you?'

Charlie nodded.

'He should have stayed to supervise, dodgy things, cardioversions. What time did you get home?'

Charlie shrugged.

'Dunno. Eleven, eleven-thirty. But yesterday was different.'

Tommy shook his head.

'Yeah, sure was, the boss's number one drug whipped off the market and just listen to him, you'd think it was good news.'

Charlie laughed. Tommy was right, but it was part of Clements' genius, the way he turned that interview around so that the focus was on the new medication. Not a mention of patient deaths, just heart 'irregularities'.

'Just watch your back, kid. I've seen how people like him operate. Don't get on the wrong side of him. Guys like that hang decent kids like you out to dry.'

Charlie met his gaze.

'I'm leaving in four weeks, Tommy.'

Tommy shook his head.

'A lot can happen in four weeks, Charlie. And remember, it could be a case of out of the frying pan into the fire. Just because Clements' brother is President of some big American cardiology association doesn't mean that he's any better than his prick of a brother. Bet they even look alike.'

Charlie smiled.

'He talks the same, anyway.'

'See, I told you.'

Charlie laughed and stood up.

'Hey, any tips for Clonmel?'

'Put ten on *Milky Way*. To win.'

Charlie reached into his pocket.

'Make it twenty. What time's he running?'

'Three thirty. I'm going to head down at lunch-time.'

'Here's forty. Back another winner while you're there.'

Tommy smiled.

'Man after my own heart. *Sine metu,* have no fear. By the way, want me to make any phone calls to our 'have a nice day' Californian broker?'

Charlie hesitated. Oh hell. It was worth a gamble. Might as well go for it. *Sine metu* and all that.

'Buy WorldPharma. Ten grand.'

Tommy arched an eyebrow.

'But aren't they in the shithouse after the Cardelia thing?'

'Exactly. They've never been lower. We're in at a good price, shithouse or no shithouse, Tommy my old flower. The only place they can go is up. And as far as the pharmaceutical industry is concerned, the market is always bullish.'

'Yeah, and what about Elan?'

Charlie smiled.

'Elan's not finished yet, Tommy. I think we should hold on for a while. Remember how they recovered last time?'

Their joint portfolio had grown substantially in the past year; the usual spread of blue chip, a solid sprinkling of pharma and a few medical biotech. At least it made keeping up with the latest clinical trials more interesting. And it had paid for the deposit on his apartments.

'Righto, Charlie, WorldPharma it is. I'll ring the States later, when they're awake. C'mon, let's grab some breakfast.'

Charlie smiled. Tommy liked phoning their Californian broker. Especially when the calls were made from Clements' office.


They sat in their usual place, near the window, on the right, third from the top. From here they could see but not be seen, exactly as Tommy wanted. He watched Tommy add three spoons of sugar to his cup.

'Here you go, Doc, we must be the only two people left in this hospital who use sugar. Bastards.'

Charlie laughed. Tommy reminded him of Homer Simpson, doughnut in hand, belly straining under his blue coat, short legs stretched out in front of him, as if he had all the time in the world. Which, of course, he had. As head porter, Tommy's role was 'supervisory' and like he often said himself, he could supervise just as easily from the canteen as from anywhere else. He had a way of assimilating and storing information and putting it all together so that it made sense. He was like the eyes and ears of St Anne's; nothing slipped past him. He knew who was pregnant, who was on holiday, and who was doing what they shouldn't be doing with someone they shouldn't be doing it with. Charlie watched him take a large bite of doughnut.

'Wonder what Krispy Crème doughnuts are like.'

Charlie grinned.

'I'll let you know. Hey, maybe we could buy the Irish franchise.'

'Christ, Charlie, that'd be the ticket. You and me, travelling the country, selling doughnuts, fleadh ceoils, football matches, festivals... Jesus, we'd have a mighty time.'

'We sure would.'

Then Tommy's smile faded.

'You are coming back, aren't you?'

Charlie punched his shoulder.

'Of course I'm coming back! Two years, three max. I should have a chance of a consultant's post by then.'

Tommy nodded.

'How are your mother and Edie shaping up?'

Charlie sighed.

'Mother's marking the days off on the kitchen calendar. And Edie won't even talk about it.'

'At least there's loads of flights now, they'll be able to get over to see you.'

Charlie smiled.

'They've already booked their flights for summer.'

Tommy reached for his cup.

'Poor Edie, she's a lovely girl, God bless her, not like all those ladettes or whatever they call them.'

Charlie smiled.

'Edie can be tough enough when she wants to be.'

Tommy smiled.

'Like her mother. I remember your Mam at the football matches. She'd invade the pitch if someone gave you a hard shoulder.'

Charlie laughed.

'I remember. Even the refs were afraid of her.'

'She's a great woman, Charlie, kept the place together, did everything she could for ye, best schools and everything.'

Charlie nodded. Clongowes and the Ursuline must have cost Mother a small fortune. No wonder there was never any money for anything else.

'Suppose everyone in Clongowes was loaded?'

Charlie nodded.

'You should have seen some of the cars. The lads would come back after Christmas on about their skiing trips. I was the only one who never went anywhere.'

'Nothing wrong with that, Charlie.'

'I know.'

Tommy was right. There was nothing wrong with being the poorest boy in Clongowes. Especially if you were top of the class and a good sportsman. But it planted a seed; a seed that had grown steadily from the day he started first year, a seed that was still growing. One day, he would have lots of money. One day, he would no longer be the poor boy.

'How does Edie feel about living at home?'

Charlie shrugged.

'Her school is only a few miles away.'

'Still.'

'They could always move to Dublin, I suppose, when Mother retires, stay in one of the apartments. Maybe Edie could get a job here.'

Tommy shook his head.

'If your mother didn't move when your father died, she's not going to move now, Charlie. When people retire, it's around familiar people and things they want to be, not a load of strangers. Anyway, I can't ever see her selling.'

An image of the Lodge flashed in front of Charlie. His mother had already turned down dozens of offers from property developers. All the other old houses nearby had sold up, clearing the way for housing estates. But not Lily Darmody. The Lodge and the gardens were still intact. Mother was not going to sell.

'Maybe you're right, Tommy.'

'Course I'm right. Why would she want to leave Clonmel? It's the nicest town in Ireland. '

He shook his head.

'What are we doing in this big, dirty city at all, Charlie, eh?'

Ten minutes later, Charlie hurried towards main reception. He watched the sea of people surging through the hospital doors; anxious visitors looking lost and dazed, staff with purposeful walks trying to make up time, patients in too-warm dressing gowns coming back from a smoke. Hospitals sure were funny places.

'Sign here, Doc.'

Charlie looked at the package. Wonder what it could be. More chocolate? But Edie would hardly use a courier service. He scribbled his signature and turned the package over. Aha! *GoldMed Communications*. He should have known! He opened the package. Jesus! Every article that was ever written on Diastora must be here! No mention of Cardelia, of course. Like a defrocked politician or last year's Miss Ireland, Cardelia was yesterday's news.

He flicked idly through the pages; most of the articles were familiar but it was handy to have them all together, saved him doing a literature search. Mind you, the management of hypertension involved more than Diastora! A note fell to the floor. Charlie bent to pick it up.

'Would really appreciate if you could start work on this asop.'

He could imagine her saying the words, her voice rising at the end of the sentence and then that penultimate smile, the mother of all smiles. Then he reached into his pocket for his mobile. Probably Edie.

'Charlie, it's Marianne.'

Speak of the devil.

'Hi Marianne, how are you?'

'Busy, busy, busy, you know what it's like. Did you get the stuff I sent over?'

'It's in my hand.'

'Good.'

He could imagine her smile; deep, red lips, bold and provocative.

'Look, I know you're up to your eyes, Charlie, but is there any chance you could get the first article in to us by Monday or Tuesday?'

'Sure.'

'You're a darling. *Medicine Now* has given us a slot for next week and I don't want to miss our place. I really do appreciate this, Charlie. Timing is everything in this game.'

A pause. When she spoke again, her voice was softer.

'How about having dinner with me on Saturday night? A little thank you from GoldMed?'

Charlie closed his eyes. Shit! Shit! Shit! He was going home on Saturday. Or maybe not... he could always ring Edie, tell her he had to work...

'Well?'

'Sorry, Marianne, I'll have to pass, I'm afraid. I'm going home to Tipp on Saturday.'

'No problem, Charlie, another time?'

'Sure, I'd love to.'

Boy would he love to. Ah shite, anyway. Like Marianne had just said, timing was everything.

# 7

Charlie swung through the gates and swerved to avoid a pothole. Home at last, thank God. Over a hundred miles away from the grating sounds of the city and the bleeps and noises that filled his every waking moment. Beside him, he could see the yellow dots of crocuses and the first of the daffodils pushing through the grass. Above him, the rooks, loud and boisterous with the fuss of springtime, were flooding home to the darkness of the grove.

The old Scots pines loomed black in front of him, with their squirrel-red bark and their branches reaching out, as if they were trying to grab you. Edie never liked those trees, said they were full of whispers, that they gave her the creeps. Strange, Mother didn't like them either, always stopped them playing there when they were children, said they were dangerous. Funny how she considered it safe to climb the big oaks and not the Scots pines. He shrugged. Mother, God bless her, had her own take on things, always had, always would.

He drove slowly, avoiding the potholes deepened and darkened after a winter of frost and rain. There was no point in filling them, the avenue needed a proper undersurface; a big job involving diggers and lorry loads of stones. And money. He sighed. Maybe next year. Right now he needed any all the spare cash he had.

He rounded the bend and a long ridge of shiny slate came into view, high above the garden wall. The new houses were flying up. He hadn't realised the roofs would be so high. He felt a tinge of sadness; the Lodge, his home, was surrounded by houses on all sides now, like a wagon train surrounded by Indians. All that separated it from modern suburbia, from reality, were its crumbling walls covered in moss. And, slowly, stone by stone, that mossy wall was gradually disintegrating.

It was as if the Lodge was stuck in a time warp; always the same, the house that refused to change. Like the people who lived in it.

As he drew nearer, he could see Edie, standing on the steps, waving like crazy. She was wearing faded jeans and an old navy sweatshirt that used to be his like about a million years ago. It looked better on her, as usual. Now she was running down the steps, Lucy at her heels, the two of them tripping over each other. He smiled and crunched to a stop. She looked so young, like a teenager, with her hair tied up in a ponytail and her shabby old Levi's. A moment later, her arms wrapped around him in a tight hug. She smelled of roses and honeysuckle. Gently, he pulled away and held her at arm's length, searching her face. Good. She looked fine; same old Edie, eyes wide and shining, dancing and daring.

'You OK?'

She fixed him with her deep blue eyes.

'What you really mean is, am I bonkers?'

He laughed and planted a kiss on her forehead.

'Well you don't seem bonkers to me.'

Her arm hooked his and they began to climb the steps, Lucy dashing madly between their legs, her allegiance divided. He bent down to nuzzle the

68

Labrador's ears. How could he even have considered not coming home this weekend?

'I'm really glad you're home, Charlie.'

He met her gaze.

'What did you want to tell me?'

Edie shook her head.

'Later, when she's in bed.'

Charlie nodded. Conversations in the Lodge were divided into two types: the ones with Mother present and the ones without. It had always been the same.

A moment later, he opened the kitchen door. His mother had her back towards him, lifting something out of the Aga.

'Smells delicious, Mother.'

Instantly she straightened and turned around, cheeks flushed from the heat of the oven.

'Charlie! I didn't hear the car! I'll just put this down.'

There was a sizzle as the hot tin met the moisture of the draining board. Then she was beside him, her arms around him, a milder, less demanding embrace than Edie's. There was flour on her cheek.

'Perfect timing. I've just taken out the roast. I hope you're hungry.'

'I could eat a horse.'

Charlie could see Edie mouthing the word 'lick-arse'. He winked across at her.

'Sit down, love, you must be exhausted. Edie, can you pour Charlie some juice and can you take the plates out of the bottom oven? Or maybe we'll open the wine now, Charlie, what do you think, would you like a glass of wine?'

Charlie caught Edie's eye.

'Sounds great.'

His mother reached behind her for the bottle of wine already open and warming behind the lid of the Aga. He watched her pour three glasses, slowly and carefully, equal measurements, like a child dividing out sweets. Wine was for special occasions and celebrations, bought one bottle at a time, carefully chosen and carefully drunk. There was never any other booze in the house; alcohol had caused enough damage in the Lodge. Neither him nor Edie ever brought alcohol home; it was something that one just didn't do, an unwritten household rule. Every bottle of alcohol was bought on demand, even the whiskey for the Christmas cake. It was all part of Mother's military budgeting, her tight hold on domestic finances.

'Cheers, Charlie.'

Edie clinked her glass and took a long, deep swallow. He could see his mother's eyes narrow. Edie raised the glass to her lips again and met her mother's gaze.

Oops. Trouble at the camp.

'Edie! Put down that glass and start mashing the potatoes! I need to finish making Charlie's gravy.'

'Charlie's gravy! I like gravy too!'

Charlie smiled. Nothing had changed, still the two of them bickering away. He glanced around the kitchen, letting his eyes linger, soaking it all in. He wanted to memorise every bit of it; his mother whisking the gravy, the foil-covered roast resting on the draining-board, juices settling and flesh firming, the old mahogany clock, solid, steady, never missing a beat.

He put down his glass. He would miss all of this; this time warp of warmth and peace. This piece of Yesterday. It hadn't changed in as long as he could remember; the cracked cream tiles over the Aga, the faded lino on the floor, the big oak table, soft and pale like a lump of bleached driftwood, the kitchen chairs, with their mismatched floral covers and their underneaths sagging with prolapsed horsehair. Somehow, it was like this room, and the people within it, had never changed.

His eyes rested on his mother, her face flushed again from straining the broccoli. Same blonde bob. Same knee-length skirt. Then his eyes travelled to Edie, mashing furiously, her brow knitted in concentration. Same long chestnut hair, same slim greyhound build, scrawny and delicate, stooped and apologetic. His Edie. She caught him looking at her and threw a spoon across the table.

'What?'

'Nothing.'

Then the familiar sound of the old school bell, calling everyone to dinner. Charlie smiled. It was one of Mother's strange little habits, ringing the bell for dinner, even when everyone was already in the kitchen.

A plate piled high with food appeared in front of him and he felt his mother's hand on his shoulder.

'Here we go, Charlie! Edie, some gravy for Charlie! Oh, I heard Doctor Clements on *Morning Ireland* last week, Charlie. I thought he spoke really well, explained everything. Such a lovely man, so concerned.'

A fork dropped and Charlie looked up.

'Sounded to me like he was making excuses for that drug they took off the market, the one that caused the abnormal heart rhythms. Another big cover-up.'

He could see his mother's lips tighten.

'That drug had nothing to do with Dr Clements, Edie! He was only trying to reassure people, get them to have their blood pressure checked.'

Edie's fingers curled around the wine glass.

'Hello! Anyone with a brain around here? What part of 'dangerous side-effects' don't you understand, Mother? The drug must have been dangerous to be taken off the market, for God's sake. What kind of abnormal rhythms did it cause, Charlie? You know, so go on, tell us.'

'Calm down, Edie, don't get excited.'

Mother's tone was slow and measured, her school principal's tone.

'Charlie?'

Edie's eyes flashed dangerously. He put down his knife. There was no fobbing off Edie with comforting sound bytes. After all, she had spent two years studying pharmacy, she knew something about pharmacology.

'It caused irregular heart rhythms in a small number of elderly patients.'

'I know that. You haven't answered my question, Charlie.'

Her eyes fixed his.

'Supraventricular tachycardias.'

'Sounds serious. Maybe you might like to explain to Mother what exactly supraventricular tachycardia can cause?'

Charlie put down his glass.

'Ventricular fibrillation.'

'Leading to…?'

He hesitated a moment.

'Death.'

Edie smiled and raised her glass.

'Nasty enough side-effect, I should think.'


The rest of the meal was OK, apart from Mother insisting he eat all his mashed potato. She said that he wouldn't be able to find any decent potatoes in the States. Pity they'd be long out of his digestive tract long before he even stepped on the plane. Potatoes were like sleep, you couldn't stock up on them. But it was pointless trying to explain that to Mother.

'Now, who's for apple tart? It's nice and juicy if I say so myself. I'll cut it, Edie, you might burn yourself.'

'Suppose I might.'

Charlie searched Edie's face. Something had happened, he was sure of it. Another row, perhaps. Maybe Tommy was right; maybe Edie needed her own space. But the thought of her alone in some apartment filled him with panic. Edie wasn't meant to be alone; not now, not ever.

'This time next week you'll be in Paris, Edie.'

A quiver of a smile.

'Where are you staying?'

She hesitated a moment.

'Near the Opera.'

'That should be handy, very central.'

He could smell cloves in the air.

'Who did you say you were going with again?'

Edie stood at the sink, her face in shadow.

'Mags Barry from Waterford, remember her?'

Charlie shook his head.

'Can't say I do.'

Strange he couldn't place her; it wasn't as if too many of Edie's friends had stayed at the Lodge. And the ones that had visited were never invited back if he paid them any attention. It was as if there was some unspoken rule saying hands off Charlie. Come to think of it, Edie hadn't had anyone to stay in ages. Maybe you just grew out of things like that.

'Her father's a dentist.'

Charlie smiled. Typical Mother, making sure the professional pedigree was mentioned. It made Mags whoever she was suddenly acceptable.

'Don't forget good walking shoes.'

She nodded and picked up his plate. His eyes followed her as she crossed to the sink. Strange how she didn't want to talk about Paris; normally she'd be all talk about where she was off to.

It was just after ten when his mother put down her reading glasses.

'Don't stay up too late, Charlie. You need a good night's sleep, love.'

He stood up to kiss her goodnight. Up close, a myriad of tiny wrinkles framed her eyes. Mother was getting old. The realisation sat on his chest like a lead weight.

'And what about me, Mother, don't I need a good night's sleep too?'

Edie made no attempt to stand up. His mother looked at him and smiled.

'Of course you do, Edie.'

Charlie waited until his mother's footsteps faded, then bent down and tugged Edie's ponytail.

'OK, out with it, what's up between you two?'

Edie shrugged.

'It's like a prison here.'

Charlie sighed. Maybe Tommy was right.

'What won't she let you do, Edie?'

His voice was soft.

'I want to take a year off, Charlie, no big deal, lots of teachers do it.'

Oh sugar. I suppose his going away had started this off.

'You're going to travel?'

He hoped his voice sounded casual. Inside, his thoughts were spinning. What if she wanted to stay with him? How could he explain that it wouldn't be a good idea? And who would travel with her? This Mags person that he couldn't remember? Edie and backpacking sent a prickle of fear down his spine. But he had to play along, to listen to her. Then gradually he might be able to coax her to change her mind about whatever daft idea had taken her fancy. That was the mistake Mother always made, jumping down Edie's throat the minute she opened her mouth, never giving her a chance, never trying to get around her in a nice way.

'I'm not going anywhere.'

He nudged a log with his foot, releasing a hissing spray of sparks.

'I'm going to stay in Clonmel.'

What the fuck. Taking a year off to stay in Clonmel? Doing what for God's sake?

'I found this place, Charlie. It's perfect.'

Christ.

'You're going to move out?'

'No! It's a shop.'

'You're going to live over a shop?'

'No, stupid, I'm going to open a shop.'

'Sorry, Edie?'

He'd obviously misheard.

'I want to open a shop, my own shop.'

She wanted to open a shop. Sweet Mother of Jesus. Just as well Mother was in bed. This was worse than he'd thought. He had to be very careful what he said next.

'Where did this all come from, hon? What kind of shop?'

Her eyes lit up.

'Sort of like a health store.'

He felt a sinking feeling.

'Go on …'

'You know, holistic stuff, supplements, organic foods, Fair Trade...'

He raised his hand.

'Hold it right there, Edie. The country's full of health food stores - there's a Nature's Way in every town in Ireland. There are probably more health food shops than pharmacies in Dublin right now.'

She looked up and smiled.

'That's Dublin. There's only two in Clonmel. And the market is growing; a lot of immigrants from the new EU accession countries are big into natural remedies. Anyway, my shop isn't just about health foods, the emphasis is more on the spiritual dimension.'

Oh God, this was getting worse.

'Meaning…'

'Psychology, spiritual resources, books, CDs, DVDs…'

'You mean that 'Power of Now' stuff?'

Edie's room was crammed with books on 'personal development'. He called it self-help. Pep talk for losers. Total waste of money.

'Don't knock it, Charlie. It works, you know. But people like you and Clements wouldn't understand that. All you talk about is salaries, property investments, ten year plans.'

He felt a prickle of annoyance. Why did it bother Edie so much that he owned a few apartments? Everyone his age, apart from Edie of course, owned some bit of property. Did she expect him to give his money away to charity?

'Money makes money, Edie. There's no point in my paying rent when I could be paying a mortgage. And what's wrong with knowing where I want to be in five years' time? You can't just drift along...'

'Like me?'

Shit. He knew what she was thinking. Almost thirty, a primary school teacher, living at home. No house, no relationship. It wasn't what she had dreamed about, no sirree.

'Look, Edie, you've no idea what it's like in hospital medicine. Fifty docs were after my rotation in St Anne's. Some guys won't even tell you which jobs they've applied to. Everyone's breaking their balls to get the job they want. You've got to keep the pressure on, to make the right moves. It's dog eat dog. One of the senior registrars across town blew his brains out last month.'

Edie closed her eyes. Damn. Why had he opened his big mouth? Edie clung to misfortune and disaster. Tragic images stayed with her for ages. First the tsunami and then Katrina. He put his arm around her.

'In the real world, Edie, it's not all Florence Nightingale or Mother Theresa. You have to play tough, fight your corner, watch your back. It's how it is, honey.'

He guided a stray strand of hair back from her forehead.

'Survival of the fittest?'

'Exactly.'

'But at what price, Charlie?'

He looked away. What was wrong with wanting to be a consultant? He'd had enough of empty pockets, soul-destroying summer jobs and bank loans, of scrimping and saving and always having to check that you had enough money before you bought something, even lunch. He knew what it was like to grow up in a house that was falling down. What was wrong with wanting a house like Clements' or an Audi TT instead of a shit-bucket Primera?

'I've busted my butt for that job in the States.'

'You mean sucked up to that creep and laughed at his stupid jokes.'

77

Charlie sighed. He should never have told Edie those jokes. He should have known she wouldn't like them. But they were only jokes for God's sake. Jesus, what was it about Clements that got under people's skin? First it was Tommy, now Edie.

'So, looks like you don't want me to take a year off either.'

Her voice was low. For a moment he said nothing. Maybe her idea wasn't that crazy after all. If it was anyone else's idea, he'd probably be all for it. And there certainly seemed to be a growing market for that kind of thing. Edie spent half her wages in health food stores. Maybe he should check out some shares in the health food business. Mind you, it was pretend medicine, all fine until someone got sick, then it wasn't very long before they were running back to their doctor. And he couldn't imagine Edie managing anything, let alone a business. OK, she was a bright kid, straight A's in her first year exams, would probably have been an honours student the whole way up. Poor kid.

He slipped off the couch and slid down beside her on the floor. She moved closer and nestled into him. He reached for a log and threw it into the fire. A spray of sparks fanned out, spitting and hissing their protests. That was another thing he would miss; the big old fireplace. Everyone else had pulled out cast-iron fireplaces, old baths and Belfast sinks but Mother had changed nothing apart from the wallpaper in the hallway occasionally.

He turned to look at her.

'OK, Edie, just say this idea of yours is a runner, and just say you find a premises, have you given any thought to a business plan? For example, how are you going to finance it? How much stock would you have to carry?'

She shook her head and smiled.

'Money, money, money, Charlie! There you go again! All I want is to pay the rent, maybe make a small amount of money to live on.'

He sighed. Christ. Imagine Edie dealing with an auctioneer. Or a builder. They'd chew her up and spit her out. And take every euro in her purse.

'Have you told Mother?'

'Only about wanting to take a year off, I didn't mention anything about the shop. We didn't get as far as that.'

Hmm. He'd partly guessed that Mother knew nothing about this. Otherwise, she'd have been on the phone straight away, looking for a script for lithium. He closed his eyes. Christ. This was brilliant; really good timing. Here he was, heading off to the States in a few weeks' time and here was Edie with some crazy scheme of opening a 'spiritual' shop. For fuck's sake.

But he had to be careful. Challenge Edie head on, and there was no way she'd back down. Like the time she refused to go to Cape Clear Irish college, threatened to swim to Baltimore if Charlie didn't come with her. And like the eejit he was, he agreed. It rained for two full weeks. And the course had been crap. But, strangely enough, he had enjoyed it.

'OK, Edie, here's the deal. I don't want you to do anything until after your holidays. I don't want you to rush into anything. Promise me that you won't do anything until we talk again.'

Edie nodded.

'Promise. Hey, remember the time I wanted to set up a bagel bar and you said no-one would be interested in bagels? Or juice bars?'

'That was different.'

She punched his arm.

'No, it wasn't! You just won't admit it.'

He turned to look at her. Her eyes were deep blue; a beautiful velvety blue, so different from his own dark brown. He blinked and nudged a log with his foot, exposing a beam of red.

'Remember Cape Clear?'

She began to laugh, and he watched the dimple above her mouth begin to deepen. Soon they were both laughing, remembering other courses, other holidays, other happy, sunny, dusty, grassy days from their childhood. It was like a floodgate had been opened.

After a while, she stretched and stood up. He felt cold without her body leaning against his.

'Better go to bed, I suppose. She'll kill me for keeping you up. She's making pancakes for breakfast.'

Charlie smiled. More food. It was Mother's way of showing she cared. There was a short silence; when Edie spoke, her voice was low.

'What do you think Dad would say, Charlie? What would he want me to do?'

He followed her gaze to the mantelpiece, to the small rectangular photograph in the silver frame. It was taken on his ninth birthday, the last birthday he had a father; him with his new football, Edie in that yellow dress with the blue spots and the two missing buttons. And Mother and Father. Or Uncle and Aunt, to be technically precise. All laughing faces, everyone happy. As if it would always be like that.

'I don't know, Edie.'

He could remember that day clearly, it seemed just like yesterday. He drank three bottles of coke and Mother never said anything, not even a word about it rotting his insides or dissolving his teeth. Father looked thin and gaunt, he could see that now. But that day, that glorious, sunny, yellow dress day, his father hadn't touched a drop. Just kept calling them his angels and giving them money to buy more sweets. His eyes rested on his mother's face. Her expression was strangely incongruous; her lips were smiling but her eyes were dark. Maybe she knew that her husband wouldn't see the next birthday, or live to see the boy they had raised as their own become a man.

'Nobody told us.'

He knew what she meant. Nobody told them that their father was going to die. He felt a painful rush of memory; starched uniforms, the pungent smell of disinfectant, shiny hospital lino. And the whispers…

Edie was beside him again. She handed him a photograph; the wedding one; men with dark baggy suits and women with hats like flowerpots, standing on the steps of Powerstown church. His parents in the middle, their young faces shining with life and hope. Beside him, the best man; Dad's brother, Raymond. Charlie's father. They could be twins, Dad and Raymond, same ropey tallness, same thin faces, same slanted grin.

'Your mother was beautiful.'

Charlie's eyes turned to the bridesmaid. His mother was beautiful, no doubt about it; wavy auburn hair, brown eyes, just like his. Aunt Ella. The woman who had given birth to him. The mother he had never known. Funny, really, how these people, his parents, were strangers to him, people he had no memories of. They had existed as parents for a brief six weeks. Both had been killed instantly in the accident. Dad was lucky to have survived. It seemed natural that his uncle should adopt Charlie. The two babies would be like Irish twins, him and Edie, six weeks apart in age, first cousins, now reared as sister and brother.

He looked at his mother's face again, straining to feel something, some sprinkle of emotional recognition; it didn't seem right to feel nothing at all.

'I can sense him sometimes, watching me.'

'Who?'

'Dad, stupid.'

'Like a guardian angel?'

Edie shook her head.

'How could he be a guardian angel? Guardian angels have never lived on earth, I've told you that before.'

Charlie smiled. Edie and her angels.

'You know I don't do angels, Edie.'

'Well, you should. Just let the angels into your life, see what happens.'

'Maybe I don't have a guardian angel.'

'Everyone has angels, Charlie, even serial killers and Dr Clements. But you have to ask them to help you.'

Charlie shrugged. Somehow he just couldn't see himself asking angels for help. Not yet, anyway.


Later, much later, he stared at the dying flames. The coals glowed orange and deep and he could feel his face flushed with heat. Edie was probably sound asleep by now. What were her words again? Something about living in the present, being in the 'Now' as she called it. Total horseshit. All his life he had escaped the pain of the present by dreaming of the future. The present was only a means to an end. The present had been a fatherless childhood, the poorest boy at Clongowes and breaking his butt at college to make the grades and hold down a weekend bar job. Why think about today when you can dream of a better tomorrow? As for the past, well, no point in going there.

His father, the man who had been father to him for nine years, the man whom he had adored and worshipped, was gone. He had left them, preferring the company of sour whiskey and smoke-filled pubs.

Edie saw it differently, of course. For her, it was just another illness, her father another victim, another casualty. Sweet, silly, forgiving Edie.

The photograph slipped from his hand and landed face down on the rug. He made no move to right it.

# 8

Edie looked around the garden and smiled. The snowdrops had merged into a snowy carpet and the daffodils had gathered numbers beneath the trees. Already the light that painted the garden was different; brighter, stronger, warmer. She reached down to knead Lucy's ears.

'Spring's here, Lucy!'

Yes. Spring was here. And with it, new life, new beginnings.

She opened the hall door and slipped the brochure into her pocket. It had arrived only yesterday and was all about learning to use the right side of your brain as well as the left. Amazing, really, the untapped potential of the brain. The trick was knowing how to open up the latent pathways. And the course was going to show her how. She'd read the brochure again later on, just before she went too bed; it made her feel she was ending the day on a positive note. Mind you, even reading it twenty times wouldn't be enough some nights; you couldn't beat Mother for a good old dose of negativity, just in case you thought you were getting ahead of yourself.

A moment later, she opened the kitchen door. Her mother was sitting at the table, the paper stretched in front of her, Sudoku on the left, death column on the right.

'Lovely day, isn't it, Mother?'

Her mother looked up, eyes big behind her reading glasses.

'There's rain in the forecast.'

Edie sighed. There was always rain in Mother's forecasts.

Then Edie noticed the small bag in the middle of the table, one of those paper bags pharmacies put your tablets into.

'Did you call to the chemist?'

A rustle of pages.

'I popped into Dr Brown to have my blood pressure checked.'

Instantly Edie felt a stab of guilt. She had forgotten to tell Charlie about Mother.

'So, how was it, your blood pressure?'

She began to flick through the post.

'A bit up, nothing major.'

Edie looked up.

'What was it?'

'One hundred and sixty over a hundred. He started me on another blood pressure tablet.'

'Not Cardelia, I hope.'

Her mother smiled.

'No, not Cardelia'.

'Did you tell Charlie?'

'I don't want to be bothering Charlie. Besides, you're right, Charlie shouldn't be treating his own family. And I don't want you telling him, do you hear me?'

Her mother's tone was firm.

'Yes, Mother.'

Edie turned away. The words 'Yes, Mother' echoed in her brain. How many times had she said those two little words? A thousand times, maybe a million? Maybe she should record 'Yes, Mother' on her Dictaphone, then all she'd have to do was press a button.

A moment later her mother stood up and straightened the tea-towels on the rail in front of the Aga. Oops. She must have brushed against them when she passed.

'I'll be away next week, Mother, what if -'

Her mother put up her hand.

'Stop fussing! I'm fine! I'll be able to get more rest on my own. It'll be nice to have some peace and quiet.'

Edie bit her lip. Is that what she was? An annoyance, a maker of noise, a disturber of the peace?

'I got you some nice Lidl chocolate on my way home, 70% cocoa solids.'

Her mother's tone was softer. She handed Edie the chocolate. Edie looked at the wrapper. 70% cocoa solids just like Mother said. And coconut. She hated coconut. Surely Mother knew that by now? Her favourite chocolate was Cadbury's Caramelo, same as Charlie.

'Thanks.'

Chocolate from Mother. It was Mother's way of saying that the subject of taking a year off was closed. Terminated by chocolate. End of story. Edie bit her lip. Not this time. This time, she was going to do what she wanted, whether Mother liked it or not. And all the chocolate in Lidl wouldn't make one bit of difference.

'I'll change my clothes.'

She reached for her backpack. It slipped off the chair and the contents spilled across the floor. Damn. Her angel cards. Here we go again.

'Don't tell me you brought those silly angel cards to school again. I'm surprised Mr Sampson hasn't banned them. They're worse than those UGIOH cards.'

Edie dropped to her knees and began to gather up the cards. UGIOH! For God's sake! Only Mother could compare UGIOH cards with angel cards.

'Beth likes them.'

'Don't mind Beth, she was always a bit daft. Went on that contraceptive train to Belfast. What about Father Tom, he's the school Chairman, what would he say?'

Edie looked up.

'He wants me to get him some.'

Her mother sighed and shook her head.

'All daft, even the priests...'

She was almost at the door when her mother spoke again.

'They're probably laughing at you.'

A familiar hotness gripped her throat.

'Nobody is laughing at me, Mother.'

'Maybe they are, but you don't know it, like -'

Her mother's voice faded, her words hanging like daggers in the air, the damage done. Edie closed her eyes. Say it, Mother, go on, say it! 'Like the last time'; they might be laughing at you like the last time. She could feel heat in her cheeks now. She looked out the window. The sky had clouded over and the naked trees swayed in fury, like they were shaking their fists at her. The mountains, an hour ago so warm and welcoming were now dark and troubled. Any moment now, it was going to rain.

'That was different. I was sick then.'

'This angel healing, this angel therapy thing, it's all rubbish, can't you see that, child?'

There was a gentleness in her mother's voice, but the words still stung like nettles. They were only cards, for God's sake! Cards!

'Charlie thinks it's all nonsense too.'

Aha! The trump card! She should have known that Mother would drag Charlie into this.

'He's hardly going to start recommending angel therapy, is he, Mother? Drugs are all that doctors deal in.'

There was a short silence.

'You don't actually see, or hear these angels, do you, Edie?'

Oh for God's sake!

'You mean am I having any visual or auditory hallucinations? First rank psychotic symptoms? No, Mother, I'm not! I don't see angels, nobody sees angels!'

But she could feel them sometimes, like a breeze on her face or a rustling at her shoulder. But best not mention this. She took a long, practised breath. Deep and wide.

'I'm not mad, Mother, or whatever word you'd prefer to use, 'unstable', I think was your favourite.'

Instantly, Edie regretted her words. Her mother's face paled, and her ash blonde hair seemed to merge with her skin. Edie moved to touch her, to tell her that she was sorry. Then her mother looked up.

'I don't know how you can be so stupid.'

Edie's hand froze. Slowly, she turned and walked away.


It was almost midnight when she turned off the light. The corners of the pillowcase were hard and ropey from rolling them between her fingers, a childhood habit. Mother had called her stupid. She had apologised later, of course. After dinner, just after pouring the tea. But it was too late; the hurt was already a handprint on her heart, along with all the other handprints of hurt. Her hand moved to touch her face, and she remembered another time.

Her cheek had been red for hours afterwards, hot and stinging like a burn from a kettle.

She must have been about twelve, first year in Thurles, her first weekend at home. Mother had found her diary. And, being Mother, she had read it. And, of course, she had found the bit about Charlie. Edie had never seen her in such a fury before; her eyes were wild and her voice all shrill and squeaky. Then her hand appeared out of nowhere. Over and back. Over and back. Then the stinging shame. After that she stopped writing in her diary.

She closed her eyes, pushing away the memories. Oh to be millions of miles away from here! This room, the bedroom that had been hers for nearly thirty years, was choking her. Even the books that filled the room threatened to suffocate her. Charlie said she owned every self-help book ever written. Like as if it was a bad thing. He probably thought she was stupid too.

She felt a hotness prick the back of her eyes. What harm did her books do, or her angel cards? She had bought them with her own money. She had never asked him, or Mother, or anyone else, to read them. She had never said that they had the answers.

She reached down and turned off the electric blanket. Even though the central heating had been on since five, the room was still cold. She pulled the duvet up around her shoulders. You just couldn't warm some houses. It was the same with people, she supposed.

# 9

Charlie opened the library door and looked around. Good, the room was empty apart from two surgical SHOs down the back, staring at their screens, probably on 'eBay' or 'MySpace' judging by the looks of concentration on their faces. Now was as good a time as any. He slipped the card out of his pocket and reached for the pen in front of him. Red pen. Always red pen and block capitals.

*'TO MY DARLING VALENTINE'*

*SOME DAY YOU WILL BE MINE.'*

It was a short and simple message, the kind of one he knew she'd like, nothing distasteful or smutty. He didn't want her to think that some creepy lech might have sent it. It was the usual type of card; nothing too fancy, the usual flowers on the front. This one had primroses and daffodils on the cover and inside, a big yellow rose. Yellow was her favourite colour. Now for the difficult bit. What had he written on last year's card? *'You are always in my heart.'* Or was it *'From a secret admirer?'* Would it matter if he wrote the same thing again? Then he smiled and began to write.

*'YOU LIGHT UP MY LIFE.'*

Perfect. He closed the envelope. Now for the address, block capitals again, of course. She'd probably analyse the envelope too, knowing her. A moment later, he sat back and smiled. Finished. Now all he had to do was to give the card to Tommy to post on his way down to Tipp. Keep her guessing. He smiled. Tomorrow, she would have her Valentine's card.


Twenty minutes later, he pushed through the doors of St Anthony's. He wasn't looking forward to what lay ahead, but someone had to do it, and today, that someone was him. The silence hit him immediately when he opened the door; no radios, no television, not even the sound of women chatting. He supposed it was how the patients showed their respect. Or maybe death hit you more when you were lying in a hospital bed. A woman looked up from her rosary beads and nodded. Then Father Kennedy, the chaplain, appeared from behind the curtains of the bed in front of him.

'Morning, Father.'

'Morning, Charlie.'

Normally they discussed the Sunday matches but not today. Slowly, he pulled the curtains closed behind him. They made less noise when you did it slowly; less abrasive, less grating.

He turned around. In front of him lay the freshly dead body of an elderly man admitted three days ago with chest pain. Sitting beside the bed, the man's wife, holding his marble hand in hers, silent tears glistening on her cheeks. Her face reminded Charlie of a broken eggshell, shattered and cracked. He'd give anything not to be here, but some-one had to talk to the family and somehow, it was usually him. He reached out and touched the woman's arm.

'I'm sorry, Mrs Kelly. We did what we could but it was a massive heart attack.'

The woman nodded. Her eyes, glazed with grief, never left her husband's face.

He remembered speaking to her briefly the night her husband came in; he remembered telling her that there was nothing to worry about.

'He seemed to be doing fine; that's why we sent him back to the ward. He was in great form yesterday; we had a big chat about Cheltenham.'

This time, her eyes met his. She smiled and nodded.

'Yes, he told me.'

Something about her reminded him of Mother. Maybe it was the tiny wrinkles fanning out from her eyes or perhaps it was the colour of her hair. Or maybe it was that opaque loneliness in her eyes; the mark of widowhood.

'The children are on their way... God love them.'

Her voice trailed off.

'My father died when I was nine.'

Charlie stopped, surprised by his sudden revelation.

'He must have been very young. What happened?'

Her voice was gentle.

'Cancer.'

Liver cancer, probably caused by alcoholic liver damage. Killed by the booze, in other words. But no point in burdening Mrs Kelly with the details. He looked away, his eyes resting on the bedside locker, on the half-empty Lucozade bottle that would now be thrown out.

'It must have been hard for your mother.'

He nodded. He had never given much thought to what it must have been like for Mother. After Dad died, she had continued on as normal, running the show, calling the shots, just like she had always done.

'At least Mikey got to see his grandchildren. Poor Mikey.'

The tears began to flow again. Charlie put his arm around her sunken shoulders.

'He didn't have any pain.'

She nodded.

'I said good-bye to him while you were resuscitating him. Wonder if he heard me.'

Her words floated in the air. Charlie touched her hand. It was important to say goodbye.

'He was probably looking down on us.'

My God, had he really said that? He was beginning to sound like Edie. Then the woman gripped his hand and squeezed it tightly.

'Thank you, Doctor Darmody, you've been so kind, right from the start.'

The woman's face lingered in Charlie's mind as he rounded the corridor towards Coronary Care. Somehow, despite the circumstances, he was glad that he'd spoken to her. He had touched on something, he wasn't quite sure what, but whatever it was made him feel good. In some small way, he'd made a difference.

A few minutes later, he pushed through the doors of CCU. Clements looked up and smiled.

'Ah, Charlie, there you are! Another free bed, I hear.'

Charlie nodded. Somehow he couldn't bring himself to return Clements' smile.

'A quick word, Charlie, if I may.'

Charlie followed him over to the window. Down below, in the car park, he could see two women hurrying towards the entrance. He could see by their shoulders that they were crying. He felt a dart of sadness. Mr Kelly's daughters.

'I've got two privates coming in later for 24 hour holter and stress testing, can you take care of it, Charlie?'

His voice was low and confidential.

'Sure.'

Wonder what VHI would say if they knew that the only thing Clements did for his fees was to shake hands and sign the claim forms. Not bad if you could get it.

'Has Marianne been on to you?'

Charlie's hand moved to his pocket.

'I must have left my mobile in the office.'

'It was about the article, I think.'

A thin, apologetic smile.

'I left it on your desk.'

A flash of teeth.

'Great stuff, Charlie! You're a dinger! I'll have a look at it straight away. Not that there's any need.'

Charlie felt a hand on his shoulder.

'You know, Charlie, you remind me of myself at your age, bursting with energy. Keep it up, and remember, no survivors.'

Charlie nodded. He knew what Clements meant. No survivors meant head down, the end goal always in sight, keep the focus, no mercy, no distractions. You had to stay on track, no matter what.

A few minutes later, Charlie flicked his mobile open. Marianne.

'Charlie! I was beginning to think you'd left the country! I suppose you were busy saving lives.'

Charlie hesitated.

'Not his time.'

'How was your weekend?'

Charlie smiled. Marianne always touched base on a personal level first. Maybe this was something they taught in communications courses.

'Great. And yours?'

'Working, I'm afraid, up to my eyes with the Diastora launch. There's never a dull day in medical PR.'

A tinkle of a laugh.

'Suppose not.'

'How's the article coming along?'

'It's finished. I'll email it to you when John has read it.'

'That's fantastic, Charlie! If only all our writers were like you!'

A short pause.

'Can I dare mention the other articles?'

Her voice was girly girly, sweety sweety.

'The risk factor one is almost done, I'll finish it tonight.'

'Brilliant! I'll touch base with you tomorrow, so.'

A golden tinkle, her arm bracelets merging with her laughter.

'Oh, Charlie, I almost forgot! There's a GoldMed presentation on Friday - *'The role of the pharmaceutical industry in medical education.'* John said you might like to come. It should be interesting.'

Charlie smiled. Interesting for whom?

'What time is it on?'

'Seven forty-five. It's a breakfast meeting at the Trinity Plaza, everyone seems to want breakfast meetings these days.'

Of course everyone wanted breakfast meetings. It shortened Friday. Most of them probably continued straight on to the golf course.

'I don't know...'

'It'll be over by nine. John says it's fine.'

Of course Clements would say that it was fine! Fine for him! But he wouldn't be the one spending the rest of the day catching up. If he went to the meeting, he could kiss goodbye to splitting early.

'Who's the speaker?'

'Me.'

'You any good?'

'Depends.'

He smiled.

'I'll think about it.'

'You have to come, Charlie! You're part of the team!'

Charlie smiled. Sounded like she really wanted him there.

'OK, but I want a proper breakfast, not yoghurt and organic muesli.'

'Rashers and sausages. And eggs, of course, any way you want them.'

Charlie laughed.

'Black pudding?'

'Loads of black pudding. I guarantee you the fry of your life.'

'OK, it's a deal.'

'Great! See you Friday, so. Seven forty-five. The Trinity Plaza.'

And then she was gone. Mission complete.


Charlie handed Clements the chart. Good, only one more patient to see. Somehow, he felt tired. Those fluorescent hospital lights always seemed to sap his energy. Or maybe it was the wards themselves; crowded, airless, choking, too many bodies, too little space. No wonder people got MRSA in hospital. Wet days like today were the worst; somehow the smells of puke and sweat and diarrhoea seemed to linger. To make matters worse, in the new part of the hospital, you couldn't even open the windows. Jumping out was no longer an option.

He looked up, waiting for Clements' nod. Then he clicked the angio film into the viewing box and stepped sideways. He could see the anxious look on the patient's face and felt a prickle of irritation. What was taking Clements so long? He'd already seen the radiologist's report; he knew the right coronary artery was almost completely occluded. It was as if he enjoyed the build up to bad news.

'Mr Cotter… your angiogram has shown a critical blockage in one of your main coronary arteries. You need an angioplasty. Do you know what an angioplasty is?'

'No, Doctor.'

'Charlie?'

Charlie moved closer.

'An angioplasty is where a special balloon device is passed into a blocked blood vessel and expanded, breaking through the blockage. Then we put in a stent, it's a kind of internal splint device to keep the walls of the artery open.'

'Is it… serious?'

Clements stepped in front of him.

'It's a complicated and dangerous technique but we get excellent results here in this unit. By doing an angioplasty, we can save your life and keep the surgeons away from you.'

A pause for the information to settle. Then the patient's low murmur.

'Thank you, Doctor Clements.'

Charlie mentally added another angioplasty to Friday's list. That made seven. The Cardiac Unit at St. Anne's did more angioplasties than anywhere else in the country. Angioplasties were big business. The biggest payout by medical insurers over the last five years. No wonder Clements liked them. It was like unblocking a drain for two thousand euro a go. Not bad for a little bit of plumbing. Just the thing he himself might get into in a few years' time. Maybe he'd do nothing else but angioplasties, then he'd really be coining it.

Finally. The ward round was over. Charlie grabbed a bundle of X-rays and hurried down the corridor. Some of the films hadn't been reported on yet and he needed to return then straight away or he'd be in deep shit with the radiologists.

Suddenly he felt a hand on his shoulder and jumped. Clements! The man had an unnerving habit of creeping up on you. He was like a thief in the dark, swift and silent. Must be his soft Italian shoes.

'Great article, Charlie boy! Couldn't have done better myself.'

Ha. Ha. Ha. An arm around his shoulder now. The smell of spicy aftershave.

'Can I email it to Marianne?'

Clements nodded.

'Please.'

Then his voice lowered.

'She's something, isn't she, Charlie? A babe with brains. Not too many of those around. If people like her were running the health service, we'd have no trolleys in Casualty.'

Or patients, thought Charlie.

'Marianne told me you're almost finished the second article.'

Charlie nodded. Word sure travelled fast.

'I need to go over it again.'

'Oh, I'm sure it's fine, Charlie. Don't waste too much time on it. After all, it's only *Medicine Now*, not the bloody *Lancet*.'

Yeah, right.

'I must say that blasted Cardelia thing took us all by surprise. Diastora wasn't due to be launched for another three weeks but luckily they managed to get the product licence pushed through.'

Charlie nodded. Yeah, very lucky.

'Don't forget the meeting tonight.'

Shit. He'd forgotten all about the Hypertension Advisory Board meeting! Jesus, any more time with GoldMed and he'd start dressing like those PR types with their tight shirts and their pointy shoes. And that was only the men.

'It'll be good for you to see how these things work, Charlie. Advisory boards are part of the course, part of every business. And cardiology is our business; we're the ones to set the agenda, to draft the clinical guidelines, to develop the educational materials. We're the doctors, Charlie, we call the shots. WorldPharma takes a back seat. Their role is purely observer.'

Hmm. Then Clements smiled. It was as if he knew what Charlie was thinking.

'Someone's got to fund these boards, Charlie, and it certainly won't be our Minister for Health, that's for sure.'

'John…'

Charlie hesitated. He had to be careful how he put this.

'Yes?'

'Has being a 'key opinion leader' caused any problems for you with your medical colleagues?'

Last thing he wanted to do was to jeopardise his chance of a consultant's post.

'Problems? Why should it? There'll always be a few jealous begrudgers but feck them. Nobody's going to tell me what to say and do. I don' t mind if a company gets mileage out of the fact I use their drug. I'm not going to use something that doesn't work, Charlie. And I've no problem mentioning something that does. Take Diastora, for example, it's a good drug, pricey, but effective. It's in the right place at the right time. I'm happy to stand over it.'

A moment later, Charlie pushed through the doors of Coronary Care. Maybe Clements was right. Feck the begrudgers. Being seen and heard was part of the course. And that was exactly what he planned to do.

# 10

Charlie slipped into a seat at the end of the table and smiled. Just in time. He reached for the bowl of mints in front of him. At least he hoped they were mints and not some bloody cardiac drug. The door opened and the room fell silent. Charlie smiled. It seemed like every man in the room was sitting straighter. There were no legs on display today, but Marianne looked very sexy in a tight black trouser suit and high, clinky heels. Her lips were shiny and moist, probably one of those lip-gloss things Edie used. She glanced around the table, her eyes resting briefly on each person in turn.

'Good evening, everyone! Glad you could all make it. Before I begin, I just want to let you know that the Diastora launch has been brought forward to the 12th of March. Our keynote speaker is Professor Kenneth Jenkins from Liverpool, whom I'm sure everyone here is familiar with.'

Charlie smiled. Last time he heard Jenkins speak was at the Cardelia launch eighteen months ago.

The next twenty minutes were a pleasant blur. Marianne did her usual patter about the board being independent blah blah increasing awareness of hypertension blah blah educating healthcare providers (he hated that word), media activities blah blah. Then she stopped and glanced down at Clements.

'Thank you, John, for an excellent interview on *Morning Ireland*. The feedback was very positive.'

A Richter ten smile.

'OK, professional tools. What has been suggested,' (Charlie wondered by whom) 'is an algorithm for treating hypertension, a stepwise approach to treatment. Anyone got any thoughts on this?'

A short cough from somewhere.

'Hasn't this been done already?'

'Not with the latest drug classes included.'

Aah! Of course! Charlie smiled. There was a short silence, then Clements spoke.

'Sounds a great idea, Marianne. Doctors could keep it on their desks.'

'Exactly, John, we could laminate it and perhaps we could do a fridge magnet version.'

A hand went up at the end of the table. It was Ted Crowley, one of the Limerick cardiologists.

'I take it that the algorithm will be in line with the latest guidelines from the *European Society of Hypertension*?'

A dazzling smile.

'Of course, Ted. Dr Darmody here is going to do the initial draft, as I know how busy you all are. Then we'll send it to every member of the board for their comments. We won't sign off on this until every one is satisfied with the content. After all, we're not doctors; you are.'

A nervous cough from down the back.

'After the algorithm has been approved, we'll send it to all the relevant professional organizations for their endorsement; e.g. The Irish College of General Practitioners, the Irish Nurses' Organization and the Irish Heart Foundation. Any questions?'

Charlie could feel his tummy gurgle. Dinner would be nice.

'Finally, the patient handout on hypertension.'

A low mumble from around the table. Then the Limerick cardiologist again.

'Surely waiting rooms are swamped with stuff like this?'

Charlie smiled. Trust Ted Crowley. Just because it wasn't his idea. He was a pompous old bastard at the best of times. Charlie looked at Marianne. Cool under fire, as usual. An even smile. Hands open, nothing to hide.

'I'm only too well aware of the vast amount of unsolicited material that doctors receive every day, Ted. That's why we're designing this fact-file as a pocket-sized leaflet that can double as a patient medication card.'

An approving nod.

'It will be short and concise; ten key bullet points. You'll all be sent a draft before it hits the printers. It will also be available on CD and can be customised on practice computers for individual patients. We also plan to get a senior RTÉ personality to host a podcast on hypertension that patients can download.'

Charlie could see the look on Ted Crowley's face. What the fuck was a podcast?

'OK... back to the articles... Dr Darmody has kindly agreed to do the first drafts.'

A smile in Charlie's direction. Then she looked away and it was like someone had turned off a light.

'Finally, because of the unprecedented demand, we did have some initial problems with distribution of Diastora but that's all sorted now. As you all know, Diastora is a new category of anti-hypertensive and obviously we need to fill an information gap. We see the launch as an ideal educational platform and are confident that we can generate a lot of noise especially since the Irish Heart Foundation kicks off their 'Healthy Heart' week the same day.'

Charlie smiled. Nice one, Marianne. She sure let nothing pass that could be useful. He wondered if she did the same with men.


Charlie put down the menu and looked at his watch. Almost nine-thirty. If he didn't eat soon, he'd collapse. Still no sign of Marianne and Clements. He wished they'd hurry up. He reached for a bread roll. Then he felt a hand touch his arm.

'Mind if I sit here?'

'No, of course not.'

He could smell her perfume, something sweet and fruity, strawberry or maybe passion fruit.

'Well, have you decided?'

'What?'

'What you're going to eat, silly.'

A soft flutter of eyelashes.

'Steak, with pepper sauce.'

It was the only thing he recognized as near-normal food on the menu. I mean, kangaroo, for God's sake!

'Man-food. I'll have the same.'

She closed the menu with a decisive little snap. Then she looked across the table and shook her head.

'I wish Dr Reynolds could decide on the bloody wine! That's the thing about connoisseurs, they study the wine list as if it was a legal document.'

Charlie laughed.

'Did you know that Dr Clements has his own wine cellar, dusty bottles, thermometers, the works.'

She nodded. 'I know.'

Suddenly she was on her feet.

'I can't wait any longer. I'm getting a G and T, want one?'

Her eyes twinkled.

'Sure.'


Snippets of conversation drifted across the table. Joe Fleming was talking holidays, the word 'Tuscany' had been mentioned a few times. Safe topic, holidays. Hard to go wrong. Prof Reynolds was still lost in the wine menu. Clements was talking shop with a Cork consultant and Ted Crowley, the Limerick guy, quiet as a lamb now, was buttering a bread roll. Suddenly he heard the tinkle of ice. She was back.

'Here you are, Charlie! Sparkling water, wasn't it?'

Their hands touched briefly. Then her eyes fixed his.

'Cheers, Charlie! To the future.'

She clinked his glass.

'Remember you promised to have dinner with me before you go? How about Shanahan's?'

Hmm. Shanahan's on the Green cost a small fortune. Still, if someone else was paying and especially if that someone happened to be Marianne…

'Sounds great.'

Her eyes were deep cornflower blue. Innocent, deceptive eyes. Killer eyes with long, curling, strangling eyelashes. Yet, her face had a certain fragile quality, almost childish, as if she needed to be protected. Like Edie. But, of course, Marianne was nothing like Edie. She didn't need to be protected. It was the other way round.

'So, you still good for Friday?'

Friday? Then he remembered - the GoldMed 'Big Breakfast', the one where Marianne was going to rally the troops.

'Sure. You promised me the mother of all breakfasts.'

She looked directly at him.

'So you like breakfast. I must remember that.'

# 11

Edie opened her eyes and smiled. She knew exactly what day it was. St Valentine's day, the next best day to Christmas Day. She slipped out of bed and tiptoed across the room. Slowly, she creaked open the bedroom door and crept down the stairs.

At the end of the stairs, she took a deep breath and looked up. A wave of disappointment hit her. The mat inside the door was empty. Nada. Zilch. Rien. She stared at it for a moment, then sank to the floor. Maybe the post was late. Or maybe he hadn't sent any card this year...

Suddenly, she straightened. She could hear noises on the landing; a door opening, closing... Oh God, don't tell me she's up! Her eyes remained fixed on the letterbox, willing something to fall through. A flush of a toilet. A door opening; a soft footfall on the landing.

'Edie!'

She hesitated a moment.

'Yes, Mother! I'm down here!'

'You're up already? Can you put the porridge on the Aga?'

'OK.'

Damn! Trust Mother to be up early today of all days; it was just after seven-thirty. Neither of them normally left home until ten to nine; it was one of the advantages of teaching locally. Reluctantly, she stood up. The mat in front of her seemed to grow in size, brown and ugly, mocking her. Suddenly, there was a flash of colour and movement, a delicious little clack, and there it was, a large pink envelope. She fell to her knees and lifted it to her chest. This time yesterday he was holding this.

She hurried into the downstairs toilet and turned the key. Carefully, she coaxed the envelope open and smiled when she saw the cover. Flowers again, this time beautiful yellow flowers, her favourite. Slowly, she opened the card. Red pen, just like before. And block capitals.

'YOU LIGHT UP MY LIFE.'

How simple, yet how lovely! She pressed the card against her chest and closed her eyes. Who was this 'secret admirer' that sent her a card every year? The postmark said Cashel. It had to be someone she knew. It had to be.

Suddenly she heard her mother's step on the stairs. Quickly, she slipped the card under her nightie. Between now and bedtime she would memorise every detail. But right now, the card was still fresh and unexplored, waiting to be discovered.

Back in the hallway, it didn't seem that cold any more. Through the oval window near the door, she could see pools of sunshine drench the budding daffodils. Everything was perfectly still. She felt a deep, warm calm. Someone, somewhere, loved her. And she loved him too.

It was just after three when Edie reached the shop. The girl with the chirpy voice that Edie imagined belonged to someone with long nails and perfect make-up, had told her that the auctioneer would meet her here at three-fifteen. That meant she had ten minutes to herself. She leaned her bike against the wall. Time for a little poke around.

First, the roof. Apparently roofs were very important, according to that property magazine she'd bought. She crossed the road to get a better view.

From what she could see, the roof looked OK; no big holes or anything. And the slates were nice; different shades that changed colour with the light, merging like heathers into a deep purple hue. The drainpipes were a bit dodgy but surely that wouldn't be a major job. And the chimney looked fine. She buttoned her coat. Wonder how much they wanted? Dilapidated and all as it was, it was still commercial. Then again, it was off the main drag and a bit too small for most businesses. Somehow she had a good feeling about this. Maybe it might just be possible.

The rain was beginning to fall now, teasing little wafts of spray that played on the breeze. Here one minute, gone the next. Like most things. Edie tightened her scarf around her neck. Not much longer now before Mr Sherry or Fitz or Doyle or whatever he was called, arrived.

'Edie Darmody?'

Speak of the devil.

'Yes, that's me.'

He was about her own age; leather jacket, black polo, very snazzy. His smile faded when he saw the bicycle. No car obviously meant no money in auctioneers' eyes.

'OK, shall we get going? I've another appointment at four.'

His tone was clipped. Edie lowered her chin; she felt like she had already been dismissed, just like those job interviews where somehow her medical history had preceded her.

Edie stepped inside and smiled. It was just as she had imagined; high brown counters, tall glass cabinets like the old chemist shops and yellow newspapers scattered on the floor.

'Best thing, if you ask me, would be a knock job, put up a townhouse, maybe two.'

Edie's hand flew to her mouth. How could he even think of knocking it down?

'What kind of shop was it?'

A shrug.

'Holy statues, rosary beads, religious things. Been shut for twelve years, bit of a downturn in that market, I suppose.'

He laughed, and Edie saw his eyes turn to the skips and cranes across the road. His kind of religion.


She followed him into the kitchen and immediately her eyes were drawn to the dresser; willow pattern mugs, books, biscuit tins, old photographs, even an old brown radio. She smiled. Life's little treasures. How lovely.

'What happened to the owner?'

'Died a few months ago in a nursing home. Left it to some niece from Limerick. She wants a quick sale.'

'What about the furniture?'

Edie's eyes returned to the dresser.

'Furniture? It's all rubbish. Full of woodworm. Nobody wants this kind of stuff anymore. She'll probably throw it in, save her hiring a skip.'

'Can I see the garden?'

A pause.

'It's raining.'

'I don't care.'

He sighed and began to fiddle with the keys.


A few minutes later, she bent down to pick a snowdrop. She was glad he had stayed inside; there was something private about this forgotten garden, something that couldn't be shared with someone who only saw houses as currency. Down at the end, she could see the fragile candyfloss of a cherry blossom tree and some apple trees, gnarled and stunted with age. The wall on her right was covered with clematis, Charlie's favourite flower.

'Like I said, plenty of space for an extension or maybe two townhouses.'

She jumped. Townhouses indeed! Save cutting the grass and weeding and pruning, she would leave this garden exactly as it was.

'I'm afraid we have to go, I've -'

'- Another appointment. I know.'

She hesitated a moment.

'How much?'

His eyes widened.

'You serious?'

She met his gaze and nodded.

'Three eighty.'

'Three hundred and eighty thousand?'

'Like I said, it's commercial, plenty of room to expand out back. Or get planning for two townhouses and sell them on.'

Edie bit her lip. Three hundred and eighty thousand euro! It was an awful lot of money.

'How much of a deposit would I need?'

A slow shrug.

'Twenty.'

Edie swallowed. She'd have to borrow from the Credit Union, say that she was changing her car. Or getting dental implants. Maybe Charlie might help her; after all, he was the one always saying that she should invest in property.

'I'll call in tomorrow after school.'

'You a teacher?'

A spark of interest.

'Yes.'

And I do have a car, actually, just like yours, except it's a year younger.

'You have any investment properties already?'

'No.'

She could read his eyes. Gee, the only twenty nine year old in Ireland without a mortgage.

'Here's my card. It's a good buy, lots of potential. You've chosen well.'

For a property virgin. Edie tucked the card in her pocket. Auctioneers were all the same, all gab and sucky-uppy if there was a deal in sight. Mother always said that auctioneers were thick as planks. She should know, she'd taught enough of them over the years. Mind you, thick and all as they were, they weren't doing too badly for themselves...

It was just after seven when Edie opened her bedroom door. Eddie Hobbs had just started which meant that Mother would be glued to the TV for the next forty minutes. Normally she watched it too; it made her feel good to know that there were people out there even worse at managing money than she was. But tonight she made some excuse about having to do corrections. She needed time on her own; time to plan what she was going to say at the Credit Union, time to think about what she'd stock in the shop.

110

She went through her list again. First the angel therapy section; books, tapes, cards, posters, little statues and stuff. Then the books; spiritual, holistic medicine, nutrition, yoga, psychology, the works. She might even put in some seating where people could sit and read, like that dinky bookshop in Schull. She'd have a health food section, of course; supplements, vitamins, the usual. She might even make her own gluten-free bread. She could use the old cabinets to display crystals and essential oils, maybe a range of burners and scented candles. Yoga mats and relaxation tapes were another thing. She smiled. There was certainly no shortage of items for 'Spiritual Me' alias 'Spiritual Miscellany' (she couldn't decide between the two).

Suddenly her mother's voice bounced up the stairs.

'Edie, it's on! The weather!'

Edie sighed. What was it with Mother and the weather? I mean, it wasn't as if they lived in a bloody hurricane zone like poor cousin Beatrice who lost everything in Katrina. And if it didn't rain today, it would rain tomorrow. Everyone knew that.

'Coming!'

But first, another quick peep. She reached under the pillow and pulled out her card. She looked at the cover for a moment, then she opened it and ran her fingers over the message, tracing every letter. Could it be Tony, that pharmacist from Cahir? He was the last guy she had gone out with, about two years ago. He still texted her; stupid blonde jokes and stuff. The only reason she had gone out with him was that he had eyes like Charlie. But he was nothing like Charlie. No sense of humour. Zero. She sighed. Silly, really, comparing guys to Charlie, but she couldn't help it. Charlie was everything she wanted in a guy; funny, kind, intelligent. At the thought of Charlie, she felt a sudden twinge of guilt. She had promised that she wouldn't do anything about the shop. And, for the first time in her life, she had broken a promise.

111

# 12

Charlie glanced around the room and smiled. One thing was certain; Marianne sure knew how to pull a crowd. There must be at least two hundred people here; drug reps, product managers, marketing managers, MDs, all rungs of the pharmaceutical ladder. At the top of the room, a giant blue screen, with the words '*Today and Tomorrow*'. It reminded him of the time himself and Killian gatecrashed a Fianna Fail Ard Fheis thinking it was a wedding.

He reached for a glass and poured some orange juice. Freshly squeezed, just as he liked it. A waiter appeared beside him and handed him a menu.

'I'll have the heart-stopper, please.'

'Excuse?'

'I mean the full Irish, please.'

He put down his glass and glanced around the room again. It was kind of ironic, really; I mean here they all were, stuffing their faces with platefuls of saturated fats, all courtesy of the world's biggest manufacturer of cholesterol-lowering drugs! His eyes rested on a balding man at the next table. The man was eating hungrily, his plate piled high with food. The two women on either side, however, stabbed the air with empty forks. Nothing seemed to reach their lips. Charlie smiled. Female drug reps were all the same. Ate nothing, zilch. All skinny, of course, totally the opposite to their male counterparts with their big bellies. Amazing, really, the difference between how men and women react to corporate hospitality. The women keep on getting thinner and thinner, while the men get fatter and fatter. It would make for a nice piece of evidence-based research.

Then he heard a familiar laugh. Marianne, a few tables away, leaning over a chair, talking to some guy in a dicky-bow. The man began to laugh and Charlie felt a dart of jealousy. He wondered what Marianne had said to make the man laugh. Then she saw him and winked; a slow, heavy-lidded, secret wink. He smiled and winked back, communication established.

A moment later, she began to weave her way towards the podium. Her suit was purple, short jacket, pencil skirt. Purple suited her, made her look kind of regal. A corporate purple princess.

Suddenly a plate appeared in front of him. Great stuff. Rashers, sausages, eggs, black pudding, mushrooms; the mother of all breakfasts just like she had promised him. Good. He liked a woman who delivered.

She raised her hand. An A1 smile. No rasher between her teeth. A sudden hush descended; even the waiters were still. Show time.

'Good morning, everyone and thank you all for coming, I know you all have busy schedules. Today, I'm going to talk to you about your world, the pharmaceutical industry; a profession under attack.'

Her words were slow and clipped, every syllable carefully enunciated. Charlie cut some more bacon; nice and salty, the way he liked it.

'Ladies and gentlemen, the pharmaceutical industry is being fired on from all quarters. It is seen as reaping excessive gains, of buying favour with key opinion leaders and of trying to unduly influence prescribers.'

A controlled murmur like the benches at the House of Lords.

'The pharmaceutical industry is accused of benefiting the developed world and ignoring less developed continents. Drug prices and profits have recently become a political story and a target for public outrage. According to John Le Carré; *'Big Pharma is engaged in the deliberate seduction of the medical profession, country by country, worldwide. It is spending a fortune on influencing, hiring and purchasing academic judgement to a point where, in a few years' time, if Big Pharma continues unchecked on its present happy path, unbought medical opinion will be hard to find.'*

A collective intake of breath. A voice somewhere to Charlie's right.

'Last time I'm buying his books. Wanker.'

All eyes were on the podium.

'According to an article in the *Economist*, 'legalised bribery' is what some drug reps call their employers' marketing. And further down the article we read: *'Drug firms are having to work harder to build relationships with doctors, repositioning themselves as providers of medical education, without this coming across as a bribe.'*

Charlie put down his fork. The room was silent.

'Ladies and gentlemen, these statements, these hostile attitudes, these false accusations, cannot go unchallenged. It is the pharmaceutical industry that fills the educational and research gaps ignored by our government. And it is time the pharmaceutical industry defended itself.'

A loud murmur of agreement.

'GoldMed, Ladies and Gentlemen, can help you.'

The lights dimmed and Charlie scanned down through the bullet points. He put down his cup. This should be interesting.

'First, show face. When something unfortunate happens, don't try to hide behind the receptionist. Get out there, show face, smile, look human. If your

MD can't do it, then hire a medical person as your spokesperson, someone who can be the acceptable face of your company.'

Charlie reached for a slice of toast. It was cold, like damp cardboard. Toast should be buttered hot. Even the hospital canteen made fresh toast.

'Next - don't think sick, think well. Nobody likes the idea of making money out of the misfortune of others. Focus on the fact that your statin is normalising someone's cholesterol so that they can lead a normal life and emphasise the health-promoting aspects of medicines. Sponsor positive health issues like running tracks, healthy diet campaigns and sports events. Let the pharma industry be the face of wellness, not sickness.'

A loud clapping from up front.

'Corporate health. Does your company promote healthy lifestyle and wellness programmes? What food choices are available in your canteen? Think in-house gym, stress management programmes, yoga, Tai Chi, Pilates. Practice what you preach, boys.'

A shower of nervous laughter.

'Next - learn how to say sorry. Meet controversy head on; apologise and get on with it.'

Charlie smiled. She made it all sound so simple. He picked up a croissant. Cold. It felt like it had just come out of the freezer. Cold toast and freezing croissants. Jesus.

'Finally, chill out, guys! Life isn't that bad! Let's lose the image of bald guys in dark suits.'

A few embarrassed coughs.

'Lighten up! Be approachable! Dress down on Friday, heck, dress down on Monday too!'

Another laugh. Then her voice became low, almost confidential.

'GoldMed can help you. This is what we do. And we do it very well. We have a good team here in Dublin. We know your business. We know the market. We know the regulatory environment. We can be your independent advisor, your finger on the media pulse, your provider of medical education. GoldMed has strong links with a number of different organizations including professional bodies, government agencies, lobby groups, NGOs and patient focus groups.'

Charlie pushed his plate away. Strange, but he was no longer hungry. So much for the fry of his life; he'd barely touched it. All around him, people were on their feet. Then he felt a slap on the shoulder, the kind of slap given by men who have played rugby.

'She should be on stage.'

Charlie nodded.

'She is.'

At the door, he turned. She was standing at the top of the room, her face flushed with success. Around her, a sea of smiling, balding, nameless men. All looking for redemption. He hurried down the corridor. Strange, but his tummy felt slightly queasy, like something hadn't agreed with him. Maybe he shouldn't have eaten that bacon.

# 13

Twenty minutes later, Charlie folded his paper and stepped on the Luas. Good. There were a few free seats. Then again, it was after nine, most people were probably already at work. A few stops later, however, the tram was crowded. Probably the Friday rush to Heuston Station.

Then he noticed the girl standing in front of him. Might as well do the gentlemanly thing and offer her a seat. Besides, St Anne's was only two stops away. He stood up and tapped her on the shoulder.

'Would you like a seat?'

Icy eyes met his.

'No.'

Even as she spoke he could see her suck in her tummy. Shit. Shit. Shit. For a brief moment he thought she might hit him; women were so aggressive these days. There weren't too many Edies around, for sure.

He caught the eye of a middle-aged woman and smiled. She reminded him of Mother, the way she held the handbag on her lap with both hands. She looked away. He shrugged and reached for his mobile; might as well check his messages. Friendly Irish, how are you. He clicked on the Inbox. Good, a text from Edie.

'Got real cool valtine card.'

He smiled and was about to flip the phone closed when another text came through.

'Hope u enjoyed presentation. Thanks for coming.'

'Enjoy' wasn't exactly the word he had in mind. Mind you, he couldn't help but feel a certain grudging admiration for the pharmaceutical industry; they sure were ahead of the posse when it came to putting a spin on things.


The round had already started when he reached the wards. Charlie hurried over to where Clements was standing.

'Sorry for being late.'

Clements looked up and smiled.

'No problem, Charlie, you couldn't help it. I suppose Marianne played a blinder?'

Charlie nodded.

'Yeah, she sure did.'

They moved on to the next patient; a middle-aged man with severe hypertension. Charlie glanced at the drug chart. He could see the thick red line through Cardelia. Diastora had been added in blue pen, one hundred mg twice daily, maximum dose.

'Blood pressure still not satisfactory. What do you think, Charlie, a low dose of an ARB perhaps?'

There was a little cough and then a woman's voice.

'Sorry, Dr Clements, aren't ARBs contraindicated with lithium?'

It was Marie-Theresa, a pretty little Filipino nurse who had joined the staff about a year ago. Charlie glanced at the drug chart. Marie-Theresa was right. The man was on lithium. And angiotensin 2 receptor blockers were contraindicated. Charlie looked at Clements. Oops.

'What about the twenty-four hour urinary catecholamines, is the result back?'

His tone was curt.

'We haven't sent a twenty-four hour collection, Doctor Clements.'

'What do you mean 'not sent'? I requested it yesterday!'

Charlie's thoughts flew back to yesterday's ward round. Yes, they had discussed sending urinary catecholamines but Clements had said that it could wait. An intern shuffled beside him. Hope he'd have the cop to keep his mouth shut. No-one spoke. Then Marie-Theresa's tiny voice.

'Sorry, Dr Clements, I must not hear you, I do immediately.'

Charlie sighed. Marie-Theresa's language skills always deteriorated around Dr Clements. Usually her English was perfect. He turned to look at her. Her head was down, her petite frame dwarfed by Clements' tallness. It was as if she was being swallowed up in his shadow. He bit his lip. It wasn't her fault. His eyes moved to the patient. The man's eyes fixed his. Charlie looked away. The man didn't understand. He didn't know the rules of this game, especially the one that said you never, ever criticise a consultant, no matter what. End of story.

Then he remembered Edie. This could be Edie. This could be Edie being bullied and no-one to stand up for her. Things like this didn't happen to Marianne, they happened to the Edies and the Marie-Theresas of this world. He cleared his throat.

'Marie-Theresa is right, Dr Clements. We said we'd wait until Monday to send off the twenty-four collection.'

All was silent. No-body moved. Even the intern with the bad cough had stopped coughing. He could feel Clements' eyes laser through him. Those Bush eyes. Unreadable, unemotional.

'Did we indeed? Well, in light of the patient's current clinical condition, let's revise that decision. There's nothing static about the science of medicine. Diagnoses and decisions need to be re-evaluated on a daily basis. That's why we do a daily ward round. Otherwise we could just do a Monday ward round, what do you think, Charlie?'

Charlie's lips parted but he said nothing. Somehow he got the feeling that Clements was trying to make him look stupid, as if he had meant that once a decision was taken it was final, which wasn't what he had meant at all. But, of course, Clements knew that.

'Sorry, Dr Clements.'

Somehow, he felt an apology was expected. It was obvious that he had pissed Clements off by sticking up for Marie-Theresa. Now he had to make up for it. And if three little words meant that he was back in Clements' good books, so be it.

Clements smiled.

'No problem, Charlie.'

It was just before five when Charlie reached the library. Nearly all the seats were taken; mainly students, heads down before the Finals in six weeks' time. He caught the eye of an attractive redhead and winked. She smiled and held his gaze. He looked away. Back to work, Charlie boy. No time for that right now, even if she is a babe.

He turned back to the screen and clicked the word count; two thousand nine hundred and fifty; still too long. Mind you, he might just get away with it. *Medicine Now* didn't seem too fussy about the length; they'd probably sold ads on the article already and would publish whatever he sent them. He clicked 'save' and yawned. Three down, one to go. The last one would be easy enough, hopefully; only a few weeks ago he'd written a similar piece for another publication. All he had to do was juggle stuff around a bit, change the introduction and summary, add on some practice points and hey presto, a brand new article!

He could just imagine what Edie would say. Lazy fecker. And she was right. But Edie didn't have to write four articles in two weeks; Edie knew nothing about time pressure. Edie lived in the secure, cosy, little world of primary school teaching where you got to stay home with a sore throat or a blocked nose and got days off for voting and confirmation. You could be on your last legs in St Anne's and you'd still have to work.

He stretched and yawned. Some day soon, he'd be a consultant; he'd be the one calling the shots. King of the hill, top of the peak. He could slip off to his rooms in the afternoon. No awkward things like central lines, stress tests and chasing results. None of the Mickey Mouse stuff. And you got a full night's sleep and your own parking space. Like Clements always said, no need to work hard, just work smart. Speak of the devil. He flicked his mobile open. Wonder what he wanted.

'Hi, John.'

'I've got tickets for the Munster match on Saturday and thought you'd like to join me. A corporate invitation.'

Corporate meant pharmaceutical, of course. Probably WorldPharma. They did all the big matches. Charlie felt a sinking sensation. Last thing he wanted was to spend Saturday afternoon at a rugby match but what could he do? He could hardly say that he didn't want to go. Clements was from Limerick, a Munster man through and through, despite Clongowes.

'I'd love to.'

'Great. You'll enjoy it.'

Sure I will. Fuck. Fuck. Fuck.

# 14

Charlie looked around the bar and smiled. Molloy's sure was buzzing; builders from the site next door, helmets on the counter, women having a quick drink after late night shopping, and, of course, the St Anne's crowd, on their regular Friday night piss-up. The talent wasn't bad, either. He caught the eye of a nurse from Outpatients and smiled. She held his gaze. He could see Tommy at the end of the bar, sitting at the counter. He winked at the nurse and she smiled. Catch you later, honey.

'God, I could murder a pint!'

He slipped into the empty seat beside Tommy.

Tommy shook his head.

'You're working too hard, Charlie.'

Charlie shrugged.

'Has to be done.'

Tommy licked some Guinness from his upper lip.

'Any news on Cardelia?'

Charlie shook his head.

'Nothing. You know there's something about this that doesn't add up, Tommy. Some of the trials are bound to have included elderly patients.'

'Are you saying that they weren't finished?'

Charlie shook his head.

'Maybe. Or maybe they were just never published.'

Tommy leaned closer.

'What exactly do you need, Charlie?'

Tommy's voice was low, like when he discussed investments.

'I need the full Cardelia datasets.'

'What about asking Clements? Didn't you say that St Anne's was one of the trial centres?'

Charlie nodded.

'Yes, about four years ago, before I started. But Clements is kind of touchy about Cardelia. And I don't want to piss him off, not now.'

'Have you tried his office?'

Charlie put down his pint.

'Are you suggesting that I go through his filing cabinet?'

'God, no, Charlie! I'd never suggest anything like that! But let's just say that you could accidentally find what you're looking for when you're looking for something else, if you know what I mean.'

Charlie laughed.

'Tommy Porter, you're a terrible man. Here, drink up, my round.'

Charlie waited until the pints were in front of them.

For a minute or two, he sat in silence, watching the blackness of the Guinness darken and quieten, then he spoke.

'Edie wants to take a year off.'

Tommy looked up.

'What's wrong with that? Sure I was thinking of taking a gap year myself that time I turned fifty. Mind you, I can't see your mother letting her go off travelling on her own.'

Charlie nodded. No point in telling Tommy about the shop thing. Anyway, with a bit of luck it might be sold by the time she got back from Paris.

'Your mother won't be around forever, Charlie. Maybe it's about time Edie was given some independence.'

Charlie shook his head.

'C'mon, Tommy, you know what Edie's like! She worries about everything, from finding a parking place to who'll turn to shake her hand at mass. Anyway, it's not as if she never gets away; she's off to Paris next week.'

Tommy looked up.

'On her own?'

'God, no; one of her friends from training college is going with her.'

They drank in silence for a while, then Tommy put down his glass.

'I was thinking about Tracy the other day. Where is she now?'

Charlie looked away.

'Broome, I think, aboriginal health. I haven't heard from her in a while.'

He knew what Tommy was thinking. But what was he supposed to do? He didn't have time for a serious relationship; not then, not now.

'You should keep in touch, Charlie.'

There was a short silence. Then Tommy spoke.

'It's a funny old world, Charlie. Sometimes we do the right thing for the wrong reasons and sometimes we do the wrong thing for the right reasons. Don't beat yourself up over it.'

Charlie looked up.

'Wouldn't it be great, though, if we could do the right thing for the right reason?'

Tommy laughed.

'Jaysus, if that was the case, there'd be no crack at all. Mistakes are part of life, Charlie, part of the game.'

Charlie put down his glass.

'What about you, Tommy, any regrets?'

Tommy shrugged.

'There was someone, a long time ago. After that, well, suppose you could say nobody else matched up ...'

Charlie nodded. He knew what Tommy meant. When you loved someone, anyone else would always be second best.

'They break our hearts, Charlie.'

Charlie put down his glass. So much for the rumours that Tommy was gay. Just because he wasn't married and liked the Eurovision Song Contest.

'True love, Charlie, is about letting go.'

'I know.'

Boy did he know. They sat in silence for a while. Then Tommy spoke.

'Wonder what the Guinness is like.'

'Where?'

'America, you gom.'

'You'll have to visit me and find out for yourself. I'll take some time off and show you the sights.'

Tommy smiled.

'Are you sure you wouldn't mind an old codger like me arriving on your doorstep?'

Charlie punched him on the shoulder.

'We're friends, Tommy. Friends visit each other. I'd love if you came over.'

It was the truth. Having Tommy visit would be great. They could go to baseball games and donut houses and drive-ins and lots of other stuff. And it would be someone to talk to.

'You know, Charlie, I was just thinking the other day. I've been in Dublin for over forty years now. I've spent most of my life in the Big Smoke.'

'What age were you when you left Clonmel?'

'Sixteen. A cousin of my mother's was a wards-maid here in the hospital, it was she got me the job. In the beginning, I used go home a lot but after the mother died, it wasn't the same. Mothers hold things together, Charlie.'

Charlie nodded.

'I still miss Clonmel. What about you?'

Charlie shrugged.

'I kind of lost touch when I went to boarding school, Tommy. After a while the lads stop ringing you for matches and stuff, especially when you're not around for training.'

'Not much hurling in Clongowes, I suppose.'

'No.'

'You're too slight for rugby, lad, I always said that.'

'Try telling that to Mother.'

He could still remember his mother's face when she found out he'd dropped training.

'Don't be too hard on her, Charlie, she didn't understand; she thought she was doing the right thing making you take it up again. Anyway, didn't you take up the hurling again at college?'

'Yeah, and I've the scars to prove it.'

His fingers moved to the bridge of his nose, deviated ever so slightly to the left.

'Sure it's part of your charm, Charlie boy. Anyway, what price a broken nose for the king of sports?'

Charlie nodded.

'It's a wonderful feeling, Tommy, running down the field, the sliotar on your stick, the wind through your hair, like you're flying.'

Tommy smiled.

'How do you think Tipp will do this year?'

'Ten to one they'll beat Clare. Not sure about Cork.'

'Don't mind Cork, they're all fancy stick work; no speed, no skill. Hey, if I can get tickets for the Munster Final, will you come back for it?'

Charlie nodded.

'You bet.'

Then Tommy touched his arm.

'Like I said, Charlie, don't worry about Edie, I'll drop in, keep an eye on things. Your mother's always delighted to see me, talks away about you for hours.'

Charlie laughed.

'Yeah, it drives Edie mad.'

'Isn't she right to be proud of you? You'll be a consultant soon.'

'With a bit of luck.'

'You make your own luck in this world, Charlie. You've worked hard, you deserve your just rewards. And don't worry about Edie, like I said, I'll keep an eye on her. You can't be too careful, when the strain is there and everything.'

Charlie looked up. What had Tommy just said? *'When the strain is there.'* He hadn't heard that expression in years, not since Aunt Nora was trying to persuade Mother not to send them to Ring. 'Don't put any pressure on them, Lily, especially when the strain is there.' Edie hadn't taken ill then, so what

127

had Aunt Nora meant? Was it Dad's drinking? Or was there a history of mental illness in the family? A grandparent, perhaps? He must remember to ask Mother. Not that he'd get too much information.

Charlie stared at the white foam ringing the inside of the glass; complete, full circles, the sign of a good pint. Or a hastily consumed pint. Or both. Memories from the past came floating back. Maybe he shouldn't have had that last pint.

'Tommy, my mother, you must have known her. What was she like?'

Tommy hesitated a moment.

'A beauty if ever there was one, Charlie, a real stunner, full of life, wild as a hare, always laughing. Herself and your mother were best friends, the two of them were always together, looked like two movie stars, they did. Your mother was going out with your father first, then Ella met Ray, but I suppose you know that.'

Charlie shook his head.

'No. She doesn't talk about it, any of it.'

He put down his glass.

'Who was driving, Tommy?'

It was a while before Tommy spoke.

'I don't know, Charlie.'

I think you do.

'Leave it be, Charlie. It doesn't matter now.'

'I wish she'd talk about him. He was our father.'

'I know lad, I know, but people cope with grief in different ways. Your mother's way is to put on the brave face, keep the show on the road. Maybe the past is too painful a place.'

'That past is mine too, Tommy, I have a right to it.'

He stood up and pulled on his jacket. Time to hit the road. Tommy was wrong about Edie. He wasn't guilty at leaving her. In fact, Edie was one of the reasons he was going; she had to make a life without him and he had to make a life without her. There was no other way.

'See you, Monday, Tommy, sure you're OK for a lift?'

'Got one sorted, Charlie. Take care of yourself, lad.'

Charlie worked his way through the crowd. He could see the nurse he had winked at earlier locked in a passionate embrace with one of the interns. Not that he cared. All he wanted right now was some time on his own.

Outside, the wind whipped his face. He wrapped his scarf tightly round his neck. It was the multi-coloured one that Edie had knitted a lifetime ago, the one with the holey bits where she had dropped stitches and the clashing colours at one end where she had ran out of wool. But it was his favourite scarf; a bit jumbled up but kind of sweet. Just like Edie.

# 15

A yellow wedge of sunshine hit the kitchen table, like a spotlight, lighting up the packet of organic muesli but ignoring the All-Bran. Edie smiled. The angels had spoken. She reached for the muesli. Behind her, a soft grating sound. Mother peeling potatoes. Or carrots. Or parsnips. Today was Irish stew. Mother liked to have it all prepared and sitting in the casserole before school so that all she had to do was put it on the Aga when she got home.

Edie turned, observing the slow, careful way her mother washed and dried her hands, like a surgeon scrubbing up before an operation. Even preparing dinner was a sterile and military operation. She watched her mother tuck the tea towel in front of the Aga and reach behind her to untie her apron strings. There now. All done. Edie could see a smile cross her mother's face. Strange how chopping could make some people happy.

Her mother turned towards her and Edie could see the smile begin to fade. Oops. She knew what was coming. She could see it in the way her mother's left eye twitched ever so slightly and the way her smile hung suspended on her face, like the thin quarter of the moon in the kitchen calendar. She took a deep breath. Here it comes. Skirt-attack.

'You're not wearing that to school, are you?'

Edie lowered her spoon.

'What?'

'That skirt!'

First her skirts were too short. Now they were too long. You just couldn't please Mother. Anyway, everyone was wearing long skirts this winter.

'What's wrong with it?'

She hoped her voice sounded casual, uncaring.

'It's too hippyish, way too long, a ridiculous length, it could get caught in the bike.'

Oh for God's sake! She could just imagine the headlines. 'Loony daughter choked by own skirt.'

'It's fine.'

Her mother's eyes narrowed.

'It's not just the skirt... the cardigan, those boots...'

Edie bit her lip. OK, it was A wear meets Champion Sports but hey, that's how she liked to dress.

'It's comfortable.'

A dangerous pause.

'It looks stupid.'

Edie sucked in. Yep, here we go again. Stupid Edie. Good old Mother, never one for arrows, no sirree, it was scud missiles or nothing. She pushed her bowl away.

'I didn't mean you, I meant the clothes look stupid.'

It was as if Mother was explaining something to one of the kids at school. Blame the action and not the child kind of thing.

'But I chose these stupid clothes so that makes me stupid too, right?'

She could see her mother's lips tighten.

'No.'

'Charlie wears terrible clothes and you never call him stupid.'

It was true. Mother never commented on Charlie's clothes, no matter what he wore, even when he wore totally clashing colours.

'Edie…'

Edie looked up. Mother's face had that familiar pained look she got when she realised she'd overstepped the mark. Edie lifted her chin.

'I'm an embarrassment to you, aren't I? I can't even dress properly.'

Her mother took a step towards her. Edie stepped back, away from her.

'I could have done Medicine, too, Mother, I had the points.'

'I know.'

A pained look.

'I got honours in my first year exams.'

Shit. Tears, for feck's sake. When the pained look doesn't work, pour on the sprinklers. She reached for her backpack.

'You haven't finished your breakfast, Edie.'

'I'm not hungry.'

She closed the door behind her. Stupid seemed to be Mother's favourite word these days.


Edie pressed hard into the pedals, as if she was crushing something. She often did this, imagining the hurt passing through her body, down her legs and into her feet and finally being pushed out into the pedals. Other episodes of hurt came flooding back; the time Mother didn't like the tapestry she had brought back from Greece, asking why she hadn't bought lace. Or the time she was being bullied in school and Mother said it was because she wasn't popular. Oh there was plenty of hurt to be dissipated, no doubt about it.

She glanced up at the sky; no sign of the sun now, of course, just when you could do with it. It wasn't fair. Charlie could do what he wanted. Golden Boy. Everyone's Golden Boy. First in everything; first to walk, first to be toilet-trained, even first to get his tonsils out. Later on, it was the same; all Charlie's student exchanges were with wonderful families while she got the families from hell.

Then she felt her anger slip away. It wasn't Charlie's fault that Mother thought she was stupid. And she could hardly blame Mother for being proud of him; he had done the business, delivered the goods, a qualified doctor, well on the way to becoming a consultant. In all fairness, Charlie always wanted to become a doctor, ever since they were children. But somewhere along the way, they had gotten to him, messed with his head. All he talked about now were drugs and research. Altruism was a dirty word these days.

Suddenly a horn beeped behind her and a car whizzed past. She could see the driver staring at her in his mirror. Must be the skirt, ballooning out like Mary Poppins. Maybe she should have worn bicycle clips or perhaps tucked it into her knickers. Then they'd have something to look at.

An image from the past flashed in front of her; Charlie, with his big mop of tousled hair and his long dangly legs, the two of them laughing, Charlie pedalling, she on the crossbar, tearing off to the football pitch, their skin bare and baking in the summer sun, Mother yelling warnings behind them. She bit her lip. Oh, Charlie.

Suddenly, out of nowhere, a feather floated down in front of her, over and back in a slow pendulum movement, snow white and pure, like it came from heaven. She smiled. A sign.

At dinner, all was velvet calm. Mother had placed a big vase of daffodils on the table, near the water jug. And there was chocolate cake with vanilla ice cream for afters. Conscience cake.

They ate in silence. When they were finished, Edie stood up and began to clear away the plates.

'Leave that until later, Edie. Sit down and have your cake.'

Her mother put a plate in front of her. Edie stared. What an enormous slice of cake.

'Sorry about this morning.'

Edie smiled.

'It's OK.'

And it was OK. She reached for her fork. Mother was right. That skirt was a ridiculous thing to wear on a bike. The minute she got home, she'd taken it off and rubbed it with Vanish soap. Then she'd left it to soak in the garage sink. Hopefully the oil stains would come out.

# 16

Edie licked a tiny blob of icing from her lower lip. Not bad for bought cake. Wonder where Mother got it. She wiped her hands on her jeans and turned back to the screen. Right. Time to get back to business. This time, the *Lancet.* She typed the words *'Big Pharma'* in the search box and pressed return. Bingo! A full page of hits! She clicked on the first one. A moment later, she reached for her mobile. Time to phone Charlie.

He answered on the second ring.

'Hi, Edie. Everything OK?'

She sighed. It was as if he was waiting for her to do something crazy.

'Yeah, course, why wouldn't it be? I've just walked naked under the Arch in Clonmel but otherwise, everything's fine.'

He laughed.

'Got a few minutes, Charlie?'

'Sure.'

'I've found some interesting stuff on the pharmaceutical industry.'

'Where? *Reader's Digest? Woman's Weekly?*'

Edie sighed. Typical.

'Actually, Charlie, they're articles from your precious peer-reviewed *BMJ* and *Lancet.* Listen to this.'

A groan.

'Do I have any choice?'

'No, actually, so just shut up and listen. And remember, these articles are written by doctors, not crackpots.'

'Most of my doctor friends are crackpots.'

'Just shut up a minute, will you please? This one's called *'The tightening grip of Big Pharma'*.

'Riveting.'

She cleared her throat.

*'Efforts by pharmaceutical companies to suppress, spin and obfuscate findings that do not suit their commercial purposes were first revealed to their full, lethal extent during the thalidomide tragedy. Although government drug regulation schemes around the world are now in place, the insidious tactics of Big Pharma have changed little.'*

She waited for him to say something.

'Well?'

'Well what?'

'It's all one big cover-up. Thalidomide, Cardelia, same thing, they just dig a big hole and bury it.'

That quietened him. Might as well keep going while she was ahead.

'All these guys agree that the pharmaceutical industry shouldn't control medical research. *"Doctors must look to existing institutions to challenge, on the public's behalf, forces of commercial bias that risk permanently staining the integrity of medicine."*

An audible sigh.

'Like I've already told you, Edie, my work is independent research in a university department.'

It was just how Mother spoke to her, as if explaining something to a child. She felt a flash of annoyance.

'Sorry, Charlie, I must have misheard you. For a moment there, I thought you said 'independent'.'

'I did.'

'You think that working in a university department somehow makes your work 'ethical' and free from commercial bias? The independent scholarly status of our universities is a thing of the past, Charlie, they're all jumping on the band-wagon like everyone else to commercialise their research.'

'Oh for fuck's sake, Edie, that's pure and utter horse-shit!'

Aha! She was obviously getting to him.

'Is it, Charlie? Or maybe you just don't like hearing the truth? You're prepared to sell your soul same as the rest of them. I heard you telling Mother about doing lectures in the States.'

'So? It's a good career move and I'd get to see the place.'

'Oh, come on, Charlie! These lecture circuits are just another big merry-go-round. It's only doctors agreed by the pharmaceutical sponsors who are invited to give lectures and chair sessions at meetings. Lectures are given on the same topic by the same speakers all over the world. Whatever happened to free debate?'

'Oh for God's sake, Edie!'

Good, he was getting annoyed, a rare occurrence. She must have touched a nerve.

'Answer me one thing, Charlie and I'll leave it at that; have you ever given a talk or a lecture not sponsored by a pharmaceutical company?'

Silence. Surprise. Surprise.

'I take that as a no.'

'My research work is a worldwide clinical trial with huge implications for cardiology.'

'Yeah, and huge implications for a certain pharmaceutical company's profits. You think that being a 'clinical trial' makes it OK? Hello? Where have you been, Charlie? What about that trial that caused those poor feckers in England to blow up like the elephant man? One guy lost all his fingers.'

A pause.

'That was unfortunate. Calm down, you're over-reacting.'

'Unfortunate? Over-reacting? For God's sake, Charlie! Government-backed research doesn't exist. The big, randomised, controlled trials are all coming from drug company research. And surprise, surprise, these trials all show that powerful drugs work well. Every new diagnosis means a new product opportunity. Doctors are like pawns, agents of big pharma, dishing out the drugs, a pill for every ill. I don't know how you can be part of this.'

A short silence.

'Like it or not, Edie, this is how things work. I can't do research on my own, nobody can. The system may not be perfect, but it's the best we've got right now.'

He was back to his reasonable voice.

'That's what worries me. Things are never going to change if nobody does anything. People like me can't make a difference; I'm just another loony from down the country.'

She paused.

'But someone like you can.'

'How, Edie?'

He sounded tired.

'I don't know, but you'll find a way, I know you will.'

She could hear a sigh.

'Any other news for me, Edie? Anything else to cheer me up before I go to bed?'

She smiled.

'No, that's all, Charlie. Sleep tight.'

She put down the phone and smiled. She'd rattled him, definitely. Then her eyes fell on the mouse-mat on the desk beside her. *'Cardelia - Today and Tomorrow.'* She shook her head. Yeah, sure.

# 17

Charlie dropped to his knees and began to rummage through the papers and journals on the floor. His mobile was here somewhere; he could hear it ringing. Oh God, what a mess! Old newspapers, coffee mugs rimmed with yellow, a pillow, a gum shield. Jesus! This place was a job for Rent A Kill. Good. There it was, sticking out from under a pizza carton. Blocked number. Fuck, he hated blocked numbers. Could be anyone. He flicked it open.

'Yoah! Charlie here.'

'Charlie, it's Marianne. Is this a bad time? I can call back later.'

Charlie smiled. Her timing was uncanny. He had just been thinking about her.

'No, it's fine. You know you're lucky I picked up; usually I don't answer blocked numbers.'

'Why?'

'Don't you think it's kinda rude? I mean, you know you're phoning me, right, but you deliberately choose to keep your identity secret.'

Her laugh tinkled down the line.

'Get over it, hon. Everyone in my business uses blocked numbers. Otherwise nobody would answer the phone to us.'

Charlie laughed.

'Have you eaten?'

'No, not yet.'

'How about joining me for a take-away?

'Tonight?'

'Of course, silly. Unless your idea of a takeaway is a breakfast latte. I was thinking Thai, or maybe an Indian if you'd prefer.'

'I don't mind.'

Shit. Why did he say that? Women like Marianne expected men to have opinions.

'How does some tempura, a green curry, maybe some prawns and noodles sound?'

'Sounds great.'

Dippy dunky love food.

'Could you pick up some beer on the way?'

Beer, of course, he should have thought of it.

'Sure. What would you like?'

'Singha beer would be great if you could get it.'

What the hell was Singha beer?

'What did you say it was called again?'

Another tinkle of a laugh.

'Singha. It's a Thai beer.'

He scribbled the name on his hand. If the lady wanted Singha beer, the lady would get Singha beer.

'What time?'

'Say eight'ish? I'm starving, I had an early lunch.'

Charlie smiled. She probably meant an early lunch yesterday.

'Where do you live?'

A shimmer of a laugh.

'I'd forgotten you haven't been here. I'm just beside Earlsfort Terrace. Number 20, Earlsfort Villas. One of the penthouses.'

Charlie smiled. He should have known it would be a penthouse; right at the very top, just where she wanted.

'Sure you don't want me to pick up the food?'

'No, I'm good. What kind of noodles you like, doc?'

Oops. Trick question.

'Any kind.'

Noodles were noodles, right?

'Egg noodles, so. You OK with prawns, not allergic or anything?'

'No, I eat anything.'

Pheasant. Sausage. Kangaroo. Anything.

'Talk soon.'

The line went dead. He glanced at his watch. Ten past seven. That gave him fifty minutes. He ran his fingers through his hair. OK. Shower, he had to have a shower, change his clothes, buy some flowers, pick up that Singha beer. He took a deep breath. Take it easy, Charlie; keep it cool. So what if you're a few minutes late? It wasn't his usual form to go running the moment a woman clicked her fingers. Not his usual form at all, no sirree. But this was different.

An hour later, he stepped out of the lift. Number 2 was just across the hall. The door was open and the smell of Thai food wafted towards him, spicy, fragrant, hot. Just like Marianne.

He knocked.

'It's me, Charlie.'

'Come in!'

Her voice sounded distant.

'Pour yourself a beer, opener's on the coffee table. I'll be out in a tic.'

She must be in the bathroom. Or the bedroom. Jesus, get a grip! What did she say again? Oh yeah, opener on the coffee table, pour a beer. But first, he had to get the flowers into water. He crossed the room to the kitchen. Oops. The sink was full of glasses. And he didn't want to start searching the presses. Maybe he'd leave the flowers in that little cloakroom he'd seen on the way in. They were lilies, blooms still closed, quiescent and composed. Full of promise, just like Marianne.

He opened his beer and glanced around. It was just like he had imagined; the kind of place you'd expect a PR chick like Marianne to live in. Open-plan, pale furnishings, funky prints on the walls, loads of glass and chrome, lots of space. And no clutter.

The couch was soft and squidgy, the kind of couch that sucked you in. A love couch. You could suffocate happily on a couch like this. Couldn't be very good for your back, though. Then again, Marianne probably didn't spend too much time here.

He lifted the bottle to his lips and took a long, slow swallow. The Singha beer wasn't bad. Mind you, it wouldn't want to be. He had to go to three off-licenses before he found it. And it had cost twice as much as Heineken.

'What do you think of it?'

Jesus! He jumped to his feet, almost spilling his beer. He hadn't heard her come in. Her lips lightly touched his cheek.

'It's nice.'

Nice? Could he not have thought of a better word than 'nice'?

'I'll get the food. You must be starving.'

His eyes trailed her into the kitchen. Even when she moved out of sight, bending down behind the island unit, he could still imagine her. Tight black leggings that showed every curve. Skinny white t-shirt. Dressing-down, Marianne style. Speckled cleavage with its dusting of freckles. And she was barefoot. Probably just finished Pilates or yoga or something. He swallowed and raised the bottle to his lips again.

A moment later, she was back, carrying a tray of steaming bowls. He jumped to his feet.

'Stay where you are. Everything's under control.'

He smiled. He didn't doubt it.

'Your hair is nice like that.'

It was out before he realised it. Another bloody 'nice'.

'You like it?'

Her fingers touched her hair.

'Didn't have time for Peter Marks so I so just tied it up.'

He longed to touch it.

'It makes you look younger.'

Shit. Talk about putting your foot in it.

'I suppose at my age I need all the help I can get.'

'I didn't mean -'

'- I know what you meant, Charlie Darmody!'

She laughed and threw him a pair of chopsticks.


He watched her as she ate. Tiny, carefully selected, thought out bites. Her chopsticks moved like knitting needles, clicking, teasing, chasing and finally snapping up their prey like a gannet diving for fish. His own movements, amplified by knife and fork, seemed clumsy in comparison. Maybe he should have opted for curry. Curry was a level playing field.

'Cheers, Charlie! To the future!'

She handed him another beer.

'To the future!'

A few minutes later, she put down her glass.

'Too many carbs in beer. And yeast. Got to watch the old 'Candeeda' as they say in America. Think I'll change to wine.'

Her hand moved to her tummy, brown and smooth. Then she began to rub; slow, circular movements. She was even skinnier than Edie.

Charlie reached for the wine bottle and began to pour, first Marianne's glass, then his own. He was on the floor now, propped against a footstool, his legs stretched out in front of him. Marianne said she'd never seen such long legs. She had taken his place on the couch, curled up like a kitten, her t-shirt rolled high on her midriff, laughing at something he'd said. His head felt light. No way could he drive now, not after all that wine. Last thing he wanted was to get busted by the cops just before heading off to the States. He'd take a taxi home and collect the car in the morning.

Their eyes met. God, she looked sexy! For months he had imagined this, but he had never thought it could happen so simply, so easily. He put down his glass. Careful, Charlie. Any sudden movements seemed to reverberate around the couch, like a water-bed, and he didn't want to spill her wine. They were only inches apart now.

'So.'

Her eyes sparkled. In them, the big question.

'Only a few weeks left. You'll be missed, you know, only bit of talent in St Anne's.'

Charlie laughed.

'What about Clements? I thought all the women fancied him.'

She raised an eyebrow and smiled.

'Apart from John, of course.'

'So, are you looking forward to the States?'

He hesitated a moment.

'Yeah, definitely.'

'But…'

God, why did women never settle for an answer like men did?

'It's a long way from home.'

'Where's home, apart from Dublin?'

'Clonmel. My mother and my sister live there.'

Strange, he thought he'd told her that already.

'Ah! A mammy's boy!'

He looked down at his glass.

'Don't know about that.'

'How old is your sister?'

'Twenty-eight.'

He couldn't tell her that he and Edie were the same age; it would lead to all kinds of questions and he didn't want to go there.

'She's a teacher, primary school, same as my mother.'

'And she's still living at home? Jesus, Charlie, the girl should get a life!'

'It's not as simple as that.'

Don't ask, Marianne, please don't ask.

'John tells me you're going to be working with his brother.'

'Yes, Professor Bill Clements.'

'What's he like?'

'I only met him once, the time I went over. He seemed nice enough. Looks a bit like John, only bigger.'

A girlish giggle.

'You know what they say, everything's bigger in America. Bet he had white teeth.'

Charlie laughed.

'He did actually, now that you mention it.'

'How long will you stay?'

Charlie shrugged.

'Two years, maybe three. Until something comes up here.'

'So you are coming back?'

He nodded.

'Handy that you were working with his brother.'

He smiled.

'Yeah, fierce handy.'

'So, what do you really think of your boss, Doctor John Xavier Clements?'

Careful, Charlie.

'Amazing. Teaching, research, meetings, editorial boards, advisory boards, you name it. I don't know how he does it.'

He turned to smile at her.

'But you know that, don't you?'

She returned his smile.

'Yep. Our kind of man.'

'And what about you, you like your job?'

'Yeah, sure, can't imagine anything else. Gives me a buzz.'

'You're fairly young to be Director of Healthcare.'

'It's a start.'

'You planning on getting rid of your MD?'

She punched his arm.

'You don't think much of us PR people, do you, Charlie?'

He shrugged and smiled.

'You think that all we do is put a spin on things, make them look good? The pharmaceutical industry is a business like any other business. And big business at that. The pharmaceutical industry employs over 20,000 people here and has invested over four billion in the last five years alone. Yet, every day, someone's on their case; NGOs, third world advocates, patient support groups, the Green Party, consumers. Everyone's complaining about the price of drugs, as if the pharmaceutical industry should develop these drugs and give them away for free. I mean, for fuck's sake!'

Charlie smiled.

'Why don't the drug companies use their own in-house communications people?'

'Some do. But using a third party like us is better, it separates the message from the apparently self-interested messenger.'

'Aah!'

'Besides, we're better at this kind of thing. It's what we're trained to do. You're a doctor. I'm a PR person.'

Charlie smiled.

'Information laundering.'

A tinkly laugh.

'Yeah, I suppose you could call it that.'

'What about key opinion leaders?'

She put down her glass.

'You mean how do we identify the right ones to groom?'

A mischievous smile.

'Look, Charlie, nobody's going to come knocking on our door offering to do talks and to write articles for us. The right people have to be persuaded, flattered, nudged along. Obviously we want reputable, well-informed spokespersons, people who know their stuff and are good communicators.'

Charlie nodded.

'Doctors do this kind of thing because they want to, Charlie. We don't force any doctor to say or do anything.'

Charlie smiled.

'That's what worries me.'

'It's not just WorldPharma that benefits when their drugs sell, Charlie, the entire economy benefits.'

'And what's good for the economy is good for society.'

'Exactly.'

He turned to look at her.

'And what do you think, Marianne? Do you think that what's good for the economy is good for society?'

A slow smile.

'Frankly, Charlie, I couldn't give a shit. I only care about what's good for me, and what's good for the economy is good for me, end of story.'

She placed her hand on his. Her touch was soft and cool.

'Know what your problem is, sweetie? You've got a conscience. Terrible handicap, a conscience. Word of advice, sweetie, lose it. Won't do you any good.'

She leaned over and took his glass. Their fingers touched. He could smell her perfume. Slowly, she uncurled and slipped off the couch. The tiny mole he had noticed previously winked up at him from between her breasts. She reached for his hand.

'Let's take a shower.'


He awoke with a start. Grey light fingered through the blinds. He turned and looked at her. She looked so beautiful, so perfect, with her hair flooding over the pillow and her skin soft and smooth as satin. Her eyes opened and she smiled.

'You look good in the morning.'

'So do you.'

He bent and kissed her on the forehead, his lips moving to find hers. If he didn't leave now, he'd never leave. He stroked her cheek.

'I have to go.'

'I know.'

At the door, he turned around to look at her. She opened her eyes.

'Be a darling, Charlie, and dump those bloody lilies in the downstairs loo. Haven't a clue who sent them; the concierge must have put them in the sink while I was out. I absolutely detest lilies, they remind me of coffins.'

He nodded.

'Sure.'


Gently, carefully, he lifted the bouquet of lilies out of the sink, their heady, sweet scent swirling around him. Lilies were Edie's favourite flower. He could just imagine them, on top of the piano, smiling down on her as her fingers danced on the keyboard.

# 18

Charlie looked out at the floodlit gates of Rockwell College and smiled. Next town was Cahir, then Clonmel. He should be home in less than thirty minutes. Amazing he hadn't crashed on the way down. He kept seeing her face, imagining the taste of her skin, the feel of her body. Earlier on, in the library, it had been the same. It was as if she had taken him over.

At dinner, he sat in his usual seat at the top of the table. Behind him, the draining board, piled high with saucepans, bowls and various size whisks. The closer it got to his departure, the bigger and more complex the dinners seemed to become.

He glanced around the kitchen. There was something different about it but he didn't know what. Then he noticed the bright yellow rectangle, halfway down the wall beside the Aga, like someone had painted it there. But it wasn't fresh paint; it was paint that had been, until recently, protected from the kitchen smoke and steam. He swallowed. The calendar. Someone must have taken it down. Edie, he supposed. Probably couldn't bear to watch Mother ticking off the days; the steady, relentless, inexorable descent towards the middle of March.

'Some Yorkshire pudding, Charlie?'

He watched his mother pour the gravy directly into the waiting epicentre of his mashed potato. Years of practice had given her NASA precision. How come it was only mothers who know where to pour gravy on mashed potato? He looked up at her and smiled. Maybe it was the light (Mother had started using low wattage bulbs in the kitchen), but he thought she looked a little pale tonight. Probably just tired. Mother wasn't a good sleeper at the best of times, and with him going away and Edie going off on holidays, she was probably awake half the night. She always fretted when Edie was away.

'You OK, Mother? You look tired.'

'We had the religious exam this week, some of them didn't know their prayers, can you imagine? After only getting Holy Communion last year? Just goes to show what prayers are being said at home.'

Charlie nodded. Best not say too much; he hadn't been to mass in years and poor Edie only went for a quiet life.

'Now, before I forget, tell me all about this presentation that Dr Clements asked you to do.'

Oops. He hadn't mentioned the presentation to Edie yet.

'It's the launch of a new blood pressure drug. Dr Clements is away so he asked me to give the keynote speech.'

Edie's fork pinged on her plate. Her eyes challenged him across the table.

'There's no such thing as a free lunch. Or a free launch. So, what are you going to say?'

Charlie shrugged.

'The usual stuff about blood pressure; diagnosis, treatment, lifestyle.'

'With drugs like Cardelia?'

'Edie!'

Mother's hand froze, the gravy boat suspended mid-air.

'Diastora is a totally different class of drug, Edie. It works in a different way.'

'So it kills you in a different way.'

'Edie! Let Charlie eat his dinner! For your information, Edie, Dr Brown started me on Diastora and he said it was a wonderful drug, very safe.'

Edie raised an eyebrow.

'And where do you think he was getting his information?'

Suddenly his mother was beside him, blocking him from Edie.

'More gravy, Charlie? Did I put enough butter in the mashed potatoes? I know you like them buttery.'

Charlie could see Edie's eyes narrow.

'You know, Mother, for someone who questions everything, from the price of spring lamb to the war in Iraq, it really amazes me how you haven't questioned how a drug can be taken off the market and so quickly replaced with another one. I can't believe how complacent you are.'

His mother put down her knife and fork.

'I may not trust the pharmaceutical industry, but I trust doctors. And if Dr Browne says a tablet is OK, and Charlie says it's OK, then I'm happy. And I can hardly be accused of being complacent, of all things. Who wrote to the Consumers' Association about the cost of schoolbooks? And who took on the County Council about sorting out that fiasco of a roundabout down the road?'

Charlie smiled. Mother, dix points. He'd forgotten how alike these two women were, always questioning, stubborn as two mules. No wonder they argued so much.

'Nobody's got any opinion in this country any more, they don't care as long as they can spend, spend, spend. They accept everything without as much as a whisper; the smoking ban, nursing home charges, decoupling. Can you imagine the French farmers being told what to do?'

Charlie smiled. Mother was off.

'Sheep, that's what we are! Must be our colonial past.'

Mother had a Republican leaning that often revealed itself at the oddest moments.

'All people care about is going to the latest shopping centre, sorry, 'retail outlet' every Sunday and spending all the money they've borrowed.'

Charlie reached for the milk. Shopping on Sunday was one of Mother's pet hates.

'Most new drugs aren't even necessary.'

Good. Edie was back, a bit late, but at least she was back.

'According to Health Action International, over 70% of current drugs are unnecessary.'

Charlie raised an eyebrow. Health Action International – who the hell were they? Probably some crazy left-wing militant group. God knows where Edie heard about these organizations.

'HAI is a global NGO that advocates rational drug use. It supports the World Health Organization's policy to distribute the 250 most essential drugs to the two billion people who don't have them.'

Charlie nodded.

'We all agree that underdeveloped countries need cheaper medicines, Edie, but we still need research to develop new products.'

She shook her head.

'Like I've already explained, Charlie, industry-funded research isn't worth the paper it's written on. They veto the publication of results they don't like, for God's sake, and you don't call that biased?'

154

'Without the pharmaceutical industry, there'd be no research. Without WorldPharma, I wouldn't have a job in the States.'

'And what are you going to be working on?'

Charlie hesitated.

'It's a new blood pressure tablet.'

Edie laughed.

'Quelle surprise! Another blood pressure tablet! To replace Diastora when the shit hits the fan there!'

'Edie!'

Mother hated bad language.

'So convenient, isn't it, that most of us get high blood pressure at some stage! Some of these new tablets are no better than a diuretic, you know that as well as I do, Charlie. Sure, they change a few little things here and there, say that the new drug is more effective, do a load of 'scientific' trials, then when the patent runs out on Diastora, they launch the new kid on the block and publish a load of dubious clinical trials that compare the drug with sugar tablets.'

He met her gaze.

'Nobody's going to influence my results, Edie.'

'Sure, Charlie! Meanwhile WorldPharma pays the bills, right? C'mon!'

Charlie put down his fork. A mountain of mashed potato stared back at him. Then he felt his mother's hand on his arm.

'More lamb, anyone? Charlie, you haven't finished your potato, I hope you're not coming down with something.'

'Poor little Charlie. Want me to get you some Calpol, pet?'

Their eyes met and he smiled. War over. That was the good thing about Edie, she never stayed mad for very long. Fast furious fights but no offence taken. Mother and Edie had it down to a fine art.

'So, Edie, all set for Paris?'

Time to talk about something else apart from the bloody pharmaceutical industry.

'Yep.'

'Want a lift to the airport?'

She looked up.

'No, it's fine, thanks, Charlie. I'll take the airport bus from Heuston.'

'Don't forget to take your mobile charger, Edie, and that foreign adapter thing. Apple tart, Charlie?'

Already he could smell the sweet scent of apples and cloves.

'Where are you staying?'

'Some hotel near the Opera.'

Charlie picked up his spoon. Funny how Edie didn't want to talk about Paris. Normally she'd be all talk about restaurant recommendations and shows, devouring everything she could find on her destination. Then again, she'd been to Paris before; she knew the ropes, where to go, what to do. Hopefully... He looked across at her. She seemed OK, yet... something in her eyes worried him. It reminded him of before.

'You are going to Paris, aren't you?'

As soon as the words were out, he regretted them. Her eyes darkened.

'I'm not going to the south of France, if that's what you mean.'

'Sorry, Edie, it's just -'

'- You're worried that I'll do something crazy? Like the last time? I didn't know what I was doing then, Charlie, you know that.'

Shit. Why had he said anything?

'You think that I'd get the same delusion again? Don't you know anything about mania or have you forgotten your psychiatry already?

Psychotic people have thousands of delusions, false thoughts, false realities to choose from, it doesn't have to be the same old Vichy psychosis!'

He could see the quiver in her lower lip.

'And, just in case you're worried, I've no intention of turning up at your dumb meeting.'

Charlie swallowed. The thought had actually crossed his mind, Edie turning up at a pharmaceutical conference, demonstrating against the evils of Big Pharma. Her and her whacko lefty friends. He felt a sudden wave of shame. Edie would never do anything to hurt or embarrass him.

Suddenly he remembered the lilies.

'I nearly forgot, Edie, I've something for you.'

A few minutes later, he handed her the bouquet.

'Oh Charlie, they're gorgeous!'

She wrapped her arms around him, almost suffocating him, like she used do when he went back to Clongowes after the weekend.

'Sure these are for me? Or did some busty blonde ditch you before you had a chance to give them to her?'

He smiled.

'Something like that.'

Edie had an uncanny knack of sensing things, things that nobody else picked up on.

'OK, I promise that I won't mention the pharmaceutical industry again for the rest of the weekend if you don't mention America. OK?'

'Deal.'

Then slowly, carefully, he helped her arrange the flowers, the sweet scent of lilies swirling round them.

# 19

Charlie looked at the number flashing on his bleep. Casualty. Another admission. This would be his fifth trip to what the interns called 'Calcutta' and it wasn't even noon. The Casualty department was airless and stagnant; it smelled of unwashed flesh and body effluents, a fetid bunker of human suffering that turned into a living nightmare at the weekends. Yep, Casualty was a great equaliser, no doubt about it.

He pushed through the doors and sighed. Not good, not good at all... there must be at least a dozen trolleys here, all waiting for a bed. And the wards were full with the weekend admissions, most of them chronic obstructive airways disease on drips and oxygen. A great start to a Monday. Yes, indeed! Looked like it was going to be one of those days; a bitch from start to finish.

He reached for his mobile. Nothing, no missed calls, not even a reply to his text. Should he or shouldn't he phone her? What would he say? He was hardly going to tell her the truth; that he had thought about nothing else all weekend but the feel of her body in the heat of the night. Damn. This would happen now, just before he went away. Edie would say it was Fate, of course. Well to hell with Fate. He wasn't going to let Fate dictate what should and shouldn't happen. You had to be proactive; you had to make things happen.

He slipped the mobile back in his pocket. Later, when he got a chance, he'd phone her, invite her to dinner; say it was his turn. He could always send her flowers, of course, but after that episode with the lilies, better not chance it.

Suddenly he jumped. An emergency bleep. The sound pierced through him. He glanced at the number flashing on the display. The Stress Test clinic. Someone must have zonked on a treadmill. Probably an arrhythmia. He grabbed his stethoscope and began to run.

Thirty seconds later, he pushed through the clinic doors. He could feel his heart pounding in his ribcage. The man on the floor beside one of the treadmills was motionless, face already dusky blue from lack of oxygen. Charlie took a deep breath. OK, remember the routine; same as always.

A. B. C. He tilted the man's jaw backwards.

A is for Airway. His fingers reached inside the man's mouth. Nothing, no obstructing foreign body.

B is for breathing – Charlie glanced at the man's chest – nothing. No breath sounds.

C is for circulation. His fingers felt the man's carotid. Nada. His eyes flew to the monitor; luckily the leads were still attached. Ventricular fibrillation, just as he thought. He nodded at the intern beside him.

'OK, Harry – let's start CPR, you do the chest compressions, I'm going to slip in an airway. Jenny, can you get a line up?'

His voice sounded surprisingly calm. He glanced at the man's face. Not one of their regular cardiology patients; must be a new patient, probably one of Clements' privates. He caught Sister' s eye.

'He's from the rooms, Charlie. Chest pain on exertion. Dr Clements wanted an urgent stress test. Poor man was only two minutes on the treadmill. No warning, just a small bit of ST elevation. Next thing he was on the floor. I've bleeped Dr Clements.'

Charlie nodded and lifted the epiglottis with the tip of the laryngoscope. Good, he could see the vocal cords glistening below him; now all he had to do was to pass the tube between them. Bingo. He reached for the Ambu bag.

'OK, guys, can someone start bagging here? We need to defibrillate.'

Charlie glanced at the monitor again. No change. The man was still in ventricular fibrillation. Next thing to asystole. Next thing to death. There was no time to waste.

'What age is he, Sister?'

'Fifty-five.'

Same age his father would have been if he hadn't died.

'OK, whose turn is it to shock?'

He looked up. Nervous eyes avoided his.

'Come on, Dave, I'll guide you through it. Charge it at 200 joules and wait for the beep...'

A short silence.

'Good. When you're ready, shout 'clear' and go for it.'

The intern held the two paddles in front of him, like they were cymbals.

'Clear!'

There was an instant scuffle backwards.

'OK, Dave, put the paddles where I showed you... good.'

The man's body twitched and all eyes turned to the monitor.

'Still v. fib. Shock again... same voltage, Dave. Sister, can I have one hundred milligram lignocaine, please. Jenny, be ready to inject.'

Charlie could see Sister flick the cap off a vial in her hand. Always one step ahead, Sister Nugent. Suddenly Jenny looked up, her eyes wide with panic.

'I can't get a vein!'

'I'll do it.'

He began to move towards her but suddenly someone pushed past him. Pinstripe trousers, shiny shoes. Then a familiar voice.

'We need intravenous access now, not next week! I'll do it myself.'

Jenny's face was roasted red pepper. Poor kid. It was never nice being bawled at by the boss. Especially in front of everyone. Charlie's eyes flicked once more to the monitor. Still v. fib. They needed to get that lignocaine in. Fast. But first, they needed to shock again.

'Get ready to clear, I'm charging again.'

This time, he took the paddles himself. He glanced across at Clements. A large purple haematoma was beginning to from on the patient's arm. Blood spattered the lino. Shit. That's one vein fucked up, anyway.

'Wait, just another second...'

'We need to shock now, John. I can't wait. Clear, everyone.'

Charlie raised the paddles. Out of the corner of his eye, he saw Sister pull Clements backwards. The paddles landed and the man's body jerked again. What was Clements playing at? Didn't he know that 'clear' meant clear unless you wanted a high voltage shock?

Clements was beside him now, a tiny bead of sweat on his upper lip.

'Call the anaesthetists, these veins are impossible.'

Charlie stood up.

'I'll try the other arm. Jenny, can you take over here?'

Quickly, Charlie tied the tourniquet. His eyes scoured the dusky skin; nothing, no visible veins at all, but that was hardly surprising seeing as the man's heart had stopped nearly four minutes ago. He glided his fingers across the skin. Yes! He could feel something! Right in the centre. Probably the brachial vein.

'Sixteen gauge cannula, please, Sister.'

He took a long, deep breath. Easy does it. Take your time. He felt a little give as the needle pierced the vein. Blood trickled into the trochar. Yes!

Quickly he slid in the cannula and withdrew the needle. He caught Sister's wink and smiled.

'OK, push in the lignocaine, give it thirty seconds, and then shock again.'

Still ventricular fibrillation. This wasn't looking good.

'Keep doing CPR, Jenny. Dave, get ready to shock, this time 250 joules.'

He looked up. Clements was standing near the door, a dazed look on his face, like a rabbit caught in car headlights.

'OK, clear!'

All eyes turned to the monitor. Then a sudden cheer and someone punched the air. Sinus rhythm!

'Yes!'

There was an audible sigh of relief.

'Close one, Charlie.'

Charlie smiled.

'Sure was, Dave. OK, guys, take the patient up to CCU. What do you want done, John?'

He looked across at Clements.

'Sorry, Charlie, what did you say?'

'What's the plan? Looks like you might want an urgent angio.'

'Yes, indeed, Charlie. Put him first on the list for tomorrow. And have the surgeons on standby. A critical occlusion, most likely.'

Clements turned to leave, then stopped.

'Good work, team.'

Charlie watched his lips stretch into a smile. He seemed to have regained his composure.

'A quick word, Charlie'.

Charlie followed him outside.

'He's a friend of mine, bank manager.'

162

Charlie nodded. Being a bank manager wasn't any good to you when your heart had stopped.

'It was pointless even trying for a vein in that arm, that silly-ninny had them all shagged up.'

Charlie opened his mouth to say something, then changed his mind. Jenny hadn't messed up anything; she hadn't even punctured the skin. Then somewhere, in the deep recesses of his mind, he could hear the unmistakeable sound of a cock crowing. It wasn't the first time.

Twenty minutes later, Charlie opened the door of the doctors' res and smiled. He should have known he'd find them here. There was nothing like an emergency bleep to give you an appetite! Jenny handed him the packet of biscuits.

'Here, Charlie, take some before they're all gone. I'll make you coffee. Two sugar, right?'

Charlie nodded and reached for his mobile. A text, from Edie, saying she was coming up after school on Tuesday to do some shopping and wanted to stay with him. She had no school on Wednesday apparently, another day off for some obscure reason. Oh, to be a primary school teacher! He smiled and sent her a quick reply.

Then he hesitated. What about Marianne? Should he text her? Maybe she was waiting for him to make the first move. It was hard to know with girls like her. 'Friday was great.' No, sounded smutty. Might as well get straight to the point.

'Would you like to have dinner with me on Friday night?'

Normally he'd use abbreviations but somehow he felt proper English was best for something like this. He read the message again, then pressed send. Done. Now all he could do was wait.

# 20

Edie opened her purse and began to rummage through the change. Coins slipped through her fingers, scattering on the floor of the taxi. No wonder Mother called her butter-fingers. Maybe she should buy a bigger purse, one like Mother's, with its wide pouches and easy to open clasp. Or maybe she could just try to be less clumsy.

Suddenly she felt her cheeks begin to redden; how much should she tip the taxi driver? Four euros? Two euros? A euro? Would a Dublin taxi driver even accept a euro tip these days? Maybe he'd laugh and throw it back at her. Shit. She could see a bunch of girls approaching, heels clacking and bracelets jangling. They looked so cool, with their big belts and their skinny jeans, probably heading into town for the night.

The fare was ten euro. All she had besides a ten-euro note was a fifty, a five and some twenty-cent coins. She could hear the laughter getting louder. She bundled the five-euro note at the taxi driver. His eyes widened.

'Thanks, luv.'

A moment later, she saw one of the girls bend down. Probably picking up some of the coins she'd dropped. Their laughter bounced behind her in the crisp evening air. It must be nice to have friends.

She closed her purse and put in back in her bag. She'd have to learn to be more careful with money, especially now that she was going to be running her own business. Ah well. Five euro wasn't the end of the world. Better too much than too little. Maybe it might be the same guy bringing her back to Heuston tomorrow and if she hadn't tipped today, maybe he might take the long way round tomorrow and she'd end up missing the train. You never know how fate can catch up with you.

She pressed the intercom and waited. The first time here, she had kept her finger on the button for ages and Charlie said that she had nearly deafened him. Hopefully it would be Charlie and not Killian, his flatmate, who would answer. She never liked intercoms; they were a disaster waiting to happen. Sometimes people opened the door without saying anything and by the time you realised what had happened, the door was shut again. She smiled when she heard Charlie's voice.

'Hi Edie! I'll be right down.'

Ten seconds later, the door opened.

'Charlie!'

His arms were around her. Already she felt safer.

'So, getting ready for Paris?'

She nodded.

'It's an excuse for shopping. And there's half-price highlights in Peter Marks.'

'Don't touch your hair.'

His fingers eased a stray strand back from her forehead.

'Just a few highlights, brighten it up…'

'It's a lovely colour, Edie, leave it alone, OK?'

She smiled.

'OK.'

'I badly need some clothes, though.'

Her eyes travelled to her faded cords.

'You know, I think women spend more money getting ready for holidays than they do on holiday.'

She laughed. Charlie was right.

'What do you want to do tonight, kid? What about a play, or maybe a film?'

'Actually, I wouldn't mind just staying in, maybe get a take-away, watch TV.'

Something changed in his face at the mention of take-away. Shit. Maybe he had already eaten. Then he smiled.

'Suits me perfectly, kiddo. But are you sure you don't want to go out, hit the hot spots?'

'Certain.'

Now that she knew Killian wasn't around, all she wanted was to chill out in front of the TV with Charlie and throw sweet wrappers on the floor without Mother tut-tutting in the background. Pure bliss.

'There's some take-away menus beside the phone, Edie. Fancy a cup of coffee while we're waiting?'

'Sure. Here, I've brought some milk and biscuits.'

'You're a star! How did you know we had no milk?'

She smiled and reached for her backpack.

'Because you never have any milk.'


Edie began her usual wander round the room, stopping now and again to touch something; a CD, a book, a photograph, usually something belonging to Charlie. It was a habit of hers, feeling and touching her new environs as if to earth herself in the present and somehow make the room her own. She could hear the sound of drawers opening and closing in the kitchen. Typical Charlie. Could never find anything. Probably looking for a spoon.

She crossed to the window. Outside, she could see cars, bicycles, even a guy on roller blades. It was a million miles away from the stillness of the Lodge. She smiled. She liked being here. It was like staying over at your auntie's house when you were seven. Only better. She wished it could always be like this.

'Here we go…'

He handed her a mug of steaming coffee.

'The place seems tidy, Charlie, tidy for you, I mean. Expecting somebody?'

'You, precious, I tidied it up for you.'

Edie smiled and reached into her pocket.

'Here, a little pressie.'

'What is it?'

'It's your own set of angel cards, Charlie. Every healer should have them.'

Charlie smiled and shook his head.

'You know what I think about all this angel stuff, Edie.'

She knew that's what he'd say.

'Well, you never know. Maybe some day you'll be glad of your guardian angel when you ask for help.'

'What do you mean?'

'What part of 'ask for help' don't you understand? If you're in trouble, you call your guardian angel, end of story.'

'How do I know his name?'

'You'll know. After a while, you'll know.'

'Right.'

She knew what he was thinking. More mumbo-jumbo.

'How do I know it was the angels that helped me? I mean, couldn't it just have been luck, or fate as you call it?'

'No.'

God, he could be so irritating.

'Do you actually see these angels?'

His voice sounded more serious now.

'Oh for God's sake, Charlie! Of course I don't see angels! Been there, done that, thank you very much. But I know when they're around.'

'As in…'

He raised an eyebrow.

'As in I feel their presence. Sometimes it's like a warm brush on my face, or a sparkle of light out of the corner of my eye and when I look again, it's gone. Once I saw a golden glow just outside the kitchen window beside the rose bush.'

'There's a dead cat buried there.'

'Charlie!'

She picked up a cushion and threw it at him.

'I'm trying here, kiddo, I'm really trying. But golden glows and sparkling lights? C'mon!'

Edie shook her head. Why did she even bother?

'They don't talk to you, these angels?'

'No. But they communicate in other ways. Like when people suddenly get ideas that transform their lives or they miraculously avoid a near-tragedy.'

'How come I've never seen or heard anything?'

'Because your mind is too busy, Charlie! You've got to quieten the mind and be more aware. Angels are always near, especially in nature.'

'I remember watching something on TV one night about these children who had photographs of angels; you could see these white shadows in the photos. It wasn't until they were old men and women that they admitted it was all a hoax.'

Edie shook her head.

'For your information, Charlie, that was fairies, not angels.'

'Fairies, angels, much of a muchness.'

She sighed and reached for her coffee. This was pointless.

'You were always into this kind of thing, Edie. I can see you now, sitting beneath the old oak, chatting away to your invisible friends, your plastic tea-set all spread out on a tea-towel in front of you.'

His hand moved to tuck a wisp of hair behind her ear.

'Actually, Charlie, if I remember, you used to talk to our imaginary friends too.'

She could remember it quite clearly; herself and Charlie, cool in the shade of the big oak, chatting away. That was before Father died, of course. After that, Charlie rarely went to the oak tree, only to gather acorns for the nature table at school. It was as if, all of a sudden, he had grown up.

'Why did you stop?'

He looked away.

'I asked them to make Father better. And they didn't.'

The silence was interrupted by the sound of the doorbell. Charlie sighed and stood up.

'Probably Killian, forgot his keys again. He's a right plonker.'

A minute or two passed. Still no sign of Charlie. Wonder what was keeping him. She walked across to the window. There was a small blue sports car parked across the road. It definitely hadn't been there earlier on; she'd have noticed a car like that.

Another minute passed. She opened the door a tiny fraction. She could hear Charlie's voice and a woman's laughter. The voices drew nearer; they were coming up the stairs. Quickly, she clicked the door closed and hurried back to the couch.

The door opened and Edie put down her cup. Wow! The girl with Charlie must be a model. Red trouser-suit, shiny long, black hair, pointy, pointy shoes. Full-on make-up. She must be on her way to a wedding. Edie could feel the woman's eyes on her, dissecting every detail, like women do. She was suddenly aware of her shabby sneakers and her faded Gap sweatshirt.

'I'm sorry, Charlie, I didn't realise you had a visitor. I just called round to drop off the final proofs.'

Edie didn't like the woman's voice. It was high and toney, Dublin four with a capital F. And it was obvious by the change in her expression that she wasn't too happy at finding Edie here.

'Don't go, Marianne! I'd like you to meet my sister, Edie.'

At the mention of 'sister', Edie could see the girl's face soften.

'So pleased to meet you! Charlie has told me all about you.'

Edie looked at Charlie. They had an agreement that he never spoke about it. Then Edie saw the woman's hand stretched out towards her. A sudden flash of rings, bracelets and red nail varnish. Edie hesitated. This woman, whoever she was, was trying to steal Charlie.

'I'm Marianne, I work with GoldMed Communications. Charlie does some work for us.'

Her hand was cool and fragile. Edie took a deep breath. GoldMed - they were that PR crowd Charlie had mentioned, the crowd that worked with pharma companies. She should have known. Must pay well anyway, judging by the clothes.

'What kind of work does GoldMed do, Marianne?'

She caught Charlie's warning glance.

'We're a public relations company, mainly healthcare.'

'So you work with doctors?'

'No, not exactly, pharmaceutical companies are our main clients.'

Suddenly Charlie was between them, handing Marianne a mug of coffee. His mug of coffee. She watched Marianne's fingers curl around the Homer Simpson mug, the one he never let anyone else use, the one she had given him last Christmas. This was worse than she thought. Time to up the ante.

'So you reposition the pharmaceutical industry as providers of medical education so that it doesn't appear as if doctors are being bribed?'

A sudden splutter. Charlie, most likely. Marianne looked totally calm, perfectly composed.

Marianne smiled. Edie could see white, even teeth, perfectly displayed in a wide smile. Probably had that teeth-whitening thing done. And veneers. And crowns. Wonder how much it cost. Now probably wasn't the best time to ask.

'I'm always interested to hear what people think about the pharmaceutical industry. What particular area do you see as having a problem?'

What area! The whole industry was a problem! Edie cleared her throat.

'Well, I suppose you could call it the 'blatant bribery' element; you know, where the pharmaceutical industry spends fortunes wining and dining doctors and 'buying' the medical opinions they want to hear.'

'Edie!'

Charlie's mouth dropped open but Marianne's smile never wavered. Edie watched her take a tiny sip of coffee.

'My, my, my! Someone's been doing a little bit of reading, haven't they! But John Le Carré would have to say that, wouldn't he? I mean he wrote a bestseller on the theme. You do realise he's a writer, don't you? Writers do anything for a bit of publicity, I know; I've managed a few. So I'm afraid John Le Carré is certainly no one to talk about vested interests!'

A burst of laughter, a wave of the hand. Edie felt her face begin to redden. It was as if she'd just been dismissed.

'It's true!'

Marianne's smile faded.

'Is it? Medicine is a very ethical profession. No one can tell a doctor what to say or do, it just doesn't happen. Ask Charlie.'

Good one, Marianne. Put the spotlight on someone else. No wonder she worked in PR.

'Biscuit, anyone?'

Now she was passing around the biscuits, her biscuits! Edie could feel a heat rise in her throat. If Marianne thought that this was over, she was wrong!

'The pharmaceutical industry often refuses to publish findings they don't like, findings that don't suit their commercial interests.'

Marianne took another sip of coffee. Edie wondered if perhaps she hadn't heard her.

'I didn't know you had such a radical sister, Charlie! Is this your sister who believes in angels?'

A high-pitched tinkle of a laugh. Edie felt as if someone had slapped her hard across the face. Charlie had told this total stranger about her angel cards! What else had Charlie told Marianne? She felt a warm flush creep up her neck. She could see her coffee, untouched, sitting on the table, the name of some drug written in big blue letters across the mug. She felt a sudden wave of tiredness. She never got it right, did she? Here she was, silly Edie, embarrassing him again.

'How long are you staying, Ada?'

'It's Edie.'

A long, thin smile.

'How long you staying, Edie?'

'I'm going home tomorrow.'

Another laugh. Had she missed something? Marianne stepped closer and for a moment Edie thought that she was going to pat her on the head, as if she was a child. Or an animal.

'Lovely to meet you, Ada. It's a nice evening, you should get Charlie to show you the sights, the spire perhaps.'

Edie bit her lip. The spire for feck's sake!

'Actually, I lived in Dublin for two years.'

Terrible to interrupt their little eye contact.

'Sorry?'

'I said I lived in Dublin for two years, I studied pharmacy for a while.'

'Did you? Pharmacy, imagine, of all things! I'm not surprised you gave it up, considering how you feel about the pharmaceutical industry!'

Edie hesitated a moment.

'It was nothing to do with that.'

She glanced at Charlie. Hopefully he hadn't told Marianne the rest of her life story. She still couldn't believe that he'd told her about the angel cards.

'We were just going to order a takeaway, Marianne, want to join us?'

Edie's knuckles glistened white on the coffee table. What? He was asking her to join them! After how Marianne had made fun of her like that? Did he not realise what a cow she was?

'Sounds lovely, but I've an appointment. A client.'

Edie could see Charlie's smile fade ever so slightly.

'That's a pity.'

'Anyway, must go. I'll give you a tinkle tomorrow.'

She turned towards Edie.

'Ada, lovely to meet you. I'm sure we'll meet again.'

'Goodbye.'

The word stuck in her throat. What did she mean by 'I'm sure we'll meet again'? Charlie had never mentioned anything about a Marianne. Normally he told her everything.

Edie waited until their voices faded, then hurried across to the window. There they were, standing beside that stupid sports car. And look at Charlie, no jacket, not even a jumper, he'd get pneumonia. His hand was on her arm. Then he kissed her on the lips. Edie closed her eyes. Damn.

Five minutes later, he was back.

'Well?'

'Well what?'

'How come you never mentioned her?'

'There's nothing to mention.'

'Yeah, right. You can't fool me, Charlie. You're sleeping with her, aren't you?'

He bent down and picked up his mug. Edie could see red lipstick on the outside.

'Charlie?'

He looked up.

'OK, OK, just one night, that's all, big deal. I'm off to the States in a few weeks.'

'But you like her, don't you?'

He didn't answer. Edie sighed. Silly, silly Charlie! A girl like Marianne would chew him up and spit him out. She didn't care about Charlie; people like that didn't care about anyone. No involvement, no commitment. Too busy making money. She watched him raise the mug to his lips.

'Jesus, Charlie! You could get glandular fever or hepatitis if you drink from that! Don't you doctors know anything about hygiene?'

He laughed and put down the mug. Then he turned to look at her, his face now serious.

'Edie, I'm really sorry about the angel card thing. Something about angels came up in the conversation and I mentioned your angel cards. That's all, honestly. I don't remember her saying anything at the time, I didn't think she even heard me.'

Oh she heard you all right, Charlie. People like her hear everything and store it up until the time is right to launch the missile.

'Sorry, sis.'

He rubbed her shoulder and she smiled.

'It's OK, lick-arse. Now how about that take-away, I'm starving.'


It was after midnight when Edie turned off the light. It had been a nice night, apart from Marianne. After the take-away, they had ice-cream; vanilla, chocolate, and strawberry. Then another bottle of wine. She touched the bridge of her nose. Her sinuses would definitely be blocked in the morning after all that red wine and ice-cream. She'd probably end up talking like Clements. She smiled, remembering Charlie's impersonations of his boss; the nasal toney voice, chin in the air, arms folded behind his back. Charlie was great at taking people off.

Neither of them mentioned Marianne again. But somehow, the evening had changed; the equilibrium had been upset. Marianne was a cow. End of story. But, of course, Charlie didn't see that. As far as he was concerned, Marianne had been perfectly friendly, especially after Edie's 'unprovoked' attack. Well, at least she'd let her have it about the pharmaceutical industry. For all the difference it made; water off a duck's back. Ada! For feck's sake!

She buried her face in the pillow. Oh, Charlie.

# 21

Charlie opened his eyes. Darkness swirled around him. A yellow chink of light peeped under the bedroom door. His eyes flicked to his mobile; six fifty. The alarm was set for seven. So what had woken him? Then he heard it; that funny out-of-tune voice that drove Mother mad. It seemed to be coming from the kitchen. Charlie smiled. Amazing how she ever got into training college; weren't teachers supposed to be able to sing? He hopped out of bed and grabbed his jeans.

'Morning, Edie! You're up early, kiddo.'

She turned and smiled. Her hair was all squiggly, like pencil toppings.

'Do you realise that I won't see you for nearly two weeks? There'll be just you and Mother next weekend. Be very afraid, Charlie. She'll kill you with food when I'm not around to stop her.'

Charlie laughed. Edie was right. Mother seemed to think that big dinners would sustain him for the week ahead, like a camel storing up water in its hump. He used to think the same about sleep. All bullshit, of course.

'She'll probably use a funnel, like they do in France for the foie-gras geese.'

She handed him a plate piled high with pancakes and bacon.

'Jesus, Edie! There's a mountain of food here! You're as bad as Mother!'

She laughed and placed a mug of tea in front of him.

'Did you sleep OK?

He nodded. He had slept well, very well, actually. Maybe it was because of Edie, or maybe it was Marianne's visit.

'What about you, kiddo, you sleep OK?'

She dropped a wedge of lemon on his plate.

'Took me a while, the traffic and everything.'

Charlie nodded. He had been exactly the same when he came to Dublin. City sounds were very different to country sounds; harsher, more threatening.

'Did you read the articles I sent you?'

He put down his knife.

'No.'

He could have lied but she'd have known.

'Sorry, Edie, I'm up to my eyes, hon.'

And Edie's articles weren't exactly top priority.

'Did you know that a lot of American research centres ask you to sign something allowing them to block publication if they don't like the results? Or that they can delay publication?'

He put down his mug. Yes, he knew that. And, most likely, he'd have to sign a waiver of publication rights, too. But he wasn't going to tell Edie that.

'And that way more money is spent on marketing and promoting a drug than on actual drug development?'

He shrugged. Yeah, he knew that. Big deal. Drugs were no different to anything else. A commodity.

'Or when pharma companies can't come up with new block-buster drugs, they just alter existing ones and launch them as 'new' drugs, but at double the price?'

She did that inverted comma thing in the air with her fingers and Charlie smiled.

'Not like that, Edie, like this.'

He wiggled his fingers the same way Marianne did.

'Whatever. Look, read that stuff I gave you, Charlie; it's dynamite. You wouldn't believe what the pharmaceutical industry does to make profits.'

Charlie smiled. Wouldn't he?

'It's a business like any other business, Edie.'

Edie put down her mug.

'No, it isn't, Charlie. We can't just continue with this 'pill for every ill' crack, these guys invent diseases for God's sake! They create a market and then, like saviours, they bring us a 'cure'. It's wrong, Charlie, and doctors are just as bad to be going along with it.'

'Doctors aren't the problem, Edie.'

She shook her head.

'Doctors know what's going on, yet they sit back and say nothing, happy to leg it off to the golf course for another round of 'pharmaceutical' golf? Even you, Charlie, off to the States on a WorldPharma sponsorship. Can't you see what's happening? They're trying to control you. You jump when that botoxed Barbie you're going out with clicks her fingers.'

There was an edge in her voice.

'I'm not going out with her.'

'Whatever...'

Charlie sighed. Edie made it sound like the bloody Mafia.

'I won't do anything I don't want to, Edie, you know that.'

She shook her head.

'But that's the problem, Charlie. You don't know right from wrong any more; it's all so subtle you don't even know you're being manipulated.'

He sighed.

'And what do you suggest I do, Edie?'

'Someone's got to speak up, someone's got to do something.'

'And you want that someone to be me, Edie?'

'Yes! I do! You're not one of them, Charlie, you're not like that. At least you didn't used to be.'

He pushed his plate away.

'Things don't always pan out the way we plan them, Edie.'

She looked away.

'No, they don't.'

Charlie bit his lip. Things certainly hadn't panned out for Edie the way she thought they would. He touched her arm and she turned towards him. The fire had gone from her eyes.

'Edie, be reasonable. I can't take on the entire pharmaceutical industry.'

'Why not?'

'It's not my war. Like it or not, Edie, I'm on that wheel, I'm part of the machine, part of the system, I need them. It's different for Bono and Geldof, they can say what they want; I'd be squashed, Edie, it would be professional suicide. I could kiss my consultant's job goodbye.'

'Ask Archangel Michael to help you, the angel of truth and fairness.'

Charlie sighed. Him and Archangel Michael versus the pharmaceutical industry. Sounded like a fair match, all right. Poor, naïve Edie.

'Oh, Edie! Give the angels a rest, OK? Come back to the real world.'

The instant he'd spoken, he regretted it. He could see her eyes darken.

'Edie, I'm sorry.'

She jumped to her feet.

'No, you're not! You're just like Mother; you think I'm stupid! What's the harm in it, Charlie, tell me? Why does a tiny bit of spirituality gets up everyone's noses in this 'oh so happy' consumer society where you're judged by your big car and your stupid boat and your latest investment property?'

He reached for her arm. She pulled away.

'It's just …'

'Let me guess… Crazy Edie Darmody talking about the angels again? The mad one from the Lodge? Don't steal the apples from the orchard or she'll come after you with a knife? I'll tell you who's mad, Charlie, you and Clements, prescribing dangerous drugs, letting PR companies twist things around, liars like Marianne and people like Mother ringing a bell for dinner or cutting out Christmas cards. Don't call me crazy!'

Her eyes blazed and her voice was shrill. Oh God. How could he go to work and leave her like this? It was all his fault; he was the one who'd upset her. He slipped his arm around her shoulders and drew her close, like Dad used to do when she was having a temper tantrum.

'You're right, Edie, guess we're all pretty crazy.'

After a while, a slow smile crossed her lips.

'Course, I'm right, lick-arse.'

He smiled. Edie could never stay mad at him for very long. Her fingers fiddled with the sleeve of his sweater, twisting it, like she twisted the corners of her pillowcase.

'You'll be late.'

'So what. I can drop you at the Green if you like.'

She smiled.

'Isn't it out of your way?'

'No, not for you, kiddo.'

She tweaked his hair.

'Charlie?'

'What?'

'I'm sorry what I said about Melissa.'

'You mean Marianne?'

A wide smile.

'Yeah, that's the one.'

It was almost nine when Charlie passed the gates of Trinity. He glanced at the sea of faces milling past the gates; faces shining with youth and hope, with their scarves and their i-Pods; their jeans dark at the end from trailing on the ground. Ten years ago, Edie had been one of them, halfway through her degree, beautiful and bright, far brighter than he could ever hope to be. Edie. He could still see that fragile face, full of shattered dreams, saddened by a world that had let her down.

A wave of students surged in front of him at the traffic lights. He smiled at the girl on the moped beside him. She looked away. Probably thought he was crazy. Just because he smiled at her. This must be how Edie felt. Treated like you were crazy just because you smiled at the world and didn't hold money as your God.

Just then, a text came through. Edie. Hopefully she hadn't left something behind or lost her purse. You never knew with Edie. He opened the message and smiled. 'Miss u already. Luv. Edie.'

Love you too, hon.

# 22

Charlie glanced around and smiled; all around him, a sea of red. And plenty of red faces too. Brawn, booze and busted cervical vertebrae. That's what Edie said about rugby. Maybe she was right. Suddenly there was a communal roar and everyone was on their feet, fists in the air. The man in front of him remained slumped in his seat. Charlie sighed. Hope the poor fecker hadn't kicked the bucket.

'Ah, ref, come on! High tackle!'

Charlie smiled. Clements hadn't shut up since the match started. Maybe it was the rugby, maybe it was the booze, maybe it was the fillet of beef with the red wine jus they had for lunch. Whatever it was, he was in flying form. Food, flattery and friendship sure were the name of the game all right. The pre-match reception lasted nearly two hours. Amazing really, how a bunch of well-heeled professionals could gorge themselves like they hadn't eaten for a week. Then, of course, there was the free bar. Lethal. Double brandies, gin, whiskey, Tia Maria for fuck's sake! At twelve noon! They reminded him of young calves out on new grass. He had overheard one man, a glass in each hand, confide to his colleagues that the secret was 'to pace yourself'. There were no women in the WorldPharma corporate box, of course. God knows what the pharmaceutical companies did with female GPs. Facials and detox days, maybe, or the odd colonic irrigation, perhaps?

'Come on, Munster! Kill the bastards!'

Charlie smiled. What was it about Munster rugby, this tribal madness where sane men lost all decorum, all politeness, and, in the case of a certain Cork surgeon earlier today, his false teeth? He felt a hand on his shoulder.

'What do you think, Charlie, boy? I told you O'Gara was fit!'

Charlie nodded.

'You were right, John.'

Clements was always right. Ronan O'Gara was the business. Munster was invincible. And rugby was the only sport. Same as what all the Clongowes boys thought. Well, most of them anyway.

Charlie turned around. Joe Fleming was sitting a few rows away, smiling his perennial smile. Joe had been promoted to marketing manager since they last met. He was now one of the upper rung; another smooth-talking, smooth-skinned corporate clone. Today was his baby, his party, his idea of some medical downtime, man-style.

Suddenly there was a familiar sound; it reminded Charlie of Saturday night in Casualty. Someone was vomiting in the aisle. Hope to God it wasn't the winter vomiting bug or there'd be no male doctors working in Dublin for the next few days.

Munster won. Clements beamed. Charlie felt himself being hugged by a number of people, the sweet scent of alcohol filling the air. If someone lit a match the entire place would blow for sure.

'OK, Charlie, looks like a celebratory drink is in order!'

It was a statement, not a request. Shit, anyway. He had hoped to slip away after the match. But it looked like he'd have to tag along for another bit. The day wasn't over yet.

Thirty minutes later, they were back at WorldPharma HQ. More drink. More food. Charlie scanned the room. Same faces, same voices, only both a bit worse for wear. Joe Fleming's smile was now so wide that it looked like lockjaw. Munster's victory, apparently, was WorldPharma's victory. Must be the factory in Ringaskiddy.

'Here you go, John, crème de menthe.'

'Thanks, Charlie boy.'

Clements' words were slow and deliberate. Carefully enunciated. And there was a new, almost benign, benevolence about him. Maybe this was a good time to ask him.

'John, the Cardelia trials, weren't some elderly patients recruited?'

Might as well get straight to the point.

Clements nodded.

'What happened the results? Weren't they ever published?'

Clements shook his head.

'Not that I'm aware of, Charlie.'

'Why?'

Clements' jaw seemed to tighten ever so slightly.

'The trials were never finished, there was nothing to publish.'

'But why were they stopped?'

Clements shrugged.

'Look, Charlie, the company calls the shots as to what gets pulled, I'm sure they had a very good reason.'

Charlie watched him play with his drink, swirling it and examining it, as if he were reading tealeaves. Then he lifted it to his lips and downed it in one swallow. When he looked up again, there was a thin smile on his face that didn't reach his eyes.

'I think it's about time we called it a day, don't you?'

Charlie stood up. Conversation over.

At the door, Charlie felt a hand on his shoulder. It was Joe Fleming; the all-dancing, all-smiling company man.

'Charlie, hang on a moment, I've something for you.'

He handed Charlie a small package.

'A little souvenir from WorldPharma.'

'Thanks, Joe.'

Amazing how anyone could keep smiling that long. Maybe it was something they taught you when you became a rep; exercises for the oral muscles, Pilates for your jaws so that you didn't get cramp. Then again, Joe Fleming had every reason to smile today. It was a good day's work. Another bunch of key opinion leaders fed, watered, groomed and primed. All ready for another day.

It was after nine when Charlie got home. He kicked off his shoes and threw himself on the couch. Then he remembered the WorldPharma present. He took the package out of his pocket and pulled off the wrapping. Well, well, well. Black boxer shorts with *'Score with Munster'* on one side and *'Score with Diastora'* on the other! This beat all, as Tommy Porter would say. And, speaking of Tommy, guess who'd be getting a new pair of underpants?

He reached down and picked up Edie's folder from the coffee table. Might as well have a quick look; get her off his back. He settled a cushion behind his shoulders. Probably all quasi-scientific bullshit; he'd be sound asleep in ten minutes. Typical Edie, she had marked bits in yellow highlighter and made little notes in the margin in her spidery handwriting. Ten minutes, that's it. He began to read.

# 23

Edie wrapped the towel tightly around her hair. She knew she was smiling but she couldn't help it. In exactly six hours' time, she would be sitting in a plane, on her way to San Francisco!

She glanced out the window. The grey sky hung sullen and silent over the Galtees, seeping into the Suir; silent and stagnating. Exactly the sort of day to be leaving Ireland! Last night's Yahoo weather showed a yellow sun and twenty-two degrees in San Francisco. Good morning, America! Have a nice day, you too, Sir! Mind you, she was glad she wasn't going to Florida; last thing she wanted was to get caught in a hurricane and spend her week cooped up in a superdome.

Her eyes travelled to the case at the end of the bed. Everything was packed; ten panties, two bras, eight t-shirts, two pairs of shorts, her khaki trousers (she was going to wear her jeans travelling), her new nighties, that new Monsoon skirt and top, flip-flops, the bikini and sarong she picked up in Dunnes, a hoodie for beach walks, a sundress and a beach towel. She hadn't bothered with rainwear. All that was left was the last-minute stuff: toiletry, purse, make-up, camera, phone, passport, tickets. And she was ready! She had her legs waxed earlier in the week and had taken Lucy for an extra long walk yesterday. She had been hoping that Mother might walk Lucy while she was away but didn't like to ask her, especially since she was still a bit under the weather with that nasty gastro bug she'd picked up at school. Thank God she hadn't caught it too. Must be that prayer to Angel Raphael.

She smoothed the duvet and plumped up the pillows. There now, all nice and neat; she liked having everything tidy when she went away. The smell of sizzling bacon wafted up the stairs and she smiled. Mother only cooked a fry for breakfast on special occasions. And today was even more special than Mother realised.

A few minutes later, she skipped down the stairs and into the kitchen.

'Morning, Edie, all set?'

Edie's smile froze. Mother's face was like a wizened lemon, waxy and sallow; as if she had been awake all night.

'You look terrible, Mother! Are you sure you're better?'

'Course I'm sure, Edie! Obviously I'm bound to look a bit peaky after that vomiting bug, it's all over the school, you know. I'll ask Dr Browne for a tonic when I pick up my cert.'

Good. At least she was going to the doctor today.

'You're very pale...'

Her mother plucked a rasher from the grill.

'I always look like death warmed up without my make-up.'

'Maybe you might ask him to take a blood test.'

'OK, if it makes you feel any better, I'll ask him to do a blood test, OK?'

'And be sure to tell Charlie that you're sick.'

Her mother cracked an egg into the pan and there was a sizzle of fat.

'Oh, didn't I tell you? Charlie phoned while you were in the shower to wish you bon voyage, said he'll phone you later. He isn't coming down this weekend, has to work on his presentation. Just as well, I don't want him

188

picking up this vomiting bug. He'll be home early next Friday though, says we might go to Chez Hans for dinner.'

Edie shook her head. Well, well, well! Chez Hans! Conscience food. So Charlie wasn't coming down this weekend after all. Little Miss Shiny Lips must have clicked her immaculate fingers and Charlie had come running. And as far as his presentation, she didn't even want to go there. Just imagine, Charlie, standing up in front of everyone, telling them about the wonderful new drug that had just become available. The bells would be ringing out for Diasphora or whatever it was called. Cameras would flash, sound bytes would be recorded for the evening news, the room would be crammed with journalists, patient support groups and elected representatives with a medical conscience. All would clap loudly and nod their heads, glad to be part of it all.

Diasphora would be cited as '*a very useful weapon in the cardiovascular armoury*' or something like that. The safest, most effective drug to hit the market in the last decade. Extensive clinical trials. Changing the outlook for cardiac disease in Ireland. Edie shook her head. Lies. All lies…

Then someone would mention the Government's commitment to tackling the health crisis and the contribution of the pharmaceutical sector to the buoyant economy and everyone would clap again and smile and wonder if they'd chance a few glasses of wine at lunch. And Charlie would be at the centre of it all, the main man, the Chosen One, right at the epicentre of the Big Lie. The latest pawn in their path to conquer.

'Are you OK, Edie?'

She blinked.

'I'm fine.'

'I'll be back in time to drive you to the station.'

'There's no need, Mother. Beth's offered me a lift. She's going to the Junction anyway to collect her daughter.'

'You sure?'

'Certain.'

It suited her better this way, being dropped by Mrs Sampson. She didn't like goodbyes, especially at railway stations. It reminded her of the train back to Thurles on Sunday evening.

'You shouldn't have gone back to school yesterday, Mother.'

'It was only a few hours, Edie; my class left for swimming at big sos. Stop fussing, I'll have all next week to rest.'

Edie reached for the milk.

'Promise me you'll call back to Dr Browne if you're not better soon?'

Her mother nodded.

'I promise. Now eat your breakfast. There'll be no free-range Tipperary eggs in Paris.'

Edie smiled.

'No. I suppose there won't.'

Nor in San Francisco either. Probably pancakes with maple syrup and cupcakes - whatever cupcakes were. Or maybe bagels and pastrami.


Edie closed the case and looked around the room. Strange, as much and all as she wanted to escape from here, there were some things that she would miss. Like her bedroom, with its faded florals and cuddly toys and the crush of books everywhere you looked. She reached for her backpack. One last check and she was ready. Then all she had to do was get dressed.

Strange how quiet the house was. Not that it was ever noisy, of course. Mother had left about twenty minutes ago. The usual carry-on, fussing about passports and stuff, slipping in miraculous medals, drenching her with holy water, putting off that final, embarrassed hug. Edie hated goodbyes, always had. Must be a boarding school thing. Or maybe it was saying goodbye to Father. She would never forget his plastic, yellow face. And so cold, cold as the marble washstand in the downstairs cloakroom. She squeezed her eyes tightly shut, blackening out the memory.

She slipped off her dressing gown and reached for her t-shirt. Her clothes were laid out on the bed beside her: jeans, sneakers, Gap sweatshirt, deck shoes. The outfit had a vague French feel to it, which seemed appropriate considering she was supposed to be going to France. She'd even brought a French dictionary. Mother had wanted to know what museums she had planned to visit. She had lied, of course, but what else could she have done? Besides, it wasn't a real lie; more like a temporary delay in telling the truth.

A few minutes later, she stood in front of the full-length mahogany mirror in her mother's room. It was the only mirror in the house that wasn't mottled with age-spots and where you could see what your bottom looked like. Perfect. With the backpack on her shoulder, she could be French. Well, almost. The bulging money-belt around the middle kind of gave the game away.

She crossed the room to the bay window. At least the rain had stopped. A single ray of sunshine bathed the tulips in a perfect circle of light. Her eyes moved skywards, half hoping, half expecting to see something, a sign, maybe. But there was nothing, just the clouds scudding across an emotional sky.

OK, one final check. Passport, money, credit card, camera, spare contact lenses, book, travel pillow for her neck. Aspirin, just in case she fell asleep and didn't get to move around the cabin. There was no point in finding out how to change your life and then dying of a blood clot the minute you stepped off the plane. Oh, she'd almost forgotten! Her VHI World Assist card, just in case she was in an accident or something. Better safe than sorry, like Mother always said. The European Insurance card Mother had given her wouldn't be much use in America but she could hardly tell Mother that.

She walked over to the writing bureau. For a moment she stood there, wondering what she should do. Mother was the only one who ever opened this desk. But Mother wasn't here. She hesitated a moment, then bent down and ran her fingers along the hem of the curtain for the key she knew was hidden there.

A moment later, she lifted the lid. She felt a sudden stab of guilt, as if she was seven again and stealing chocolate from the pantry. Quickly, she began to flick through the folders; school reports, insurance certs… Christmas card list… Feis Ceoil and Leinster School of Music piano results. Mother always held on to everything, even their summer camp certificates. Then a folder marked 'Medical' caught her eye and she lifted it out. Bingo! There it was, this year's VHI receipt. She removed the page and slipped the file back where she had found it. A place for everything and everything in its place.

She was about to close the lid when she noticed a plain brown envelope on the floor at her feet. It must have fallen out of the medical file. She bent down to pick it up. The words *'For Edie. Private and Confidential'* were written on the front. Looked like her mother's writing. There was nothing to indicate what it might be, unusual for Mother who marked the hot-press with 'fitted singles' 'double flat' and 'summer duvets'. She hesitated a moment, turning the envelope over in her hands. Whatever it was had been here for quite a while judging by the faded colour of the envelope. And whatever it was had something to do with her. Maybe it was a copy of the committal form Mother had signed the day they took her away. Or maybe it was the psychological assessment she had to get done before being accepted into teacher training college.

She took a deep breath and opened the envelope. Inside was a report of some kind and another, smaller envelope with 'Edie' written on it. She opened the report. Sorry, Mother. It was some kind of official document. At the top was her father's name Daniel J. Darmody, The Lodge, Ardfinnan Road, Clonmel. And then, in big, black capitals, the words *'Post-Mortem Report'*. Her heart skipped a beat. Her father's post-mortem report. But why did Dad have to have a post-mortem when they knew he had cancer? Why did they have to violate his body in death also? Typical medical profession, no consideration.

She was about to put the report back in the envelope when she stopped. What type of cancer did Dad have? Was it really liver cancer, like Mother said? Or had they found cancer elsewhere in the body? Sometimes cancer can spread to the liver from elsewhere in the body. They called it metastatic cancer or hepatic secondaries. Well, this was her chance to find out. She turned the pages and skipped down to the last paragraph, the one marked *'Summary'*.

OK, here we go. She took a deep breath and began to read. *'The patient had a history of manic depression and alcohol abuse necessitating frequent psychiatric in-patient treatment.'*

Manic depression, Dad had manic depression? She didn't know that! Her eyes swung back to the page. The words began to swirl in front of her and she sank to the floor. Her fingers moved to her throat. It was like someone was squeezing it, squeezing it so hard that she could hardly breathe. No! This couldn't be true! This was all a terrible mistake! Her father had died from cancer, not this lie! Her father had cancer! She checked the name again; maybe this was someone else's report, not Dad's, maybe they mixed him up with someone else. But no, the date of birth was correct, so was the address. She lowered her head to her knees.

'Dad!'

She began to rock back and forth. We loved you, Dad, Charlie and I loved you. It didn't matter how sick you were or how often you were away; we loved you. You shouldn't have done it. You shouldn't have.


Edie pressed the backpack tight against her chest, her eyes on the ground. Faces and bodies swirled and twirled around her. Voices came and went. *'Boarding now.' 'Departed.' 'Mind your bags.'* The last few hours were a blur. Mrs Sampson had collected her. She had boarded the train. She had taken the bus from Limerick to Shannon. She had checked in. Then she must have gone through security. And now, here she was, in the departure lounge, waiting for her flight to be called.

She buried her face in the backpack. Mother had lied to her. Dad hadn't died of cancer. He had hung himself in the garden shed; the one Mother knocked down the week after he died. Now all that stood in that corner were the old Scots pines, with their whispers and their shadows and where the breeze blew cold and sharp, even in summer.

She closed her eyes. Suddenly it all made sense; the conversations that suddenly stopped when you entered a room, the whispers at school, the way Mother always had to 'have a chat' with people first when Edie went anywhere, like boarding school or Irish college.

The paper cup she was holding collapsed in her hand and water trickled down her jeans. How could Mother have let them grow up thinking their father had died from cancer when, all along, he had taken his own life?

Memories came flooding back; the days Dad spent in his bedroom, saying hardly anything at all, even when you brought him the paper. Other times he would be great fun, swinging herself and Charlie high in the air, taking them to the merries in Youghal; ice-cream, candy-floss, whatever they wanted, spend, spend, spend. It was as if there was no tomorrow.

You knew by Mother's tightened lips that she didn't like those trips to Youghal. Father took no notice of her, just kept on handing them coins until there were no more coins, and then they all trooped home, the smell of the bumpers on their skin and chips in their hair, tired and happy.

Did Mother think that they would love him less for taking his own life? Did she think she could protect them from mental illness by pretending it wasn't there? Or was it just typical Mother, with her à la carte approach to everything, ignoring bits of life that she didn't like, pretending that some things never happened?

'You OK, love?'

She looked up. It was the cleaning lady again. Must be the rocking. Stop rocking, Edie.

'I've just had some bad news.'

The woman's face creased with concern.

'Somebody in the family sick, love?'

'He died, my father died. He killed himself.'

'Jesus, love! I'm sorry!'

She reached out and touched Edie's arm.

'Look, I'll just clean this up first and then I'll get you a nice cup of tea.'

Clean what up? Edie looked down. At her feet was a carpet of tissues, torn up in tiny pieces like confetti, like they had been shredded. Just like her.

A moment later, the woman handed her a cup of tea.

'Thanks.'

'No bother, love.'

She gripped the polystyrene cup with both hands and held it tightly against her chest. Its warmth was vaguely comforting. She could feel someone looking at her and looked up. Instantly the man looked away. She could guess what he was thinking; look at that crazy girl with the shredded tissues and the crushed paper cups. Maybe he was right. She was crazy; she had been crazy. And she would be crazy again. Mother had always reassured her that it was an isolated bout of hypomania; it could happen to anyone under pressure. She had been working too hard, studying too late. Everyone said how hard that second year in pharmacy was. It wouldn't happen again.

But now, of course, things were different. Her father had suffered from manic depression, severe manic depression. He had killed himself, for God's sake. Some day, would she, too, do the same? Was that why Mother watched her like a hawk, waiting for the day when the black cloud would roll into town and engulf her?

She squeezed her eyes tightly shut. Poor Dad. What must it be like to feel a weight so unbearable that you just can't stick it any more? To hate yourself so deeply that you inflict the ultimate of violent deeds on your unworthy body. What did a pain like that feel like? Worse than the time her own thoughts tortured and exhausted her? How worse?

She couldn't get those words out of her head; those cruel, treacherous words: '*strangulation marks below the cricoid cartilage... signs of asphyxia caused by strangulation, the method being hanging...*'

She could see him swinging slowly in the darkness, like a pendulum, all alone in the woodshed, in the shade of the old Scots pines.

Suddenly, she felt someone touch her arm. It was the cleaning lady again. All around her, people were on their feet.

'The flight has been called, love, you OK?'

Edie nodded.

'I'll say a prayer for him, love.'

A few minutes later, she stood at the top of the steps, waiting to step inside. It was cold out here with the wind whipping around her ears but she didn't care. Cold was good. At least she felt something. She turned and looked back at the green fields and the muddy sky. Things would never be the same again.

# 24

Charlie licked some butter from his lips. This was the business all right; the *Saturday Telegraph,* a pot of tea and a toasted rasher sandwich. Perfect. He took another bite. Edie liked toasted sandwiches too. Maybe he should get her one of those panini maker things. Or maybe not. She might burn herself and besides, Mother hated gadgets: said they were a waste of money. The last 'gadget' that came into the Lodge was a washing machine and that was ten years ago. He smiled and reached for his mug. When he had his own house, he'd fill it with gadgets; plasma screens, smoothie-makers, waffle-makers, ice-machines, the entire shebang. He'd buy exactly what he wanted. And more.

Outside, a trail of silvery jet-smoke snaked across sky, dipping low over Dublin Bay. Edie should be at the airport by now. He'd phoned twice that morning; the first time she was in the shower and later there was no answer; they must have left early for the station. Mother liked to be early. He'd tried their mobiles too but no joy there either. Edie's was probably switched off for the flight and Mother had probably forgotten hers. Oh well. He'd try again later.

He switched off the TV. Edie said that watching Saturday morning TV was sad. Then he smiled, remembering their last conversation. You'd think by Edie that Mother was on death's door. But, of course, that was typical Edie, always worrying. Two alarmists, that's what they were, Mother fretting about Edie, and Edie freaking out any time Mother got as much as a head cold. Women were all the same, all panickers. Except Marianne. Nothing could panic Marianne. She had phoned him last night, wanting to know if he could come to another meeting. Noon on Saturday. Today. The Diastora product manager was back from Zurich and anxious to go over the launch. Of course he'd come, he had been planning on going into town anyway. And she had laughed that long, smoky laugh that made him remember.

They were going out to dinner in Roly's tonight, their first proper date. Tonight was going to be special.


It was just before noon when Charlie arrived at WorldPharma HQ. Marianne hurried towards him. God, he had almost forgotten how beautiful she was.

'Charlie! Thanks for coming, especially at such short notice.'

A dazzling smile, her hand reaching for his, a finger lingering to stroke his palm. Charlie nodded at the familiar faces around the table; the usual WorldPharma bunch, looking exactly the same as the last time he'd met them, not a hair out of place. Greg Harris, the Diastora product manager, looked tanned and relaxed. Must have been on a ski junket in Switzerland. Lucky docs, whoever they were.

'OK, I promised I'd have you all out of here by one at the latest. So let's get the party started.'

The next ten minutes were a blur. Charlie tried his best to concentrate but all he could see was her body beneath him. Here and there, snippets filtered through, something about pre-empting competitor activity, communicating key messages. Then she turned around and their eyes met. He smiled and winked. She continued talking, something about favourable effects on blood lipids.

Maybe he shouldn't have winked. He took a deep breath and looked at the screen. OK, Charlie, focus. Trial data to be presented by key international speakers. Position WorldPharma as a leader in heart health education.

*'WorldPharma has a strong heritage in cardiovascular health and we must build on this.'*

A collective nod, mutterings of approval. Good, it was over. Or was it.

'As you know, we can't advertise directly to the public under IPHA guidelines, but what we can do is develop media hooks that indirectly draw attention to our product. For example, we could set up speaker platforms at big events such as the National Ploughing Championship or we could target workplace health, say in a big organization like Dell.'

'Great idea, Marianne.'

'The launch press packs have already been posted. Hopefully the health sections will pick up. We're also going to do some heart health information leaflets. These could generate a lot of noise if done correctly, like distributing them by a mime artist on a Saturday, some-place like Dundrum Shopping Centre or Mahon Point in Cork.'

Charlie could see Greg Harris reach for his pen.

'The next bit is yours, Charlie. I've outlined the key prescriber messages.'

Charlie nodded. He'd already done some general slides on hypertension. All that was left were some specifics on Diastora and by now he knew the drug like the back of his hand. He glanced at the screen. No surprises there. Diastora the number one choice in the newly diagnosed hypertensive… Eight million US patients successfully treated with Diastora… Diastora the newest and most advanced anti-hypertensive available…Excellent safety profile demonstrated in extensive clinical trials and confirmed in numerous post-approval clinical settings…

'You OK with this?'

He nodded. He'd have to tone it down a little, of course, so that it didn't appear so promotional, but overall, the facts were correct.

'The last slide is to remind everyone of what GoldMed can do for you.'

Charlie smiled. As if they needed reminding. He scanned down the bullet points. *Co-ordinated and strategic product positioning. Targeted scientific communications. Strong KOL/Third party relationships. Proven track record of creative and award-winning health programmes.*

'GoldMed has strong relationships with every key health correspondent in this country. We know these people, their likes and dislikes. We know how they want material presented to them, when they want it, and how best to get it to them. We can tailor press materials to suit specific media, and specific topics to specific journalists. These people answer the phone to us because we know them, we understand them. Just like we understand you.'

A Richter nine smile. A flurry of red nails. Nods of agreement from around the table. Marianne, dix points. She caught his eye and winked. He winked back. Well done, babe, see you later.

# 25

Traffic was crazy but so what. It was Saturday, the sun was shining and he had a date with a beautiful woman tonight. He reached for the volume and began to sing along.

*'Sha la la la la la la la…'*

He liked that song. He liked Dublin on a sunny Saturday afternoon; pretty girls sipping coffee at pavement cafes, pretending it was summer. And he liked Marianne.

His fingers drummed on the steering wheel and he turned to smile at the girl with headphones cycling beside him. Surprise, surprise, she smiled back! That was the thing about sunshine, it put everyone in better form. Marianne was wearing shades today; huge white designer ones perched on top of her head like Gillian Bowler. He could just imagine her, sitting behind the wheel of her Mazda sports, cream suit, low black top, thick gold chain circling her throat. Gorgeous.

Wonder what she'd wear tonight. Probably a sexy little black number. Well he wouldn't be looking too bad himself for a change! He glanced at the Brown Thomas bag on the seat beside him. The new clothes had cost a small fortune but he badly needed them. It had been painless enough, really. The sales assistant had been very helpful, racing around the shop picking up bits and pieces, saying things like *'let me just throw this at you, Sir'*. It was probably obvious that he hadn't a clue. Twenty minutes later he was sorted; Gant sweater, some shirts including a brightly coloured one he was still a little uneasy about and two pairs of Dockers trousers. He'd even bought some ferociously expensive aftershave and some striped boxers. Just as well Edie wasn't with him! She'd have insisted that he wait for the States, Gant was much cheaper there. But he couldn't wait three weeks; he needed something to wear tonight. He was taking a beautiful lady out to dinner.

A sign for Buds and Blooms suddenly caught his eye. Would he chance buying her flowers again? The lilies had been a disaster. Roses? No, too smarmy. Daffodils? Too cheap. Hey, what about something for her rooftop terrace? A small bay tree, maybe, trimmed into a nice shape, in one of those wooden planters you see outside restaurants? Or maybe a shrub would be awkward; she'd have to water it and take it in during the frost. Maybe he should check with her first, ask her what she'd like.

He reached for his mobile. Strange. No answer. Marianne and her mobile were usually inseparable. Then he smiled. Why not drop by and ask her? Her apartment was just around the corner; it would only take two minutes. And he could always give her the Lindt chocolates as an early present.

Yes, great idea, Charlie boy! He reached down and turned up the volume. *Sha la la la la la la la...'*
He indicated and switched to the outside lane. Next right. Nearly there...
*'Sha la la la la la la la...'*


Right, now to find a parking space. Hell, he'd park on a clearway if he had to. They could give him all the penalty points they wanted, he was out of here in a few weeks' time. Hang on... that blue car was pulling out... come on, Missus… you can do it, great stuff, you're an angel. Double yellow lines but so what. This would only take a jiffy. Good, her car was here.

He sprinted up the steps two at a time. He was almost at the door when he stopped. That car, the one parked behind Marianne's; he knew that car… 2007 D. Silver Merc. It had to be. It was. Clements' car…

For a moment, he stood perfectly still. Then he took a long, deep breath. OK, let's get the picture here. Clements' car is parked outside Marianne's apartment. Which probably means that Clements is visiting Marianne. On Saturday afternoon at five o'clock?

He turned around, then stopped. Hang on, Charlie, this could be totally innocent; don't jump to conclusions. Clements hadn't been able to make the meeting; one of the kids had a rugby match. Maybe he had called in to find out how the meeting had gone. He was WorldPharma's right hand man after all, their key opinion leader par excellence. He and Marianne were in daily contact.

His finger hesitated a moment before settling on the buzzer.

'Hi. It's Charlie.'

'Charlie!'

A significant pause.

'I was just passing.'

The words sounded wooden.

'I'm just out of the shower, I'd invite you in but I'm on my way out.'

Charlie held his breath. Not good, not good at all. Out of the corner of his eye, he could see the glint of polished German steel. Then he found himself talking again, slow, even, normal sounding words, as if someone else was speaking.

'Can I talk to you?'

'Hang on, I'm on my way down.'

He waited. A few minutes later, the door opened. She pulled it closed. Her hair was loose and damp. She obviously hadn't been lying about the shower. Her lips brushed his cheek.

'Could you be a darling and give me a lift into town? I can't face driving again today.'

He looked into her eyes. Edie was right. She was a liar. He grabbed her arm.

'Is Clements here?'

Her smile faded.

'Dr Clements? No, why do you say that?'

'His car is here.'

Immediately her eyes sank to the kerb. He could hear the sharp intake of breath. Then a silence that confirmed what he already knew. He turned and began to walk away. A clatter of heels on the pavement.

'Charlie, wait! It was nothing! It's finished.'

He turned to look at her.

'You're right, it was nothing. And it is finished. Go back to him, you two are perfectly suited. Oh, by the way, it was me who brought you the lilies.'

It was after six when he finally got home. For a while, he had driven around, not caring where he was going. He had considered going to a pub, getting totally locked. Then he changed his mind. Alcohol solved nothing, he should know that by now.

He glanced at the Brown Thomas bag on the passenger seat, mocking him. What a fool, what a stupid, stupid fool he had been! How she must have laughed at him, letting him think she actually liked him, when all along she was comparing him to rich lover-boy. Playing with him, that's all she was doing, playing with him for a few weeks, knowing that soon he would be gone, out of her hair and out of her life.

He closed his eyes and slumped over the steering wheel. He should have listened to Edie. She had seen through Marianne from the very beginning. Oh Edie! He felt a sudden urge to hear her voice. He reached for his mobile. Eight o'clock French time. She was probably on her way out for dinner.

He waited a while, then pressed redial. Nothing. Just that stupid message saying that the person you have dialled has their mobile switched off. Strange. He checked his text messages again. Nothing apart from the one earlier in the week, the morning after she stayed over. He stared at the phone in his hands, willing it to ring. Switch on your phone, Edie! I need to talk to you, honey.

# 26

Charlie glanced around the living room and sighed. Funny really, how things change. This same room, which had been so bright and full of life when Edie was here, now seemed cold and empty. Outside, the stray rays of sunshine had disappeared, leaving a thick blanket of cloud smothering the rooftops. Hailstones scudded past, pinging on the roofs of cars. He tried to imagine what they might feel like on his skin; tiny little laser shafts of pain. Even nature was fickle; one minute sunshine and the next, frozen rain.

It was strangely quiet without the TV on. Even Killian's slurping or his constant changing of channels would have been welcome. But Killian had gone home for the weekend and wouldn't be back until Monday.

He wandered into the spare room, Edie's room. It was a tiny little box room, barely big enough to fit a single bed, but she liked it, said it was cosy. Then he noticed the book on the bedside locker. *Angel Therapy.* He sighed and lay down on the bed, burying his face in the pillow. It was the same old story. Over and over again.

Suddenly he jumped. Edie! He looked at the number and felt his heart sink. An 052 number, Tipperary, but not the Lodge.

'Charlie! Glad I caught you! Tim Browne here from Clonmel.'

Dr Browne was their family doctor. Charlie had spent two weeks with him in fourth med and had really enjoyed it.

'Hello, Tim! How's the golf going?'

A laugh at the other end. Charlie could just imagine him, sitting behind his big mahogany desk, his glasses sliding off his nose. He was a warm, kindly man who had stitched Charlie's hurling injuries and visited him every day when he had glandular fever. Probably ringing to wish him luck. No doubt Mother had told him about Johns Hopkins. Him and everyone else in South Tipperary. Or maybe he was looking for a locum; Charlie often put ads up for him on the hospital notice board. Poor man didn't get away too often.

'It's your Mother, Charlie, now no need to panic or anything.'

Shit.

'She was in this morning for a blood pressure check and I didn't like her colour, so I dropped in to see her again on my way home. I think she looks a bit jaundiced.'

'Jaundiced?'

'It's very mild.'

Charlie hesitated. Jesus Christ. Secondaries in the liver. Ever since Father, the ugly spectre of cancer had always lurched on the horizon, ready to pounce.

'What do you think, Tim?'

'To be honest, I'm not sure, Charlie. I don't think it's gallstones - she hasn't any pain, but she's not eating and has been feeling a bit nauseated the past week or so, so it might be hepatitis.'

'Edie mentioned that Mother picked up a gastro bug at school but when I was talking to Mother yesterday she said she was fine.'

'You know your mother.'

'Is there hep A around?'

He dare not even consider hepatitis C.

'Not that I know of, Charlie, we'd have been notified and the school would be closed.'

'Could it be her meds?'

'The only new tablet she's on is Diastora and it doesn't cause any liver problems as far as I know, but you'd know more about that than me, Charlie. Diastora's not associated with any liver problems, is it?'

'Don't think so, Tim.'

But you never knew. You might think you knew, but you knew nothing where drugs were concerned. Or where anything was concerned.

'Charlie, I think your mother needs to be admitted, bloods, ultrasound, the usual work-up. Do you want me to get her a bed in St Joseph's or maybe you'd like her in St Anne's?'

Charlie hesitated a moment. St Joseph's in Clonmel was a good hospital with three excellent physicians. They would take good care of her there. But how would he visit her?

'Here might be easier, Tim, I might be able to speed things up and have her home before Edie gets back.'

He hesitated a moment.

'Actually, Tim, did Mother say anything about Edie?'

'She mentioned something about Edie forgetting to switch her phone back on. Speaking of Edie, I hear that she's entering the property market.'

Charlie's heart skipped a beat.

'Sorry, Tim?'

'My neighbour, Mrs Hally, her son works with Sherry Fitzgerald down town, says Edie's buying a little commercial property.'

Charlie closed his eyes. Oh Edie! She'd promised not to do anything!

'Edie hasn't mentioned it, Tim, so best say nothing to Mother.'

'Oh... Sorry, Charlie! I didn't realise.'

An awkward silence. Tim was a stickler on confidentiality.

'Is Edie OK, Charlie?'

'I hope so.'

Shit. His voice was cracking. For a moment he felt like opening up to this kind elderly man whom he had known all his life. He wanted to tell him that he was worried about Edie, not about now, but about the future and about what would happen when Mother was no longer around. That he hated being away from her. And all the other crazy stuff. Instead, he cleared his throat. Time to get a grip.

'I'll arrange a bed in St Anne's, Tim. Pat O'Mahony's on call tonight, he's one of the gastroenterologists here. I was in school with him.'

Maybe there was something to the old schoolboys' network after all.

'Great stuff, Charlie. Maybe it's just as well. The medical ward here in Clonmel is closed because of that blasted winter vomiting virus.'

'I'll let you know what's happening, Tim. Thanks for all your help.'

'Least I could do, Charlie. I was a good friend of your father's, God rest him.'

His voice was gentle.

'Well I hope it's not the same as Dad anyway.'

'Pardon?'

'I hope it's not cancer.'

A pause.

'I'm sure it's not, Charlie. I'll phone you Monday, see what the story is. She's not too keen on going into hospital, you know your mother.'

Charlie smiled. Mother had a thing about picking up MRSA and SARS, not to mention the winter vomiting bug and legionella. She'd probably arrive into hospital with her own bottle of disinfectant. And then, of course, there was the hospital food thing; Mother stopped eating chicken and mince years ago. And farmed salmon was another big no-no. Not that she'd be getting any salmon in St Anne's.

It was almost ten when Charlie turned off at the Cahir roundabout. Ninety minutes, not bad. That new bypass was magic. In twenty minutes, he would be home. Home. He took a deep breath. Tim Browne was a good clinician; he may not know exactly what was wrong, but he always knew when something wasn't right, when somebody needed to be investigated. He called it 'seat of your pants' medicine. He said Charlie had it too.

Cahir was quiet for a Saturday night. Then again Cahir was always quiet. There are certain towns in Ireland that, in spite of hundreds of new houses, still manage to look sleepy and sad, as if they could do with a good dose of Prozac. Cahir was one of those towns.

His eyes rested briefly on the group of girls huddled on the steps of Cahir House, smoking. God love them in this weather; they'd get pneumonia in those mini skirts. Last time he'd been at Cahir House was at a hunt ball with Tracy. Mother had bought the tickets; somehow she liked the idea of her son going to a hunt ball. She had hired his dress-suit, bought him new black shoes, even wanted him to wear one of those naff white scarves for God's sake. He smiled at the memory.

Mother was fond of Tracy, too fond, picking out bridal flowers kind of fond. Edie said it was Mother's fault that they split up, said that Mother had interfered too much. But she was wrong. It had nothing to do with Mother. Besides, interfering was what mothers did. Somehow, though, he couldn't help but feel that Edie was secretly glad.

He dimmed his lights at an approaching truck. Trass' apple farm or the 'German' farm as Mother called it (despite being told hundreds of times that it was Dutch) looked as pretty as ever, still and quiet in the cold night air. He wondered if the apple trees had started to bud yet. The campsite was closed but the farm shop stayed open all year round. Normally he'd pick up a crate of cookers and a case of apple juice for Edie; she loved the 'German' apple juice.

Suddenly, there was a flash of yellow; daffodils, hundreds of them, in the middle of the roundabout. You had to hand it to Tipperary South Riding; they had excellent landscaping, fair play to them. Suddenly, something lit up the sky; a flash of some kind, like sheet lightening, only it couldn't be, the night was cold and frosty. Maybe it was some sort of security lighting from that new factory or disco lights from one of the hotels. He searched the sky; nothing, no beams, no flashes, nothing but the stars and the moon slicing through the sky. He sighed and smiled. If Edie was here, she'd have said it was the angels. They won't come if you don't ask them, was what she said. And he hadn't asked them. Not yet. But it couldn't do any harm, could it? Besides, nobody need know. He took a deep breath. Who was the healing guy again, Raphael, wasn't it?

'Archangel Raphael, take care of Mother and Edie.'

There now, he'd done it. Edie would be proud of him. Now all he could do was wait. Strange, he was more worried about Edie than Mother. At least with Mother, you had a tangible problem with a tangible solution. With Edie, it was different; more a free-floating anxiety. He couldn't help feeling that something was wrong.

Ahead, he could see the line of old horse chestnuts that shaded the gates of the Lodge. The roofs of the new houses glistened darkly in the moonlight, towering above the high garden walls, as if they were waiting to pounce. Mother said that the Lodge was the last fortress, the only piece of Clonmel that the developers hadn't gotten their hands on. He sighed. Not yet, anyway.

The crunch of limestone gravel on the driveway brought back a string of childhood memories. Football, tree houses, queen cakes, Christmas. The smell of conkers and pine needles, fresh hay and honeysuckle. Then the house came into view and he could see a light in his mother's bedroom. Probably fussing about, packing her case, cleaning windows, maybe even washing the floors. Or vacuuming; Mother always vacuumed before going anywhere.

He knocked twice, his usual knock. Then he opened the door.

'Mother!'

She was lying in bed, wearing a pink nightdress and the old blue cardigan she normally wore for gardening. Her face was gaunt and stretched, like a Halloween mask, murky yellow, with eyes that were stained with bile. She lifted her hand and smiled.

'I'm such a nuisance, Charlie, bringing you all the way down and you so busy. I told Dr Browne it could wait until Monday but he wouldn't listen.'

Even her voice was different, it lacked its usual authority.

'I've a bed arranged for you in St Anne's, Mother.'

Best take the firm approach straight away.

'Can't it wait until morning? You could have an early night and we could get up early tomorrow.'

'No, Mother, might as well take the bed while it's there. I've told Pat O'Mahony you're coming in tonight.'

'Pat O'Mahony? He was in Leaving Cert when you started in Clongowes, wasn't he? Does he still play rugby?'

'I think he trains the school kids at Belvedere.'

'Does he? Isn't that nice? You should think about doing that, Charlie, training the younger ones.'

Like hell he would.

'So you'll go in tonight?'

'OK, so.'

No argument, no refusals. Just 'OK, so.' She must be sick. He reached for her hand. Her fingers felt like cold cutlery. Up close, her skin was shrouded in a myriad of tiny wrinkles, like the apples withering in the pantry.

'Any word from Edie?'

Damn.

'Charlie?'

He met her eyes.

'No.'

So much for not worrying her.

'We'd surely have heard by now if the plane had crashed or anything.'

He squeezed her hand.

'She's fine, probably tucking into a big dinner this very minute.'

'Has she texted?'

He shook his head.

'Maybe she lost her phone, you know Edie, always losing things.'

Shit. Why had he mentioned losing things? He remembered the time Edie lost her passport in Malaga. Now that had been some mess. Best change the subject.

'I'll get the case down.'

A nod.

'Thanks, Charlie.'

A moment later, he placed the battered case on the end of the bed. It was the one he had for school, held together by an old leather belt, the leather cracked and worn. He swallowed. Next week he'd buy her a new case; one of those Samsonite ones with wheels. The best money could buy.

'Shall I pack?'

A nod.

He lifted the bundle of clothes and gently placed them in the case. Something about the soft velvet of her slippers against his hand caused his breath to catch. All the Sunday evenings came back to him; Mother folding his clothes, packing them neatly into this case, making sure everything was ready for boarding school. Now he was doing it for her.

When he was finished, she touched his arm.

'What do you think, Charlie?'

Her voice was low, confidential.

'It's probably just a virus, Mother, nothing to worry about.'

'I suppose the other thing wouldn't come on as sudden.'

He squeezed her hand.

'No, it wouldn't.'

Or maybe the symptoms were so gradual that she just hadn't noticed them.

'Before we go, Charlie, I want you to have a quick cup of tea. I bought one of those cakes you like in Hickey's this morning.'

He felt a tightening in his throat. Sick and nauseated as his mother was, she had stopped at his favourite bakery in Clonmel to buy his favourite cake. It was pink sponge covered with a soft pink icing. Edie called it his pink shitty cake. Neither Mother nor Edie liked it. Mother only ever bought it for him. He felt a sudden wave of guilt. Wonder how many of Hickey's cakes hit the bin over the years when he failed to show.

He opened the kitchen door and a wave of sadness hit him. Everywhere he looked reminded him of Mother; the sieve drying behind the Aga, the neatly folded tea towels, the bell she rang for dinner. He cleared his throat and reached for the tea caddy. This was one Barry's moment he could do without.

She was sitting at the edge of the bed when he returned. He handed her a cup of tea.

'Would you like some cake?'

She shook her head and smiled. A few moments later, he put down his cup. Strange how pink shitty cake always made him feel better.

'What do you want me to do before we go?'

She reached for the piece of paper beside her on the bed.

'Can you phone Mrs Hennessy and ask her to feed Lucy? Then you might put the heating on the timer so that it kicks in for a few hours every night. Last thing I want is a burst pipe. Oh, can you go through the fridge and throw out anything that might go off and check all the windows?'

Ten minutes later, he was back.

'All done, we might as well hit the road.'

She smiled and stood up. Her legs were thin and birdlike, ready to snap. He slipped his arm under hers.

'Here, let me help you.'

He took his time. By the time they reached the car, she could barely stand. Slowly, gently, he eased her into the front seat and fastened the seatbelt.

'I'll get a rug or something.'

He ran back into the house and bounded up the stairs. It would take a while for the car to heat up. He'd grab one of Edie's fleeces, maybe a duvet.

He smiled when he opened the door of Edie's room; the room was neat as a pin; she must have done one of her major clean-ups before she went away.

Navy fleece, fluffy socks. Perfect. Now all he needed was the duvet. Something slipped to the floor and he bent to pick it up. An envelope with his name on it, Edie's writing, the letters uneven, as if written in a hurry. He smiled. Probably more stuff on the pharma industry. He stuffed it into his pocket and hurried down the stairs.

He drove slowly, avoiding the potholes, conscious of his mother's silence. Her face was turned away from him, looking out, as if she was memorising every bush and plant in the garden: the hypericum at the bend, the variegated ivy near the steps, the big horse chestnut near the gate with Edie's old tree house in its lower branches. It was as if she was saying goodbye.

# 27

Charlie opened his eyes and blinked. Light streamed in through the open curtains but a familiar nausea told him he couldn't have slept more than a few hours. He glanced at his watch. Nine-thirty.

The duvet slipped to the floor and he could see that he was still wearing his jeans. Memories of the night before came flooding back; the drive up to Dublin, waiting for Mother to be admitted and then waiting for all the blood results to come back. As he had guessed, all her liver function tests were up; alk phos, transaminases, bilirubin, the works. Full blood count was normal, no retics; she wasn't haemorrhaging or haemolysing. It looked like some kind of acute liver damage. Hope to God it wasn't hep C…

Something had been niggling at him ever since Dr Browne's phone call. Could it be Diastora? OK, there was nothing in the product information about abnormal liver function but then again, there was nothing in the Cardelia product information about acute arrhythmias and sudden death, was there? After calling to see Mother, he was going to go to the library. If there was even one reported incident of Diastora causing liver abnormalities, he was going to find it.

He reached for his mobile. Maybe Edie had texted while he was asleep. Damn. Nothing; no missed calls, no texts, no voice mail. He felt a stab of worry. This was strange. Edie normally phoned or texted at least once a day. Something was wrong, he knew it; the same way he knew it the last time.

An hour later, Charlie sat at Sister's desk. The ward round should be over any minute now. The shop trolley trundled past, piled high with newspapers. Wonder what was happening in the outside world. When you worked in hospitals, it was like your own little eco-system; it was difficult to imagine that there was a whole world out there with people going about their happy, healthy lives.

At least Mother was no worse this morning. And back in normal fighting mode. The poor woman nearly had a canary when she realised that the mass from the chapel wasn't broadcast on the wards any more. It wasn't politically correct to make everyone listen to a Catholic mass in a multi-cultural Ireland. She was furious, said that if she went to Saudi, she'd have to cover up and that Catholicism was our primary religion and we shouldn't be ashamed of it. He smiled. Good old Mother.

A door opened and a swarm of people, all shapes, sizes and colours, spilled into the corridor. Good, the ward round was over. And Pat O'Mahony was walking towards him.

'Morning, Charlie. We're still none the wiser, I'm afraid. It looks like some kind of diffuse inflammation. The alk phos would probably be higher if it was obstructive. The hepatitis antigens won't be back until tomorrow. Do you know if she ever had a blood transfusion?

Charlie shook his head.

'No, and even if she had anti-D, it wouldn't have been during the at-risk period.'

'Right... and she doesn't drink... any risk of leptospirosis?'

'She was gardening last week.'

'I'll check a leptospira titre anyway just to be on the safe side.'

'Could it be a drug reaction?

'Well the biochemical picture would certainly be in keeping, but she's been on her usual meds for years. Diastora is the only new medication and it doesn't cause any liver problems as far as I'm aware.'

Charlie hesitated a moment.

'Would you mind if Diastora was stopped? Just to be on the safe side?'

'Good idea, Charlie, sounds the sensible thing to do. Anyway, her BP is fine and she's going to be in bed, so she'll manage fine without her meds. I'll stop the others as well. That's all she's on, isn't it?'

Charlie nodded.

'Are today's bloods back yet?'

A nod.

'They're much the same as last night.'

Charlie nodded. At least they weren't any worse.

'We'll continue with IV fluids and do an ultrasound and CT tomorrow. I'll give you a buzz as soon as we have the results.'

'Thanks, Pat, and thanks for coming in so late last night, I really appreciate it.'

'Look, Charlie, I know you'd do the same for me. It's the only perk of the job.'

Charlie smiled. It was one particular perk he could do without.

Charlie awoke with a start. He looked around and felt a rush of panic. Then he saw the rows of books and relaxed. He must have fallen asleep while he was researching Diastora. He glanced at the clock, almost five. He had slept for over two hours, Edie would be proud of him.

He leaned back into the chair, raising the front legs, the way Mother hated, said it wrecked the chairs. He had called to see her again after lunch; she had been in good form, reading the papers and drinking Ballygowan from the glass she had brought from home. He smiled. You should have seen her locker; disposable gloves, cutlery, a bottle of bleach and, of course, her own thermometer. She was watching the cleaners like a hawk, making sure they did a proper job. Just as well Sister had a sense of humour.

He reached into his pocket for the bar of Caramelo he had bought earlier. He found its velvety caramel strangely soothing. Maybe he should start using it on the wards, cross out Valium and instead write *'one bar of Caramelo twice daily, to be taken after food'*.

He turned back to the screen and sighed. Still nothing. No clue, no little nugget from the journals that could set him on the right path. One thing was certain, though, Mother's biochemical picture matched other cases of hepatotoxicity. It definitely seemed to be some kind of acute insult to the liver, viral or toxic. If the viral screen came back negative, then it had to be Diastora, no matter what they said. Mother's clinical picture, the lab results, the timing, everything fitted exactly.

Except for one little problem. He had gone through the Diastora product information with a fine toothcomb. The drug was squeaky clean; there wasn't even a hint of liver toxicity. It was licensed for use in liver failure for God's sake, even though other classes of anti-hypertensives were contraindicated! He rubbed his eyes. This was hopeless. Maybe he should go straight to the horse's mouth, ask WorldPharma if they knew anything about Diastora and liver damage. It was a long shot but at least it was worth a try.

He reached into his pocket for his wallet. Greg's card was here some place, he'd told him to call if he needed any more information on Diastora. Well, he did, but for a different reason. Bingo. Here it was, *WorldPharma*

*International, Greg Harris, Diastora Product Manager* - a work number and a mobile. It was Sunday, but worth a try; these corporate guys were as bad as doctors, always on the job. It answered on the third ring.

'Greg Harris here.'

'Hi Greg, this is Charlie, Charlie Darmody.'

'Hi there, Charlie! How come you're not at the match?'

Not another rugby match. Wonder who was playing.

'Actually, Greg, my mother's in hospital.'

'I'm sorry to hear that, Charlie, I hope it's not too serious.'

'Hope not. Look, Greg, the reason I'm phoning is that my mother has jaundice and we don't know what's causing it. She's been taking Diastora for the past few weeks and I know that it's highly unlikely but I was wondering if you guys have ever come across any liver problems with Diastora?'

Charlie bit his lip and waited.

'I wish I could help you, Charlie, but there's no evidence anywhere that Diastora causes any liver abnormalities. I've seen all the trials, every single one, even the phase one trials showed nothing hepatic. It's one of the few products licensed in liver dysfunction.'

Charlie sighed.

'I know, Greg, that's what I thought. What about any unpublished trials, any way of checking those out?'

This time, a short silence.

'All trials are published in their complete state, as they should be.'

Oops. Trials were obviously a touchy subject.

'Of course. Look, I really appreciate your help, Greg, and I'm sorry for phoning you on Sunday afternoon.'

'No worries, Charlie, glad to be of any help. If it was my mother, I'd do exactly the same thing.'

Charlie raised an eyebrow. Would he? Or would a true company man like Greg sacrifice his mother for the good of Big Pharma? Probably.

'Thanks, Greg.'

'See you on Saturday, so, Charlie. Best of luck.'

Saturday? Charlie closed his eyes. Shit! The Diastora launch! Oh what the hell. He could always wing it. After all, he knew everything there was to be known about Diastora. Well, almost everything.

He sighed and closed his eyes. According to Greg, Diastora didn't cause liver problems. All the clinical trials showed no evidence of liver damage. So why did he think Diastora might be causing his Mother's hepatitis? Because he believed no-one any more, least of all the pharmaceutical industry. And the weirdest thing of all was that in a few days' time, he was going to stand up in front of his peers and the medical media and tell them about a brilliant new drug called Diastora that had an excellent safety profile! He sighed. How could he extol the virtues of a drug that he suspected of damaging his mother's liver?

It was after nine when he got home. He looked up at darkened windows and sighed. Killian must have decided to wait until morning to come back. Oh well. At least he wouldn't have to watch that stupid wrestling channel.

A beer would be nice. He opened the fridge. Good. A solitary bottle of Rolling Rock glowed green on the bottom shelf. The one that got away. It was almost to his lips when he remembered his mother's comments about leptospirosis. Best use a glass. He opened the press; nothing but some tiny wine glasses and a cloudy-looking pint glass that Killian had whipped from some party. Maybe he'd take his chances with the bottle.

He took a long, deep swallow. Then he felt his heart skip a beat. There was a light blinking on the answering machine. He pressed the button and waited. A wave of disappointment washed over him. It wasn't Edie. It was Jack, an old friend from UCD, wanting to know if he could visit him in the States.

He took another deep swallow and reached for his mobile. He needed to talk to Edie before someone told her about Mother. Knowing her, she'd be on the first plane home and he didn't want that, not yet, anyway. He sighed and put down the phone. Still no reply. What the hell was going on? Why was her phone still switched off?

A moment later, he opened the cupboard. Cornflakes would be nice. With hot milk and loads of sugar. His kind of comfort food. Then his eyes fell on the Brown Thomas bag on the floor and he shook his head. So long, Marianne. Beautiful, smiling, manipulative, Marianne. He wished he'd never have to lay eyes on her again but unfortunately, that wasn't possible, not with the launch coming up.

He reached for a bowl. Yep, he'd meet her all right, no problem. But no more mister nice guy. If she wanted to meet him, she could bloody well come out to St Anne's. Why should he have to trek all the way across town? Lover boy could drive her in his big shiny Merc, the two of them laughing their beautiful heads off.

He lifted his beer and began to drink, deeper and deeper until there was nothing left. Then he remembered something - Edie's letter, the one she had left on her bed. Maybe it had the name of her hotel.

For a moment, he sat perfectly still; nothing but the sound of his breathing and his heart banging on his ribcage. Then, as the words began to roll and thunder in his head, he felt something explode inside him. His fingers closed tightly around the bottle in his hand and sent it crashing against the wall.

'No!'

After a while, the anger faded, like the embers of a dying fire. Now all he felt was a gnawing, empty pain deep inside him. Dad hadn't died of cancer. Dad had killed himself.

He let his head drop into his hands. Everyone knew except him and Edie. No wonder the children at school talked behind their backs. No wonder Mother was so evasive about the 'cancer' that killed his father. It all made sense now; how quiet Dad used to be sometimes, his roller-coaster moods, why they weren't allowed to visit him in hospital, why nobody had told them that their father was going to die.

And it explained what Tommy meant about 'the strain being there'. Why hadn't Tommy told him? He felt another flash of anger, then watched it rise and pass, like a wave on the seashore. It wasn't Tommy's place to tell him; it was nobody's place but Mother's. What was she thinking of? How could you lie about something like this? Pretend that it never happened? It wasn't fair, especially to Edie. She was his daughter; she deserved to know. After all, Edie might have inherited the strain, as Tommy put it; that mental fragility, that unwelcome genetic coding for bi-polar illness. Maybe he had too; he was a nephew, after all, fairly close in the genetic tree.

He closed his eyes. Edie. He could just imagine her, wandering around Paris, crying her eyes out. Would she understand that it wasn't her father's fault; that sometimes, at the height of the darkness, people don't know what they are doing, that their thinking becomes so disturbed that they carry through that final, ultimate act of self-hatred? Would she, could she, understand? Or would she only see that the father she loved so much had left her? The thought that some day, she too, might commit suicide had surely crossed her mind.

He jumped to his feet. He had to go to Paris and find her. Then he sighed and slumped back into the chair. He didn't know the name of the hotel. He'd have to contact the family of the girl from Waterford. Mother would surely have their number; she had everyone's number. He glanced at his watch. Ten fifteen. Hopefully, she might still be awake.

All the way in to the hospital, he thought about what he was going to say to her. Emotions boiled up in him; anger, resentment, betrayal and a deep, deep, sadness. He wanted to hurt her, to have her feel some of the pain he was feeling now. And he wanted to talk about it, all of it, all the details. He needed to know. He needed to know everything. Then he sighed. Tonight wasn't the night. It would have to wait. First, he had to find Edie.

His mother looked up when he opened the door, her eyes wide.

'Charlie! I thought you'd gone home. Any word?'

'No.'

He hoped his voice sounded normal.

'I was thinking of phoning her friend.'

A nod.

'That's a good idea, Charlie. I'll get my diary, I have her home number someplace, I got it the last time she visited us, that must be two years ago, funny we haven't seen her in the meantime...'

A moment later, she looked up and smiled.

'Here it is, Margaret Barry! It's an 058 number, Waterford.'

He could feel her eyes on him.

'Is everything OK?'

Trust Mother not to miss a trick.

'Fine, everything's fine. I'll phone in the morning, it's a bit late now.'

She smiled a watery smile.

'You'll let me know if you hear anything?'

He nodded.

'Goodnight, Mother. Try and get some rest.'

He had been going to say sleep but changed his mind. Mother wouldn't get much sleep tonight. And neither would he.

# 28

Charlie pulled back the curtains. It was almost bright; the morning fresh and dewy, the birds already in full song. Edie loved mornings like this; she often set her alarm for dawn and went off on a long ramble over the fields with Lucy, walking miles and miles before coming back to drag him out of bed for breakfast. The few times she had managed to persuade him to join her, he had actually enjoyed it. Maybe he should have done it more often.

He switched the radio on. Christ. Traffic was crazy already. There was a time when six-thirty was considered the middle of the night, now it seemed as if half of Dublin was up and about at that hour. People were getting up earlier and earlier, soon they wouldn't even bother going to bed.

Outside, the air was fresh and fragrant, like country air. Strange how spring could permeate the city, even with all its buildings. He took a deep breath and began to walk. Mother was right; things were always better in the morning. Today was a brand new day.

Twenty minutes later, he pushed through the doors of the canteen. Good, Tommy was here. Tommy liked to come in early, pick up the papers and 'debrief' the night porters before they went off duty. Charlie often wondered why he bothered going home at all.

'Morning, Charlie. You're in fierce early.'

Charlie nodded.

'It's Mother, Tommy, she's in hospital, here in St Anne's, on the medical side. Jaundice. She was admitted on Saturday night.'

Tommy put down his mug.

'Sweet Jesus! What ward is she in? I'll call in straight away.'

'St Mary's. She's having an ultrasound and a CT this morning.'

'Any diagnosis?'

Charlie shook his head.

'No, not yet.'

'Viral hepatitis?'

Charlie nodded.

'Could be.'

'I'll bring her down to X-ray and make sure she's not hanging around. I'll phone you as soon as we're back and you can get a verbal report.'

'Thanks, Tommy.'

There was a brief silence.

'What do you think it might be, Charlie?'

Charlie shook his head.

'I'm not sure, Tommy. I've a funny feeling that the new anti-hypertensive she's taking could be causing it but there's no evidence anywhere that the drug causes liver damage.'

'Well you never know with those guys, do you? Speaking of dirty drugs, any news on Cardelia?'

'Nope. I've asked Clements, no joy there. He said the elderly trials were never completed but wouldn't say why, said he didn't know.'

'Do you believe him?'

Charlie shrugged.

'Dunno. It's hard to know who to believe these days.'

Charlie put down his mug.

'There's something else, Tommy. I'm worried about Edie. She hasn't phoned since she went to France on Saturday. Not even a text.'

'That's not like her.'

'Something... something upset her before she went away.'

Tommy leaned closer.

'Go on.'

'She found something...'

Charlie swallowed.

'She found... she found my father's post-mortem report.'

Tommy's mug clattered to the table.

'Does your mother know?'

'Don't think so.'

Charlie looked up.

'You knew, Tommy, didn't you? And you never said anything.'

Tommy nodded.

'It wasn't my place to tell you, Charlie, you know that. And don't go blaming your mother either, she thought she was doing the right thing. It was her way of protecting you.'

Charlie felt a flash of anger.

'Protecting us from what, Tommy? It didn't stop Edie's breakdown, did it?'

'No. It didn't.'

There was a short silence, then Tommy spoke.

'Poor Edie, it must have been some shock, finding out like that, out of the blue. And you've heard nothing at all from her since she went away?'

Charlie shook his head.

'She's not answering her mobile and we don't know where she's staying.'

'Who's with her?'

'A girl called Mags Barry from Waterford. They were friends in training college. I have her parents' number here, I'm going to give them a call.'

Tommy held out his hand.

'Leave that to me. You go see your mother. And don't say anything to her about this until she's a bit better, OK?'

Charlie nodded. It was nice to have someone take charge.

A few minutes later, Charlie stood in the doorway of his mother's room. She was sitting on the edge of the bed, looking out the window, as if she was searching for something. He could see the mobile phone in her hand, just like last night. She'd probably slept like that.

'Morning.'

'Charlie! I didn't hear you come in.'

Her face reminded him of candle wax. Then he noticed the large purple bruise, livid against the white of the sheets.

'Your arm...'

She waved a hand in the air.

'It's nothing, Charlie. They took a load of blood this morning.'

'How are you feeling?'

'Better, I think. Not as nauseated.'

'Good.'

'Any word from Edie?'

'No.'

Her face crumpled.

'I've been thinking about it all night. She was acting a bit strange lately, as if there was something she wasn't telling me.'

Charlie bit his lip. Maybe he should have tipped Mother off about the shop. But there wasn't much point in bringing it up now.

'She seemed fine on Saturday before I left; a bit quiet maybe, but you know Edie, she doesn't like saying goodbye.'

Then she lowered her voice.

'Remember the last time, how it just kind of crept up on her? I thought she was just a bit wound up over the exams.'

Charlie nodded. He still felt the occasional stab of guilt. He had ignored all the signs; the rapid speech, the boundless energy, the way she'd stay up all night, those wild plans for her summer in France. Christ, had he been blind or what? He should have known she wasn't right.


A few minutes later, he opened the door of Sister's office. Pat O'Mahony wanted to see him.

'Morning, Pat.'

Charlie smiled. Only consultants were allowed the privilege of plonking their butts on Sister's desk.

'Morning, Charlie. I just saw Tommy Porter whizzing your mother down towards X-ray like she was the president, all they were missing were the flashing lights.'

Charlie smiled.

'The good news is that the LFTs are down today, Charlie. At least it's a step in the right direction.'

Charlie felt his heart begin to quicken. So it could be Diastora.

'So, here's the deal, Charlie… we do the ultrasound and CT and wait for the viral antigens to come back. And we keep our fingers crossed that liver function continues to improve.'

Charlie nodded. It had to be Diastora. It had to be.


A few minutes later, he looked at the number flashing on his bleep and felt his heart begin to quicken. X-ray.

'Morning, Charlie! Tom Kennedy here. Good news! I have your mother's scan and CT in front of me and they're both clear as a whistle. No gallstones, tumours, cysts or nodules. You can come down and have a look yourself if you like.'

Charlie closed his eyes and breathed a sigh of relief. Thank God. It wasn't cancer.

Just then, he noticed Tommy round the corner. Probably coming to tell him the good news. Then Charlie's smile faded. Tommy was walking fast. Tommy never walked fast. He hurried towards him.

'What is it, Tommy?'

'That girl Mags didn't go on holiday with Edie. I spoke to her a minute ago, she hasn't heard from Edie in over a year.'

Charlie felt a sudden light-headedness.

'Christ, Tommy.'

'Take it easy, son. Edie's a good girl; she wouldn't do anything to hurt you or your mother, you know that. She'll get in touch, I know she will. There's no point in you going to Paris; you wouldn't know where to look.'

'Maybe she's not even in Paris.'

Tommy nodded.

'She might even be back in Clonmel. I'll ask the brother to call round, see if there's any sign of her.'

Charlie ran his fingers through his hair.

'Tommy, is there anything else I should know? My back is to the wall here, is there anything else that Edie and I don't know about, something that could help me find her?'

Tommy hesitated a moment.

'Maybe you should talk to your mother, Charlie.'

'So there is something! Jesus, Tommy! You have to tell me!'

He grabbed Tommy's arm.

233

'You know who was driving the night of the accident, don't you? It was Dad, wasn't it?'

Tommy nodded.

'They went out for a drink the night of the christening. Your mother went home early. The car skidded off the road. They didn't have a chance; nobody wore seatbelts in those days. Poor man, I don't think he ever forgave himself for what happened. After the accident, things went from bad to worse. He was in and out of St Joseph's every second week. When he was out, he'd drink Clonmel dry. It wasn't easy; nobody could blame her.'

Charlie blinked.

'Blame her for what? What do you mean, Tommy?'

Tommy looked down.

'Tommy, for fuck's sake! I want to know!'

He knew he was shouting but he didn't care. He'd lived a life of secrets and lies; he had to know the truth.

'There were rumours, Charlie.'

'What kind of rumours?'

He tightened his grip on Tommy's arm.

'Look, Charlie, it was just gossip, you know Clonmel.'

'Please, Tommy, I need to know! It might help me find Edie.'

Tommy shook his head.

'No, it won't, son. If it would, I'd tell you. And don't go asking your mother, not until she's better. Another day or two won't make a difference.'

Charlie sighed. Tommy was right. His chat with Mother would have to wait. But finding Edie couldn't. He reached for his mobile. First, he needed to check with Aer Lingus that Edie had actually gone to Paris. Then he'd book the next available flight. He'd find her; even if he had to walk every street in Paris, he'd find her.

# 29

Edie knocked and waited. It was time to get this sorted for once and for all. After a while, she knocked again, this time more loudly. She knew they were in there; she could hear voices. Finally, the door opened.

'Yes?'

It was the scrawny woman with the fuzzy hair who had met them at the airport.

'I want to talk to Terence, please.'

'I'm afraid that's not possible.'

'I've paid for a private consultation.'

'The private consultations are on Friday.'

'But that's too late! I want to see him today.'

'Like I said, Ma'am, I'm afraid that's not possible.'

She felt a wave of annoyance.

'Why not? He's here, isn't he?'

'I can't divulge that information, Ma'am.'

Edie bit her lip. For fuck's sake! She was sick of this. Who did Terence think he was? George bloody Bush? Here she was, two days into the course, and she'd hardly set eyes on him, let alone spoken to him. And, as for the course itself, it was a joke. Not in the slightest bit scientific. All mumbo jumbo psycho-babble. Makey-up science. All they'd had so far were some 'focusing' workshops and 'visualization' classes. Apparently all she had to do was to wish for something hard enough and she'd get it. Yeah, right. Want a new job? Go on, wish as hard as you can! Hey presto, a new job!

She would always have considered herself fairly open to new ideas but this was ridiculous. Cutting edge psychology my backside. She should have known the minute she arrived that it was a rip-off. First, there was all the hassle with the room. She'd booked a private room, had even paid the single supplement before she came. But when she arrived, they'd told her that all the single rooms were gone and that she'd have to share. And it was no use complaining; they'd only one room left, end of story. Geraldine, the woman she was sharing with, seemed nice enough, apart from the snoring and the fact that she never shut up about Terence. They had, according to Geraldine, 'connected' at the meeting in Dublin.

Oops. Scrawny face was closing the door. Time to up the ante.

'Can you tell him that Edie Darmody wants to talk to him urgently?'

'In connection with?'

'Everything, actually. My room, to start. It's tiny. You couldn't swing a cat in it. Then there's the food, or rather, the lack of it. Nobody told me we were going to be on a calorie restricted diet. I'm starving. The least you could do is to give us some fruit, I mean, we're in California, for God's sake! And I don't think that sleep deprivation is a very good idea. How can we learn anything if we're exhausted all the time?'

'Sleep deprivation helps you get to a higher level.'

Edie sighed. There was no point in going through all of this with scrawny face. She had to find Terence. And that was exactly what she was going to do. She knew where he lived; Geraldine had pointed out his villa to her on their sunrise walk.

She stood on the steps and looked around. Terracotta tiles, hanging baskets, marble statues. Nice place, Terence, fair play to you.

At the door, she hesitated. Should she knock or not? If any of the staff answered, there was no way they'd let her in. She tried the door handle. Locked. But there must be another door.

She followed the fence around the side of the building, towards the trees at the back. Voiced floated towards her. A splash of water. A swimming pool! Must be nice to go for a swim in this heat. Ahead, the fence dipped ever so slightly, just enough to allow her look over if she stood on tiptoe.

Aha! There he was! Sitting under a large canopy, eating lunch. There was a girl in a white bikini sitting beside him. Edie's eyes widened. Just look at what they were eating! What she wouldn't give for a nice juicy steak and a few chips! Then she noticed the bottle of red wine. So much for the fasting, abstinence, and being a vegetarian! Terence obviously had his own way of getting to a higher level.

Suddenly, a shadow across her path. A hand on her shoulder.

'What are you doing here, Ma'am?'

'I want to talk to Terence.'

'This is his private residence.'

'Well, I want to see him now.'

'I'd like you to leave now, Ma'am. This is private property.'

'No!'

She felt a flash of anger.

'You listen to me! I'm tired of playing mind games. I want my money back and I want to go home.'

Out of the corner of her eye, she could see a gate open under the trees. Terence. He must have heard them.

'Is everything OK, Jeff?'

'Fine, boss, this young lady seems a little lost.'

Edie swung around.

'Terence! I need to talk to you!'

Suddenly she felt a hand on her arm, holding her back, pinning her. Then Terence was gone. Instead, two more muscle guys.

'Oh for fuck's sake, I'm going!'

'We'll escort you back to your room, Ma'am.'

'I don't want to go to my room.'

'We think it best you go to your room, Ma'am.'

A hand on her elbow.

'Is that a threat?'

'Of course not, Ma'am. Terence thinks it best that you do not attend the group meeting tonight.'

'Does he? So much for free choice. He's a fraud, this is all one big fraud.'

'That's a very serious accusation, Ma'am.'

'Twenty thousand euro is serious money.'


A few minutes later, they opened the door of her bedroom and stepped aside to let her pass. Suddenly, she felt a wave of panic.

'Don't lock it, please!'

'I'm afraid I have to, Ma'am. It's orders.'

'Please! I promise I'll stay, just don't lock the door. Please!'

For a moment she thought she saw a flicker of sympathy on his face. But when he spoke, his voice was the same as before, even, emotionless.

'I'm sorry, Ma'am.'

He closed the door. Then that awful sound. Click. Click. Click. She was a prisoner. Locked in a room on the west coast of America. Locked in, just like before. And nobody knew where she was. Not even Charlie. She felt a shiver run through her.

Suddenly it was all happening again. The last time they locked her up. The screams. The shouts. The smells. The swirling and the twirling of those terrible days. Caged, like an animal. No escape. The moans and groans of nearby strangers. The cigarette smoke. The slurping of soup. The shuffling gaits. Jesus.

She ran into the bathroom. Bars on the windows, same as the bedroom. She hurried back to the bedroom and began to bang on the door with her fists. She had to get out of here. If she had to knock the wall down with her bare hands, she was going to get out of here.

After a while, the door opened. For a moment, she thought of trying to run past them, but there were three of them, blocking her path. One of them was holding a tray.

'You wanted food.'

Without looking at it, she pushed the tray out of his hands. As if she was going to touch anything.

He sighed and shook his head. Then he bent down and began to pick up the pieces of food and broken crockery scattered on the floor.

'My brother Charlie is probably on his way here this very minute. He'll come looking for me when I didn't phone. He knows exactly where I am.'

The door closed again. Click. Click. Click. Locked in again. She slipped to the floor and began to cry.


After a while, she stood up and began to walk around the room. She had to stay awake. God knows what might happen if she fell asleep. She looked at her watch. Nine-thirty. The other guests should be back in their rooms by now. If she made enough noise, surely someone would hear her. She hurried into the bathroom and picked up a can of spray deodorant. Just as well that Geraldine didn't give a shit about the ozone.

A moment later, she began to bang the can against the wall. Then she took a deep breath and began to shout, loud and deep, from the bottom of her lungs. As if her life depended on it.

'Help!'

A few minutes later, she heard voices in the distance. Good. Now for the next bit. She picked up the bedside lamp and flung it at the window. The sound of breaking glass always had a certain urgency. Now the bathroom window. Crash. Voices on the corridor now, directly outside.

The door opening. Scrawny face and muscle men. Then she felt her heart skip a beat. Scrawny face was holding a syringe! Oh God, no!

'Help!'

Her voice echoed in her ears, high-pitched, unreal.

The door closing. Arms reaching out for her. Her own hands and legs lashing out, hitting and kicking.

'No!'

Strong arms holding her, pinning her. Making her fall to the floor. Her screams, loud and feral, coming from somewhere deep inside. Then the sting, the burning pain. After soon after, nothing.

# 30

It was after two when Charlie called his last patient. For once, he was glad of a busy clinic. Listening for murmurs, checking blood pressure, writing scripts, reading ECGs; it kept his mind occupied, stopped him thinking. Aer Lingus was going to get back on to him when they'd finished checking their passenger lists. Until then, there was nothing he could do. Might as well go to the library and gather up his notes. There was no point in even trying to do anything. All he could think of was Edie and what might have happened to her. Maybe she was cold. Maybe she was hungry. Maybe someone was holding her some place against her will. Oh Jesus.

He was just about to switch off the computer when suddenly he stopped. Strange, he could have sworn that he'd been on the *BMJ* website when he left. In fact, he was certain. He looked around. Everything was as he left it; his briefcase, his Homer Simpson pen, even his bar of Caramelo. He picked up his A4 pad and flicked through it; the pages with his scribbled notes were still there. Not that he'd found very much. Then he shrugged and reached for the mouse. So what if someone had been sitting at his desk? Probably some med student checking her horoscope.

He looked at the screen again. There was something familiar about that blue and yellow logo... Then he felt his heart begin to quicken. The WorldPharma website. His eyes flicked to the title bar: *'Clinical Trials.'* Jesus. His eyes skimmed down the page. Holy cow! The Cardelia datasets! Including one that he hadn't come across before that involved sixty elderly patients. Oh, my God! Three deaths, one resuscitation, two emergency cardioversions. *'Elderly cohort trial abandoned for logistical purposes.'* He took a deep breath. Logistical purposes my backside. Cardelia had killed those patients.

A few moments later, the printer whirred to a stop. He scribbled down the URL *'Clinical trials/Members@World Pharma.com.'* Obviously a restricted part of the website, accessible only by password. He hadn't even known it existed until now. He looked around the room; only a handful of students, two of them sound asleep. But someone must have seen something.

He caught the eye of the med student sitting at the nearest table.

'Did you see anyone sitting here before I came in?'

'No. But I'm only here about twenty minutes.'

It was the same story with the surgical SHO doing Sudoko in the corner. No one had seen or heard anything.

Suddenly he had an idea. What if he pressed the back button, would he see the password? He held his breath and waited. Damn! Five stars! He should have known! He glanced at his watch; three-thirty; time for Tommy's afternoon scone. He might just catch him if he hurried.

'Hey, there, Charlie boy, how's she cutting?'

Charlie pulled out a chair.

'Tommy, I know this sounds crazy, but someone's put the entire Cardelia datasets on my computer.'

'The ones you were looking for?'

Charlie nodded.

'Who?'

'I thought you might know.'

A loud laugh.

'Ah, Christ, Charlie! You think Tommy Porter here could pull off something like that? I'm flattered, but nope, it wasn't me, though I wish it were. I'm not too hot on the technology side of things. Who else knew you wanted that information?'

'Clements, WorldPharma, maybe Marianne.'

'Somehow I don't think it was WorldPharma.'

'It must have been Clements.'

Tommy shook his head.

'Clements isn't exactly the Good Samaritan type. So, what did you find?

'Some heart irregularities that were never followed up. And fatalities. The trial was stopped early.'

Tommy's eyes widened.

'And they just brushed it under the carpet?'

Charlie nodded.

'Deliberately?'

Charlie shrugged.

'Maybe, or maybe it was just plain incompetence. Either way, it shouldn't have happened.'

'Did you find anything on Diastora? '

Charlie felt a sinking sensation. Oh Christ! He had been in the privileged section of the WorldPharma clinical trials website and he hadn't checked Diastora! He jumped to his feet.

Outside the library, he paused for a moment to catch his breath. Please God, let the computer be still on! He opened the door and breathed a sigh of relief. He sat down and took a deep breath. OK, best be very careful. Once he got out of the site, he might never get back in again. The password winked at him invitingly. He clicked return.

Good, he was back in the clinical trials page again. He skimmed down the list and stopped at Diastora. Click. Click. He could feel his heart pounding. Twelve trials in all. He checked the titles. Nothing new here; nothing that he didn't know already. He knew these trials like the back of his hand. They all showed that Diastora was a safe drug, without even a whisper of cardiac or liver problems. He felt a wave of disappointment. They had covered their tracks well. Edie was right. They were a shower of bastards; lying, cheating bastards. Diastora caused liver damage. And he was going to prove it.

He looked around the room again. How come nobody had seen anything? No matter how sleepy they were, you'd think the med students would have noticed a consultant. They all knew Clements; he was one of their lecturers, for God's sake. And if it was Marianne, well, you'd want to be dead not to notice someone like her come into a room. She wasn't the type of girl who blended into the background, no matter how hard she tried. There was one other possibility, of course, one that Edie would have suggested from the very beginning. He pushed it out of his mind and hurried down the corridor.

# 31

Edie opened her eyes. So sleepy, so very sleepy. And her head, pounding, pressing, pulsing. Beside her, scrawny face, her face tunnelling in and out of focus, like some horrible kaleidoscope.

'Where am I?'

The words were thick and slurred.

'The airport, you're going home.'

The car door opened and hands reached in for her. Jesus, what had they given her? Her legs crumpled under her, as if they were made of paper. Then she felt herself being lifted into a wheelchair.

'I've told them you're just out of hospital and need to go home urgently. Just keep your mouth shut if you want to get out of here, OK?'

Edie nodded. Scrawny face was bending over her now, pinning something to her t-shirt.

'My passport...'

'I have it. And your wallet. That's all you need. Jeff grabbed a few things from your room.'

She handed Edie a plastic bag. Suddenly, Edie felt a flash of panic.

'My ticket, it's for Saturday!'

'We've changed it.'

Scrawny face's voice was flat and detached, same as muscle man.

'We've got to hurry. Your flight leaves in less than an hour. Remember what I said and keep your mouth shut.'

A moment later, they were inside the Departures lounge. Edie breathed a sigh of relief. People. Everywhere. Lots of people. They could hardly try and kill her now. And if she wanted to, she could escape. She pressed hard into the armrests and tried to stand up, but it was no good. It was like her limbs were asleep, as if she was paralysed. Maybe escaping wasn't such a good idea after all.

A few minutes later, the wheelchair came to a stop. She could see scrawny face handing her passport and some pages to the girl behind the check-in desk.

'No luggage, Ma'am?'

'No.'

'Boarding for Shannon is in twenty minutes. Have a nice flight, Ma'am.'

Now they were moving again. Edie turned around. A young woman in uniform was pushing her now. Must be airport staff. There was no sign of scrawny face. She was gone. Vanished. Like she had disappeared into thin air.

The next twenty minutes were a blur. Edie could vaguely remember the woman taking the plastic bag and placing it on the security conveyor belt. No beep. Good. Funny how she always expected it to beep, even when she knew that it shouldn't.

A few minutes later, they were at the gate. Someone said something about priority boarding and soon she was moving again.

She could see the door of the plane now, an airline steward walking towards her.

'I'll help you to your seat. It's not far.'

The moment she stood up, she felt dizzy, as if she was going to faint. A strange anaesthetic feeling. A stupid feeling. Awake but not awake. Asleep but not asleep.

After that, she couldn't remember very much. Someone fastening the seatbelt. Opening the plastic bag, finding the socks and sarong, struggling to put them on. The person beside her blowing up her neck pillow. Fixing it around her neck. Eyelids heavy, like lead. Arms like jelly. Legs, can't feel them. Must be gone. No legs. No legs so no blood clots in legs. Ha. Ha. Laughing out loud. People looking at her.

She closed her eyes and the swirling, twirling faces began again. Round and round until suddenly they are all one big, happy blur. So tired, but can't sleep. So many thoughts, chasing in her head. Her heart thumping in her chest. Her mouth, dry and parched. Voices nearby, threatening her. Hands over ears, head on knees. Go away. Leave me alone. Don't hurt me.

# 32

Back in the apartment, all was frozen quiet. Charlie sighed. He could have done with a bit of company, even of the Killian kind. The coldness of the room sliced through him and he began to shiver. It had been a hard winter; even now, almost March, it was still hitting zero. For the first time in years, he felt the searing pain of loneliness. It was like that first month in boarding school all over again; no Mother, no Father, no Edie, all alone in a cold, empty cubicle.

He threw himself on the couch and reached for the remote. An image of trolleys and nurses flashed in front of him; looked like an Accident and Emergency department. Not a funny *Green Wing* one, but a real one. Must be some sort of documentary or *Prime Time* special. It could be Casualty anywhere. War zones the lot of them.

He checked his mobile again. Nothing. He closed his eyes and sighed. He could just imagine her beside him, wrapped up together in the duvet, sharing a bar of chocolate. He felt a deep, raw pain in his throat, like an ulcer pain. Except that this wasn't an ulcer pain. And the worst thing about it was that there was nothing he could do. At least with Mother, he had been able to do something. With Edie, it was different. He didn't know where she was and what she was thinking. She could be anywhere. She wasn't in Paris, that much he knew. The airline had checked the passenger list for their Paris flights on Saturday. Edie's name wasn't on it. Nor on Sunday's or Monday's. It would be tomorrow before they could tell him if she had even boarded an Aer Lingus flight. There was nothing for it but to sit and wait.

Life wasn't a straight line, was it? It was a circle, a mill wheel of crises; up, down, up, down. First there was the four of them, the Darmody family. Then Dad died and things were rough for a while. Just as things were getting better, Mother sent them off to boarding school. But the big wheel went round and for a while they were happy again, him in medical school, Edie in pharmacy, the two of them together again in Dublin.

Then Fate turned around and slapped them right in the face. Another blow for the Darmody's just when they thought that things were going to be OK. Edie had a breakdown and the wheel went down, down, dark and deep. But even then, the wheel kept on turning. Edie improved and went to teacher training college and he qualified with first class honours. The wheel wasn't high but it had cleared the water. Silly of him to think that it could stay that way.

Just when he thought that the Darmody family had finally reached an equilibrium, that maybe they could at least feign happiness, along came Fate again with its slings of fortune. His mother was ill and Edie was missing. No half measures, for sure, no sirree; the wheel was down, down, down, in the deepest, darkest, blackest place.

He turned off the light and buried his head in the pillow. Images from the past came flooding back. Mother, all young and pretty in a summer dress and sandals. He hadn't realised until today how small she was, small and weary and wrinkled with care, like linen that had been sat on all day. It couldn't have been easy, surviving on a teacher's income, repaying the debts that must have accumulated from Dad's drinking. But she had managed, watched the pennies, ran the show, even managed to pay the boarding school fees. And done all the other stuff, like going to all the Clongowes things, driving up on her own from Clonmel, roaring at all the rugby matches, arranging their student exchanges to France, inviting their friends for the weekend, even doing the baking for their twenty-first parties. Every responsibility, every decision was hers. Including the decision not to tell them how their father died.

He was nine when Father died. But for a long time before that, Dad had been sick, in and out of hospital for weeks at a time, quiet and distant when he returned. Charlie used think that somehow it was his fault, something he had done, perhaps. Maybe he had kicked the football too hard against the wall. Maybe he had dirtied the hall with his muddy boots. He must have done something. God knows what Edie thought. She was always very quiet when Dad was sick. Sometimes, she would sit for hours on the porch, silently twisting the corners of a rug or a cushion. Hour for hour she matched him, Dad in his room, Edie in the porch, both staring into space, in some sort of mutual, silent empathy.

After he died, Mother didn't talk about him. Oh they said prayers and masses and visited the grave on Sunday, but they never talked about the happy days when Dad was well; the laughing, the trips to the seaside, the kind of stuff himself and Edie talked about when Mother wasn't around. Sometimes he wondered if the happy days had ever happened. Or maybe they had just imagined them.

He used to think that the reason Mother didn't talk about his father was that it upset her too much. Later, when he was older, and had asked about his father's illness, she had been vague and hesitant. Now, of course, he understood.

After what seemed like hours twisting and turning in the darkness, he switched on the light. It was hopeless. Every time he drifted off, he saw his father's face, puffed and purple with wild and bulging eyes, horrible stuff. He tried to remember his father's face in the photographs back home, but it was no good; it was like it had been erased from his memory.

He reached for his mobile, his link with Edie. Still nothing. He felt a wave of panic. Had Edie become hypomanic again? Or worse, had she gone the other way, depressed, even suicidal? He squeezed his eyes tightly closed. It didn't bear thinking about.

Suddenly he jumped. His mobile. It had to be Edie, it had to be.

'Is that Charlie Darmody?'

His heart sank. It was a male voice, a strong Dublin accent.

'Yes, this is Charlie Darmody.'

'Sorry for waking you at this hour, this is airport security. I've a girl here who has your number written on a piece of paper.'

Jesus.

'Edie!'

'Yes, that's her, do you know her?'

'She's my sister! Where is she?'

'Terminal one, Dublin airport. Arrivals, near the baggage reclaim. I'm head of security here and one of the lads called me over.'

'What flight was she on?'

'San Francisco. Delta airlines.'

Charlie took a deep breath.

'Is she OK?'

A pause.

'Look, I'll be honest with you, son, your sister was wandering around the luggage carousel, picking up whatever bag she could find. There was a bit of a brouhaha. The lads called me over, thought she might be drunk but I could see straight away that it wasn't booze. God knows how the Yanks let her on the flight, they're nuts on drugs.'

'Edie doesn't take drugs.'

'Well there's something wrong with her and it's not alcohol; I see enough tanked up customers to know the difference. She's strung out on something. I was going to call the airport police but she started crying and showed me your number.'

Charlie closed his eyes. Edie would die of fright if the police arrived. Ever since the last time she had a thing about guards.

'Edie had a breakdown a while ago.'

'I see... so how come, if you don't mind me asking, if her nerves were at her, that she was let off on her own like that?'

'She was fine last week.'

Or was she?

'Where did you say you got my number?'

'It was pinned to the front of her jacket. She keeps going on about 'the Leader', says she wants to talk to him.'

Charlie took a deep breath. What was Edie doing in San Francisco of all places? Who was she with? And who the fuck was 'the Leader'?

'I'm on my way. Could you stay with her until I get there, make sure nothing happens her? Tell her Charlie is coming.'

'Sure thing. Poor misfortunate, I doubt she even knows where she is. And me thinking she was a druggie.'

Charlie grabbed his jeans. A cold fear gripped him. Sweet Jesus. This couldn't be happening; not again, not after she had been so good. It was ten years for God's sake; she had been fine for ten years. He glanced at his watch. Almost five. Hopefully, Tommy might be up. And his house was on the way.

Fifteen minutes later, Charlie knocked on the door of number six Dorset Gardens. Blue door and yellow curtains: Tipperary colours. A moment later, Tommy's face appeared at the window. Instantly the door opened. Good, he was dressed.

'Charlie! What is it?'

'It's Edie, Tommy. She's at the airport; she's just arrived back from the States. She's not well. Will you come with me?'

Without saying a word, Tommy reached for his keys and pulled the door closed behind him.

Twenty minutes later, they were at the airport. Charlie sighed. He hated Dublin airport at the best of times; too much traffic, diversions, traffic cones, everyone doing their best to stop you going where you wanted to go.

'In there, Charlie, swing in there, that Mondeo's pulling out...'

'It's set-down only.'

'Fuck them. This is an emergency. It's miles to the bloody car park. Have . you got one of those doctor stickers anywhere?'

'There's one in the glove compartment.'

'I'll sort it. You go.'

'Thanks, Tommy.'

A moment later, he was on the tarmac, running through the rain, swerving to avoid the puddles. Oops. Looked like he'd just splashed someone.

'Sorry!'

Behind him, he could hear a torrent of what sounded like Japanese. Oh, get over it. There are worse things than water.

# 33

Inside the door of the Arrivals building, Charlie paused to catch his breath, then he began to run again, weaving his way through the trolleys.

Then, as if in slow motion, the nightmare of ten years ago began to unfold in front of him. It was May, just before his last paper. Edie too, was almost finished, just one exam to go. She had been a bit irritable for a while. All that week she'd been constantly on the phone to him, babbling on about some summer job or other. He hadn't paid too much attention; hadn't really listened to what she was saying. To be honest, as long as they both passed their exams, he didn't mind what she did for the summer.

The details came floating back. South of France, some place near St Tropez. She was going to work in a street stall selling Vichy skin creams that she was going to bring with her from Ireland. He remembered commenting that surely Vichy was available in France and Edie explaining that it cost twice the price. At the time he thought it a bit strange, the fact that Vichy was more expensive in France, especially since it sounded like it was made there, but he said nothing, never checked it out, just listened while she went on about only needing to sell three hundred bottles to cover everything; flights and a three week holiday. She talked about camping on the beach. He had laughed, said that he wouldn't mind sleeping on a topless French beach himself. But he never asked her the details, never checked out how advanced her plan was, thought it was just a passing idea. One of the mad notions she sometimes got.

It was only when the bank phoned Mother that he became worried. Edie had taken out a student loan and had spent thousands of pounds on Vichy products. She had bought up all the Vichy creams in the nearby pharmacies and department stores. She had even managed to buy some directly from the wholesalers. Worse still, she had set up a stall in Grafton Street, recruiting people to join her in her business enterprise.

He would never forget that awful day. The guards had phoned him; told him about Edie's stall and asked him to come and get her. Said they weren't going to press charges. When he arrived, Edie was standing alone behind a makeshift desk, a big banner behind her, sea and seagulls; it looked like she'd painted it herself. All around her, people were laughing, laughing at the crazy girl with the wild eyes and the wild hair and the torrent of speech that wouldn't stop. Vichy. Vichy. Vichy. Vichy. Vichy. Vichy.

The guards had been very nice. They had seen people like Edie before. They knew she needed a hospital and not a prison cell. They had even bought her pizza and coffee and given her a jacket to cover her bikini top. They stayed silent when she shouted and screamed on the way to the hospital. Let me go! Let me go! Let me go! Then they had shaken hands with Charlie, their eyes full of sympathy for the young med student with the crazy sister who should, that very day, have sat her last exam in second year pharmacy.

For a full month, she had stayed inside that grey building surrounded by the high walls. Soon she stopped mentioning Vichy. Her speech slowed down and the waterfall of words dried up, leaving her sad and silent. Like a dried-up fruit. And when she crossed those gates again, she was a different person. Gone was the light in her eyes, the spring in her step, the joy, the brightness, the wild spirit that was Edie Darmody. Instead, was a silent shadow, subdued and defeated, her spirit broken and her dreams crushed and crumpled.

She stayed at home for the rest of that year. Every two weeks, Dr Browne checked her lithium levels. After a while, her anti-psychotic medication was reduced and she began to smile again. Mother got in a sub for five months that winter so that she could stay at home with Edie. All those months, she didn't let Edie out of her sight, not even for twenty minutes. Even if they were down town shopping, Mother would wait outside the changing room in Clinton's while Edie tried on something. For once, it was what Edie wanted; the desserts she liked, her favourite TV programmes, the films she wanted to see.

The following summer, Edie was better. Mother suggested that she apply for training college. Nobody need know about the breakdown; she could just tell them that she didn't like pharmacy. After all, Irish had always been Edie's best subject.

So Edie became a teacher. He knew it wasn't what she wanted, he knew it wasn't perfect; but it was a job, it was secure and it got Edie back working and living again. And it meant she could live at home with Mother.

After that, Edie had been fine and the lithium was eventually stopped. No more weird thoughts, no more fancy ideas, no more false realities. No funny notions at all until that shop thing. That was probably the start of it and he had ignored it, just like he'd ignored it before, another budding delusion that he had failed to pick up on, and all because he was so wrapped up in his own little world and his precious Marianne. He bit his lip. If Edie was anything like the last time, even a fraction of what she was like ten years ago, out of contact with herself and with reality, no wonder the security guards thought she was on drugs… he felt his heart skip a beat.

Thank God they had found her. She could have been in prison or lying in a gutter in San Francisco, not knowing who she was or where she was. Even in Dublin, people stepped over you on the street and refused to meet your eyes. As if you didn't exist.

Ahead, the automatic doors and a security guard sitting at a desk. The man who phoned said to give his name and they'd let him through.

'My name is Charlie Darmody. I've come to get my sister.'

He paused to suck in some air.

'In you go, son. They're over the far side, belt number ten, near the phones.'

Straight away, even through the sea of faces, he could see her, standing beside an empty luggage carousel. Oh dear God! He began to run again.

# 34

As he drew nearer, the tightening sensation in his throat became stronger, almost choking him. Edie! No wonder they thought she was a druggie. There was some kind of cushion hanging around her shoulders, like some strange sort of life-jacket. Then he realised it was one of those neck support pillows people use on flights, all lop-sided, hanging low over one shoulder. Her hair was long and loose and tangled like it hadn't been brushed in days. She was standing beside a phone, lifting and replacing the receiver. Up, down. Up, down. Dollar bills floated to the floor. He watched her bend down to gather them up, her movements fast and frantic.

And her clothes... he felt the lump in his throat grow bigger. Oh, Edie. Loud clashing colours. Crazy woman clothes. Bright pink sarong over khaki trousers, a price tag dangling on her hips. On her feet, pink plastic sandals. One red sock. A piece of brown cardboard pinned to a stained white t-shirt with his name and number written on it, in thick felt pen.

He could see her face more clearly now. She was crying.

'Edie!'

She looked up.

'Charlie! You've got to help me! I can't get the money in! The door was locked and now I can't find the meeting room and nobody will bring me there.'

His eyes filled. Sweet Jesus. This was worse than the last time.

'I'll take you there, Edie'

He put his arms around her.

'Don't you have to go back to Clongowes?'

'No, Edie.'

She nestled into him. He could feel her thin frame against him, trembling, cold and fragile. She'd lost weight. He turned to the security guard.

'Thank you. God knows what would have happened if she left the airport. Did she have any luggage or anything?'

'No, nothing. We've checked. All the bags have been picked up. Wonder how she got through security in San Francisco. Someone must have been with her, right up to boarding.'

Charlie nodded. No way would she have managed to get through check-in and security on her own, not in this state.

'Is there any way we could check? We don't know where she's been the past few days. We thought she was in France.'

'You could talk to airport police here, they might be able to get video footage from the States.'

Charlie nodded.

'I'll do that. Thanks again.'

'Don't mention it. Such a pretty girl, reminds me of Julia Roberts, such a pity.'

Tommy was waiting outside the doors, a wheelchair in front of him.

'Hello, Edie! How's my girl?'

His voice sounded perfectly normal, like Edie was coming back from a holiday and he was there to pick her up.

'Tommy! Are you going to the meeting too?'

'Sure am, honey. Just sit in here and I'll take care of you.'

Charlie eased her gently into the wheelchair and bent down in front of her. He could smell ketones from her breath; she must be starving. God knows when she'd last eaten.

'You hungry, Edie? Would you like some breakfast?'

A silent nod.

'Tommy, why don't you and Edie have breakfast? I'll join you in a few minutes.'

Tommy nodded and touched Edie's shoulder.

'Sound as a trout. C'mon, Edie, don't know about you, but I'm starving.'

Then Charlie bent down again.

'Just a second, Tommy.'

Gently, he opened the safety pin and removed the piece of cardboard from Edie's t-shirt. No more labels.

'There now, off you go, Edie. I won't be long.'


He stood for a moment, watching them, the small, plump man and the beautiful, frightened-looking girl with the tangled hair and the weird clothes. In a strange sort of way, they looked perfectly normal together; Tommy with his slippers and brightly patterned jumper, Edie with her neck pillow and that silly sarong. He took a long, deep breath. At least she was home. She might not be well, but at least she was home. He felt a sudden wave of anger. He would find out what had happened. He would find out who this 'Leader' was and he would ask him what they had done to her. He would not let them get away with this, whoever they were. And Edie, he would fix her, even if it took the rest of his life; he would fix his little angel and make her well again.

# 35

Charlie glanced around the room. It looked the same as any other waiting room; colourful prints on the walls and vases of flowers on the windowsills. Except, of course, that these were plastic vases... The radio was on, Gerry Ryan. Must be after nine. Memories of his Final Med clerkship in the locked wards of a large mental institution came flooding back: smells of urine, soup and cigarette smoke. Then there were the sounds: the screams and shouts and high-pitched yells and the sound of breaking glass. Psychiatric hospitals had come a long way in the last ten years.

The door opened and a nurse came in. She smiled and bent down in front of Edie.

'Hello, Edie, I'm Kate.'

Edie looked at her for a moment, then looked at Charlie.

'It's OK, Edie.'

'Can you and Charlie come with me, Edie?'

He hooked Edie's arm and helped her to her feet. For a moment he felt like scooping her up in his arms and carrying her; she felt so light and fragile. Tommy said she'd almost fainted at the airport.

Halfway down the corridor, a door opened and a young girl appeared, a nurse at her side. The girl's eyes shone like beacons in a thin, ghost-like face and her elbows protruded like daggers at her sides. Anorexia nervosa. They needed to be watched at all times, even when they went to the bathroom, to make sure that they didn't start vomiting. Or exercising. He had seen what anorexia could do. Only last year a girl arrested in Casualty because of a low potassium. She was only sixteen. He bit his lip. Mental illness was a terrible thing. You had no idea what it was like; you thought you knew until it happened to you or to one of your family, then you realised you knew nothing. Absolutely nothing.

Other memories came back to him. Mike, his friend from primary school. When Mike was sixteen, he began to hear voices through his television telling him that his neighbours were going to kill him. It wasn't long before he was bundled into a squad car and brought screaming and roaring to St Luke's where he stayed for the next four months. Paranoid schizophrenia had been the diagnosis. He had improved all right; no more voices, no more death threats from his neighbours. He lived on his own now, in one of those little sheltered houses out the Kilkenny road. Occasionally Charlie would see him walking on the pavement outside Dunnes in the Oakview shopping centre; a slow shuffling gait, eyes to the ground, a shadow, an echo of what might have been. At least the Gardai hadn't shot him in some misinterpreted and tragic stand off. With Edie, thankfully, it had been different; she had gone back to a 'normal' life. Until now, that is.

Dr Hill's office was painted bright yellow, the colour of sunshine. More flowers, more happy prints on the walls. Wonder if it made a difference.

After chatting to Charlie for a bit, Dr Hill turned to Edie and smiled.

'So, Edie, tell me about your holiday.'

His tone was casual, relaxed, like a hairdresser. Edie looked at Charlie.

'It's OK, Edie, you can talk to Dr Hill, honey.'

He squeezed her hand.

'Did something upset you in America, Edie?

Edie's replies were jumbled. After a while, Dr Hill stood up.

'You sit here and finish your tea, Edie, we'll be back in a minute.'


Outside, in the corridor, Dr Hill shook his head and sighed. Then he put his hand on Charlie's shoulder. Charlie swallowed. A hand on the shoulder always meant bad news.

'I'm going to have to admit her, Charlie. She's very disorientated.'

Charlie nodded. There was certainly no doubt about that.

'She will be OK, though, won't she?'

Dr Hill nodded.

'It seems to be more an acute confusional state than a true manic episode, probably aggravated by sleep deprivation. Right now, she needs sleep and sedation.'

Charlie hesitated.

'Something upset her just before she went away.'

He began to explain about the post-mortem report. Dr Hill began to nod.

'It could have triggered it, I suppose, but there's probably something else too. We have to find where she was and what happened there.'

Charlie nodded.

'I'll go down to Clonmel, see if I can find anything.'

'Was Edie hanging out with any strange people before she left?'

Charlie shook his head.

'No, not that I know of.'

Hand on shoulder again.

'Go home, get some rest, Charlie, you look shattered.'

Charlie nodded.

'I'll just say goodbye to her first.'

Edie was sitting in exactly the same position, as if she was afraid to move. He bent to kiss her forehead.

'I'll be back in a little while, Edie, I promise.'

She grabbed his hand.

'I have to go to the meeting room! You must bring me, Charlie!'

Suddenly the nurse was beside them.

'Come with me, Edie. I'll take you there, luvvie, just hold on to me.'

Charlie stepped back. Edie was in good hands, she was safe here.

'Bye, Edie, I love you.'

She didn't turn around. It was as if she hadn't heard him. He repeated the words in his head. Bye, Edie, I love you.


A few minutes later, he stood at the door of his mother's room. She was sitting on the bed, facing the door, pages of newspaper scattered on the floor.

'Charlie! Tommy told me. How is she?'

Her eyes were pools of fear.

'She's very confused.'

She grabbed his arm.

'I want to see her! Can I see her, please, Charlie!'

He shook his head.

'She's asleep now, Mother. She's exhausted.'

Her eyes met his.

'You knew she wasn't in Paris and you didn't tell me.'

He sighed.

'I didn't want to worry you.'

She looked away.

'How bad is it?'

264

'She hasn't got pressure of speech or flight of ideas like the last time. But she's confused, doesn't know where she is or what's going on.'

Her eyes closed.

'What in God's name was she doing in America?'

Charlie shook his head.

'I don't know. I'm going to go down to the Lodge to see if I can find anything in her room. There must be something.'

'She must have planned this trip ages ago, probably bought that ticket months ago. Did you check with the bank?'

Of course, the bank! Why hadn't he thought of it? He could check her statements and find out what she had paid for, and more importantly, whom she had paid.

'I'll do it now.'

He looked at her for a moment, wondering how to begin. It was time.

'There's something else.'

'What?'

Her eyes darkened.

'The day Edie went away, she found something.'

He could see the blood drain from her face. She closed her eyes.

'The bureau.'

Her voice was a whisper.

'Tell me, Charlie.'

'She… she found Dad's post-mortem report.'

She closed her eyes again and moaned; a long, low moan, like an animal in pain. Then her body went limp, as if all the life had gone out of it. Maybe he should go now. But he couldn't leave without saying what he wanted to say, what he needed to say.

'You should have told us, Mother.'

She opened her eyes and shook her head.

'You were only children, somehow it seemed easier to let you think your father had been taken from you, and not that he... had taken himself away from you.'

'We had to find out sometime, Mother.'

'I know, Charlie, and I was going to tell you, I really was. Then Edie got sick and I couldn't... I kept putting it off.'

She grabbed his hand.

'The letter, Charlie, did she find the letter?'

'What letter?'

When she spoke, her voice was faint.

'She has it.'

He sat down beside her.

'What letter, Mother?'

She shook her head.

'I need to talk to Edie first.'

Tears glistened on her cheeks. Charlie swallowed. Mother never cried. He stood up.

'I'd better go.'

She grabbed his hand again.

'Don't judge me, Charlie, please don't judge me. Things are never what they seem.'

Yeah, he was beginning to realise that. Marianne. Cardelia. How your father died. The list went on and on. What other secrets had she kept from them?

'Tell her I love her, Charlie.'

He turned around.

'Maybe you should tell her that yourself, Mother.'

A few minutes later, he rounded the corner for Coronary Care. Good, the team was still here. He took a deep breath and walked over to where they were standing.

'Dr Clements, can I have a quick word?'

Clements looked up. A slow smile crossed his lips but his eyes were cold.

'Charlie! Welcome back! We were just beginning to wonder what had happened to you. Would you care to tell us?'

Oh shit. Now he was going to have to explain in front of everyone.

'My sister is sick, she's in hospital.'

Clements arched an eyebrow.

'Sorry, Charlie. I'm a bit confused here - I thought it was your mother who was sick?'

'She's sick too.'

A nervous giggle from one of the interns. Charlie felt a heat rise in his throat. He'd be damned if he was going to discuss Edie's medical details in front of everyone.

'I see... you'd want to mind yourself, Charlie, looks like you could be next.'

Steel grey eyes fixed his. Charlie blinked. Then Clements smiled.

'No problem, Charlie, I knew you'd have a good reason for missing the round. C'mon, we're finished here, let's take a coffee.'

Out on the corridor, Clements stopped and turned towards him.

'You look fairly rough, Charlie.'

Charlie looked down. He'd forgotten that he was wearing his denims and that faded old rugby shirt he sometimes wore in bed. And worst of all, he was wearing sneakers; dirty, wet, sneakers that squeaked when he walked. No wonder everyone was looking at him. Clements was a stickler on what he called 'appropriate' dress.

'I was up all night.'

'In that case, go home, get some sleep.'

Then Clements' phone began to ring. Typical. The ring tone was Mozart. No Simpson's signature tune for Fancy Pants Clements. Charlie began to walk away; he could hardly stand there listening to a private conversation. But Clements' voice followed him, loud, nasal and crystal clear.

'Great. Eight-thirty. I know, I know, you told me, two blocks away.'

A moment later, Clements was beside him.

'One of the kids, wants me to pick him up from rugby.'

Charlie looked away.

'If you don't mind, I think I'll skip on the coffee, it might keep me awake.'

'No problem, Charlie. Hope your sister is OK. What did you say was wrong with her again?'

'Appendicitis.'

A dismissive snort.

'Mind those surgeons, bloody butchers.'


A moment later, he reached for his mobile. Blocked number. Well fuck her and her blocked numbers. Already today he'd had five text messages; all the same old rubbish. 'Charlie, call me. I can explain.' 'I need to talk to you.' La de fuckin' da. Forget it, Marianne. I don't do explanations.

Suddenly he remembered the words of a Leonard Cohen song. *So long, Marianne*. It was one of Edie's favourite songs. Yep. So long, Marianne.

He took the shortcut across the grass to the car park. Moisture seeped through his Asics and his feet began to tingle. It was a strange but comforting feeling, as if he was being earthed or something. Then his mobile rang.

'Hi Charlie, Dan Hill here. Just letting you know that I'm going to get a CT, bloods and toxicology screen done on Edie, just in case it's anything organic.'

Charlie bit his lip. He hadn't even considered an organic diagnosis like encephalitis or a brain tumour! Instead, he had dumped the poor girl into an acute psychiatric ward just because of her history! Christ. What had he been thinking? Maybe Edie had fallen and hit her head? What if, this very minute, there was a sub-dural haematoma pressing on her brain, slowly and steadily killing her?

'I've given her a small dose of risperidone but I'll hold on the lithium for another bit. Let me know what you find. I have my hunches.'

Thirty minutes later, Charlie passed the Red Cow roundabout. He knew it was crazy, driving without sleep, but it wasn't the first time and it probably wouldn't be the last. OK, he was tired, but he wouldn't be able to sleep until he found something. There would be plenty of time for sleep later. Right now he was going to Clonmel. There had to be some clue, somewhere, about Edie's trip. And he was going to find it.

He jumped at the sound of his ring tune. Blocked number. Guess who? He flipped it open. Might as well talk to her, get it over with.

'Charlie! At last! Marianne here.'

'Yes?'

'Just touching base about Saturday. When would you like to go over your presentation?'

For fuck's sake!

'There's no need.'

A short silence.

'Well, we'd like to have some idea of what you're going to say.'

Aha! They didn't trust him. Well, well, well.

'I'm going to talk about hypertension.'

Another silence. He knew what the next question was going to be. Go on, Marianne, I'm waiting.

'And Diastora?'

'Obviously I'm going to mention Diastora.'

Or maybe not.

'You're still mad at me, aren't you?'

'Nope. I've other things on my mind.'

'Oh yes, I heard about your sister, how is she?'

'Fine.'

Clements must have told her. Same way he told her everything. Pillow talk.

'Charlie, I just want you to remember that Saturday's launch has nothing to do with you and me. We're both professional people and I'm relying on you. WorldPharma has invested huge money in bringing Diastora to market.'

To market, to market, to buy a fat pig.

Home again, home again, jiggedy jig.

'Don't worry; I'll give Diastora plenty of airtime. There's no such thing as a free launch, so they say.'

A high-pitched laugh. He realised he never liked her laugh.

'Don't forget to mention the advantages of Diastora over its competitors.'

'I won't forget anything.'

Including a full side-effect profile.

# 36

Charlie pulled the door closed behind him and knelt down to rub Lucy's ears the way Edie did. He nuzzled his face into her warm fur and stroked her back. Poor old girl must be wondering where the hell everyone had gone. Poor Lucy. Uncomplaining, uncomplicated, forgiving Lucy. If only humans could be the same.

He opened the kitchen door. Lucy rubbed against him, looking up at him, her big brown eyes begging permission.

'OK, Lucy, you can come too.'

Normally Mother never left Lucy past the hall. But today was different. Everything was different now. He lifted the lid of the hot plate and a surge of heat rose up to meet him. He stayed like that for a moment, soaking in the heat, feeling it calm and comfort him.

After a while, he went upstairs, Lucy at his heels. Funny how strange Edie's bed looked without the duvet, like it had been violated or something. He sat down on the edge of the bed and touched the pillow. He could hear Lucy's low whine at his feet and bent to rub her. I know, Lucy, I miss her too.

He looked around. Where would Edie hide something? Of course! A book. It was her usual hiding place when they were children. Might as well start with the pile on the locker. He reached for the first one; Louise Hay's *Feel the Fear and Do it Anyway*. Leader of the pack. He began to flick through the pages. Suddenly something floated to the floor and he bent to pick it up. It was a brochure; a course in San Francisco. Mind training. He smiled and put it in his pocket.

He was about to close the door when he remembered that Edie needed clothes. She could hardly wear that silly outfit she had been wearing at the airport. He opened the wardrobe door. Typical Edie, everything was stacked in neat piles - t-shirts, jeans, jumpers, shirts… even her old hockey skirts. He touched the nearest one. Memories of her scoring that winning goal for the Ursuline in the Senior A Cup Final came flooding back. It seemed just like yesterday. Then he noticed something, a little bundle, hidden among the t-shirts. He lifted it out. It was a bunch of Valentine cards, neatly tied with a red velvet ribbon. This year's card, the one with the yellow flowers, was at the top. Gently, he put the cards back where he had found them and blinked away the tears.

It was almost five when Charlie got back to St Anne's. Hopefully, he might still catch Dr Hill. He circled the car park a second time, looking for a space. Nothing; he'd have to park on the kerb. The new lab must have opened; no wonder the place was crazy. Suddenly he jammed on the brakes. That white van had driven straight out in front of him! Bloody lunatic! Hope to God they stuck in some speed ramps before someone had an accident.

Charlie knocked and opened the door. Dr Hill looked up and smiled.
'I partly guessed you wouldn't go to bed.'
Charlie handed him the brochure.

'I found this.'

After a while, the psychiatrist looked up.

'Just as I thought, but I didn't want to say anything until I was sure. It's one of these 'personal development' courses. Have you heard about them?'

Charlie shook his head.

'Mind technology, the power of positive thinking. *Strategy for success - how you can change your life.*' You pay these guys a fortune and they show you how to train your mind and achieve your goal.'

Charlie nodded.

'Edie's big into it, she's got loads of books about that kind of thing.'

Dr Hill leaned forward.

'Books are one thing, Charlie, but these courses are a different ball game. Mind games can be very dangerous for some people. And Edie was in a very vulnerable state to begin with.'

Charlie nodded.

'It's like brainwashing. I wouldn't be surprised if they used stimulants, maybe sleep deprivation.'

'Who runs these courses, is he a psychiatrist?'

A short laugh.

'No, far from it, I'm afraid. The guy who runs these courses is a self-styled guru called Terence Roberts. You might have heard of him.'

Charlie shook his head.

'He's Irish originally but he lives abroad now. Apparently he has some quasi-doctorate degree in psychology from some American college nobody's ever heard of. The guy's a millionaire; he owns property all over the world. You can be sure that Edie paid him at least twenty grand, maybe more.'

Charlie's mouth opened.

'Twenty thousand euro? You can't be serious!'

'I'm afraid so, Charlie. Most people who go on these courses are looking for something and they're often desperate to change their lives. We're talking women who've been dumped by their husbands, men in mid-life who've just lost their jobs. They all want to change things and they think that this guy will show them how.'

'Yes, but when they realise that it's all a load of rubbish, why doesn't anyone complain? Why doesn't someone expose this, you know, like Charlie Bird?'

A shrug.

'Some do, but can't prove anything. Some are too embarrassed to do anything. They don't want their families finding out how much they've spent. Notice there's no mention of price in the brochure?'

Charlie nodded.

'Some of the people who go on these course become recruiters themselves, arranging meetings, promoting the courses, telling people how it changed their lives. These guys are good, Charlie, they can pick out someone vulnerable a mile away.'

'Like Edie.'

A slow nod.

'It's not her fault, Charlie. Her only crime is wanting to change. There's nothing wrong with that.'

Charlie looked down.

'She told me a few weeks ago she wanted to open some kind of holistic shop, you know, health supplements, books, spiritual stuff. She wanted to take a year off school.'

'That fits. She was probably hoping that the course would help her.'

Charlie sighed.

'Can anything be done about this guy?'

'It's not so simple. You've got to have proof; it's got to be able to stand up in court. You've got to be careful, too, a guy like this would sue you for defamation at the drop of a hat. Terence Roberts probably has a dozen top American lawyers in the palm of his hand. The man has huge charisma, Charlie. I've seen sensible women leave their families because of him and hand him their life's savings.'

'And there's no screening before these courses?'

'No, the only thing they screen is your bank balance. Apparently, if you want one-to-one life coaching from the man himself, you pay another ten grand, maybe even more.'

Charlie shook his head.

'I can see how Edie fell for this, she's into this kind of thing, but what about all the others?'

'You'd be surprised how vulnerable we all are, Charlie, when it comes down to it. My cousin's marriage broke up because of this 'saviour'. This Terence guy is like the Dali Lama. They believe every word that comes out of his mouth and nobody can voice any dissent. It's hard to find out exactly what goes on inside his compounds. Security is huge, no cameras, no mobile phones, no taping devices. They search you when you arrive.'

'So that's why she didn't answer her mobile.'

'Throw in a fragile mindset, lack of sleep and food and a highly emotional atmosphere and you can see how Edie might have become upset. Or maybe she challenged them and they wanted her out of there as quickly as possible.'

Charlie waited a moment, delaying the inevitable question.

'Will she be OK?'

A nod.

'Some rest and tender loving care and she'll be fine, Charlie. She'll need some psychological support to help her through this, but we can arrange that in Clonmel.'

'So she won't have to go back on medication?'

'No, Charlie. All she needs is time. Sometimes that's all any of us needs.'

Charlie nodded. Time was the one thing he didn't have.

'Go easy in the car park, Charlie. Those courier vans are dynamite.'

Charlie smiled.

'I know.'

When he opened the door, his mother was sitting in her usual spot, on the edge of the bed, facing the door, waiting. He moved his chair so that he was facing her. Slowly, he told her what had happened. She listened in silence. When he had finished, she shook her head.

'I knew she wanted to take a year out but I wouldn't listen. It's all my fault.'

He looked away.

'I didn't listen, either.'

She shook her head again.

'How can people be so cruel, taking advantage of vulnerable people like that, especially someone like Edie?'

'Money, Mother, it's all about money.'

'Edie showed me an article about that Terence fellow. I thought he was some kind of healer or something, I didn't even know that he charged for what he did.'

'Oh he charged all right, Mother! These spiritual guys are sure into the money. Dr Hill said that he probably doesn't even pay tax because he's not an Irish resident. His followers get commission for recruiting people on the courses.'

'Like pyramid selling?'

'Exactly, and that's been illegal since 1980.'

'We should do something.'

He nodded.

'We will.'

It was after six when Charlie finally climbed the steps to the car park. He closed his eyes and rested his head on the steering wheel. Thirty hours without sleep. This was a new record. But boy, was he shattered. When he opened his eyes he saw that a rainbow had formed in the sky overhead. He watched the colours grow and deepen, shimmering in the rain. Then, all of a sudden, it was in front of him, right on top of the bonnet. He smiled. Edie said that being under a rainbow was special; it meant that the angels were near.

A moment later, he reached for his mobile. Time for action. His first phone call was to Philip Manning, an old friend from Clongowes, and now a senior producer at RTÉ. Ten minutes later, he closed the phone and smiled. Mission complete. Next, Mrs Sampson. But what was he going to say?

'Mrs Sampson, I'm sorry for disturbing you, Charlie Darmody here.'

'Hello, Charlie! How is your poor mother?'

'She's improving, thanks, Mrs Sampson. It's about Edie…'

'Don't say another word, Charlie. I partly guessed Edie might not be in next week. She's going to want to take care of your mother when she comes out. I'll book a sub for the next two weeks and we can take it from there.'

Charlie smiled. Problem solved. Must have been the rainbow.

'Give your mother my regards, Charlie. And would you tell Edie that the herbal supplement she gave me cleared up my sinuses in no time.'

Thirty minutes later, Charlie kicked off his shoes. He opened the fridge and closed it again. Even eating seemed too much like work. All he wanted was sleep. A moment later, he switched off the light and pulled the duvet over his head. Then suddenly Mrs Sampson's words came floating back to him -'tell Edie the herbal supplement she gave me cleared up my sinuses in no time'. He opened his eyes. Of course! How could he have been so stupid? He'd totally forgotten about Mother's non-prescription medication, all that herbal stuff! God knows what kind of mixture she was taking. He'd have to go back to Clonmel. But first, he needed sleep. He glanced at his watch. Eight twenty. He set his mobile for four. Tomorrow morning, he'd go down to the Lodge. There was something he needed to check. And it was sitting on the second shelf of the kitchen dresser.

# 37

It was just after eight when Charlie opened the door of his mother's room. Tommy was already there.

'How is she?'

'Sister said she's better this morning. I'll call over after the round.'

'What about you, did you get some sleep?'

'Yeah, loads.'

'Too much sleep is bad. Sleep is the nearest thing to being dead.'

Charlie smiled. Maybe Tommy had a point.

'I went down to Clonmel.'

'What?'

Charlie smiled. Tommy always liked to know exactly where Charlie was; he was like Charlie's own satellite tracking system.

'This morning. I'm just back.'

He turned to his mother.

'You forgot some of your medication, Mother.'

She shook her head.

'I brought it all in, Charlie, like you told me.'

'Not quite everything, Mother.'

He reached into his pocket and took out three bottles, all white plastic, all with the same yellow buttercup logo. He placed the bottles on the bed-trolley in front of her.

'But they're only supplements.'

'It's still medicine, Mother.'

He picked up the nearest bottle.

'OK, first off we have black cohosh.'

'It's supposed to be good for the menopause.'

Her voice was low; she was probably a bit embarrassed about mentioning menopause in front of Tommy.

'Did you know that you should only take this for a short time? It can cause hyperstimulation of the lining of the uterus.'

Her eyes widened.

'Are you sure, Charlie? It didn't say that on the label.'

'Well the label doesn't exactly say very much.'

He picked up the next bottle.

'Ginseng - no major problem apart from some very well-documented drug interactions and the fact that some preparations are impure. Last year, trace metals and pesticides were found in a number of herbal supplements.'

A look of alarm flashed across his mother's face.

'But everyone's on ginseng!'

'Everyone was taking hormone replacement therapy too, Mother, until they found out that it can cause heart disease and stroke, not to mention breast cancer. The whole area of herbal medicine is a minefield, Mother. It's not regulated the same way conventional medicines are. Valerian might help insomnia, but we don't know anything about its long-term safety. Even something like comfrey can damage the liver.'

'But I'm not taking comfrey.'

'No, you're not. But you're taking this.'

He reached for the last bottle.

'Kava-kava, used for anxiety, stress and tension - a 'natural' tranquilliser. And a well-documented cause of toxic hepatitis.'

His mother's hand flew to her mouth.

'Oh my God! You think that it might have caused my jaundice?'

'It's possible. How much were you taking?'

'Three capsules before I went to bed, to help me sleep. I know the bottle said only one, but I didn't think it would do any harm taking a little bit extra, especially since it was just a herbal thing. Sometimes I'd take two capsules during the day as well, if I had had a stressful day at school.'

'So some days you took twice to three times the recommended dosage. How long have you been taking it?'

'Six months, maybe longer.'

He reached into his pocket and pulled out a piece of paper.

'Kava-kava or *Piper Methysticum*, from the roots of a species of pepper plant, is indigenous to many Pacific Island cultures. In Europe, kava-kava is recognised as a relatively safe remedy for anxiety. It can also be used as a muscle relaxant, an anti-convulsant, an anaesthetic, and an anti-inflammatory agent. Excessive sedation can occur if kava is combined with other sedative medications. Kava has been known to cause toxic hepatitis and liver failure. It should not be used in people who have liver problems, nor should it be used in patients who are taking multiple medications that are metabolised in the liver or by people who drink alcohol on a daily basis. Liver tests should be routinely done in individuals who use kava on a daily basis, and patients should be counselled on the signs and symptoms of liver toxicity. Kava should not be used for longer than four months.'

Charlie looked up. His mother's mouth was open. Even Tommy had stopped chewing.

'It explains why your liver tests have improved, you haven't been taking it since you came in.'

'Have I done permanent damage to my liver?'

Her voice was faint.

'You're getting better, not worse. And you don't drink alcohol. If it was Tommy here, it might be a different story.'

Maybe best not tell her that a few more weeks of kava-kava and the story might have been very different.

'The Guinness is the only supplement, loads of iron, the safest one of the lot of them. What I can't understand is why these things are allowed on sale.'

'The thing is, Tommy, health shop vitamins and herbal supplements aren't regulated the same way prescription medicines are. Nobody knows what's on sale and where it came from. And supplements aren't standardised, you might be getting half the dose you're supposed to be getting or you might be getting ten times the amount.'

'What do I do now, Charlie?'

'Get plenty of rest, drink lots of fluids and you'll be fine.'

And she would be fine. So, hopefully, would Edie. And that was all that mattered.

# 38

Charlie slipped his bleep back into his pocket and groaned. Another pneumonia in Casualty; that meant 12 admissions already and it wasn't even noon. If this continued, there wouldn't even be a free trolley by night-time. Suddenly he heard a familiar voice and turned around. Marianne. She was wearing black, her hair shimmering under the lights, heels clicking as she walked towards him.

'You didn't return my calls.'

He shrugged.

'I'm busy.'

She stepped closer.

'Can we talk?'

'We're talking, aren't we?'

'Can we go some place private, your office or something?'

'I don't have an office. This is a hospital, not a PR company.'

'Look, Charlie, I'm sorry. He meant nothing to me, honest.'

Charlie sighed. Was there any end to this? Did the girl not even know when she was lying?

'Haven't you mixed up your tenses, Marianne? I think the word is 'means'. You're still seeing him, aren't you?'

She nodded. At least she hadn't lied.

'It's over. He just won't listen.'

She was silent for a while.

'About the launch...'

Aha! Conversation over. Small talk out of the way. So this was about work after all. He'd obviously spooked her yesterday. There was a lot of money riding on Charlie Darmody and Diastora; she had to make sure he came up with the goods, that he delivered.

'Yes?'

'I hope that what happened between us won't affect your presentation.'

He held her gaze.

'Why should it?'

'Greg Harris said that you phoned him about Diastora, some safety query, liver toxicity, I think.'

It was a question, not a statement. Demanding clarification. Charlie smiled. The jungle drums sure beat loudly in the pharma world.

'Just checking all the facts. We don't want to leave any stone unturned, do we?'

'He said that you thought Diastora might have caused your mother's jaundice.'

Charlie took a deep breath. So much for a confidential conversation. With Big Pharma, everything was up for grabs. Wonder if they knew about him and Marianne.

'My mother's jaundice had nothing to do with Diastora.'

Not since six o'clock this morning, it hadn't. Not since he'd found the kava-kava.

'I'm glad.'

Bet you are.

'How's your presentation coming along?'

'It's finished.'

Done and dusted. No need to look at it again until Saturday morning. All pruned and polished. As tight as could be. All he needed now was the balls to deliver it.

She held out her hand.

'No hard feelings?'

He stared at her hand, the way the big rings made her slim fingers look so fragile, the nails, perfectly painted in shiny red varnish. He could imagine them clicking on her laptop. Or scratching someone's eyes out. He held out his hand and smiled.

'No hard feelings, Marianne.'

Strangely enough, he meant it. Archangel Michael, angel of forgiveness and love, would be proud of him.

He watched her sashay down the corridor. So long, Marianne.

Then a familiar voice behind him...

'If Miss Glamour Puss falls off those heels, she'll break her ankle.'

Charlie laughed.

'Well, she's in the right place, anyway.'

'You still have a soft spot for her?'

Charlie smiled. Tommy didn't miss a trick.

'Nah.'

Then Tommy touched his shoulder.

'You can still sort it out with Tracy, you know. Don't let happen what happened me, kept my mouth shut too long and then it was too late.'

'And you never met anyone else?'

Tommy shook his head.

'When you've found the right person, Charlie, everyone else is second best.

Charlie nodded. Tommy was right. You might try to forget, you might convince yourself that you liked someone else, you might even put her out of your mind for a few hours, but in the end, it was always the same. If you loved someone, you never stopped thinking about them, no matter what, even if it had to be your secret for the rest of your life.

# 39

The door opened and Charlie stepped back to let someone pass. He stood for a moment in the doorway, watching her. She was sitting in an armchair, her knees pulled up in front of her, her face turned to the window. After a while, she turned around and saw him. She smiled, that wide, lopsided smile, the old Edie smile. He knew, even before she spoke, that she was back. He could see it in her eyes, the way they darted and danced and shone with brightness. The sedation had been tailed back to just a small dose at night and Edie was beginning to remember bits and pieces about the trip. Dr Hill was right, all it had taken was rest and time. She would need some counselling, more like a debriefing really, so that she could, as they say, gain closure. But attending a psychologist was no big deal; half the country was in counselling these days.

He felt a lump in his throat when he thought of what might have been. Edie was one of the lucky ones; her experience hadn't triggered anything. Apparently not everyone was that lucky. Charlie shook his head. Yes, indeed. Mind-altering and life-changing was what the brochure said. They were right.

He wrapped his arms around her, burying his face in her hair. It smelled nice. They'd washed it for her yesterday. And she was back in normal Edie clothes, the ones he'd brought up from home. Levis and a navy sweater. He kissed her on the forehead. Welcome back, Edie.

'How are you, kiddo?'

She smiled.

'Fine. When can I go home?'

'Soon. Saturday.'

Her eyes searched his.

'When is Mother coming to see me?'

He hadn't told her about Mother yet. No need to worry her.

'Today, I think.'

'Is she very mad at me?'

'No, hon, she's not mad at you.'

She touched his arm.

'I'm sorry, Charlie, I should have told you.'

'Why didn't you?'

'I was afraid you'd try to stop me.'

He smiled.

'You were right.'

He squeezed her hand.

'What happened, Edie, can you remember?'

She nodded.

'We only had about four hours sleep and practically no food.'

He coaxed a strand of hair behind her ear. Dr Hill was right; first sleep, then food deprivation - these guys had it down to a fine art.

'They locked me in my room. Oh Charlie! I was so frightened! I thought they were going to kill me and then I remembered that nobody knew where I was...'

Charlie squeezed her hand. He could just imagine what it must have felt like being locked up in a strange room in a strange place. No wonder she freaked out. The poor girl probably thought she'd never get out of there.

They sat in silence for a while and the room grew dark around them. When she spoke, her voice was low.

'Did you find the envelope?'

He nodded. For a while, neither of them spoke.

'First I was angry with him, for doing what he did. Then I was angry at Mother, for not telling us, for not telling us everything.'

'I know.'

He'd felt the same. Then he remembered the letter.

'Mother mentioned a letter. Do you have it?'

A slow nod.

'What's in it?'

'You'll have to ask Mother.'

'Please, Edie!'

'No, Charlie, she has to tell you.'

He knew that it was pointless pleading with her. He'd have to ask Mother. And this time, no excuses. He wasn't going to leave until she told him.

'Can't I go home tomorrow? I'm fine, really I am.'

'It's only another day, Edie. I'll collect you after the presentation.'

Her eyes widened.

'I'd forgotten about your presentation! It's a God given opportunity, Charlie, to say something, to speak out.'

He sighed.

'It's not my call, Edie.'

'It's everyone's call. Do the right thing, Charlie, do it for me.'

'I can't risk it, Edie. I can't risk throwing it all away.'

'You don't have to. You'll find a way. Ask the angels to help you. They'll guide you, I know they will.'

'They'll think I'm a crackpot.'

She smiled.

'Like your sister?'

'I didn't mean it like that...'

'I know you didn't. Remember, they called Galileo a crackpot. And the first people who talked about global warming. We both know that Cardelia killed people. You can't just say nothing, pretend it never happened.'

'This isn't the right time.'

She touched his hand.

'It's always the right time, Charlie.'


He sighed. All his life he'd said nothing; head down, mouth shut, never ruffled any feathers, did what was expected of him. Never once had he put his head above the parapet. But Edie was right. Somebody had to say something. And this was his chance to do the right thing. All he needed was the courage to do it.

# 40

Charlie opened the door of his mother's room. Good. No doctors, no nurses, no visitors. Not even the cleaning ladies. Just him and her and the secret that lay between them. This time he wasn't going to scuttle sideways like his star sign, the crab, sidestepping and skirting the truth. This time, he wasn't going to leave until she told him.

He watched her reach for the cup on the bedside locker, the one she had brought up from home. She took a tiny sip, a pretend kind of sip, and placed it back down again. She knew why he was here.

Outside, in the corridor, he could hear the clatter of trolleys and the soft whirr of the vacuum cleaner. Hospitals were noisy places at the best of times. Noise was good; it made things seem normal. He cleared his throat.

'What was in the letter, Mother?'

She looked away.

'What did she tell you?'

'Nothing. She said to ask you.'

A long, deep, sigh.

'Close the door.'

A minute or two passed. It was as if she'd forgotten about him. He was just about to say something when she turned towards him.

'Your father and I, Charlie, it wasn't easy.'

He nodded. It was never easy being married to an alcoholic.

'I should never have married him, I suppose. I knew he drank too much.'

Her voice was flat, detached.

'I was a fool to think that I could change him. Every day, every single day, he drank.'

Her eyes drifted downward and she was silent for a moment.

'There was a local guard, sometimes he'd bring your father home'

She hesitated a moment.

'We became friends.'

Charlie waited. Here it was.

'We had an affair.'

He could see the whites of her knuckles on the bedspread.

'I became pregnant.'

She closed her eyes.

'Pregnant with Edie.'

Charlie nodded. In some strange way, he had always known this.

'Where is he now?'

'He died before Edie was born, knocked off his bicycle by a drunk.'

He could taste the bitterness in her voice.

'Did he have other children?'

'No, he wasn't married.'

'Did he know about Edie?'

A pause. When she spoke, her voice was choked.

'No. I never got the chance to tell him.'

'Did Dad know?'

She looked into the distance.

'He never said anything, but I think he knew. The day of the christening, I cried all day. That night he insisted we all go out. I've never seen him so drunk. I couldn't stick it any more and phoned a neighbour to bring me home.'

Charlie swallowed. The night of the accident.

'That was the last time I saw your parents alive.'

'He was driving, wasn't he?'

She nodded. Charlie looked away. Deep down, he always knew that Dad had caused the accident. This man, the only father he had known, the man who had brought him to Kilmallock to get a hurley specially made for him, the man who had taught him how to fish on the Suir and shoot a pellet gun, this man had been the cause of his parents' deaths. Yet he could feel no hate.

'After that, things went from bad to worse. The guilt seemed to eat away at him. He was no sooner out of hospital than he was in again. And, of course, he kept on drinking which didn't help. It was like he was trying to drink himself to death.'

Except it wasn't fast enough. Charlie closed his eyes.

'Why did Edie ever have to know that he wasn't her father? You know how much she adored him.'

He could see her flinch. He hadn't meant to raise his voice. Shouting did no one any good, that's what Edie always said.

'Because she needed to know that he wasn't her real father.'

Charlie nodded. He was beginning to understand. Mother wanted Edie to know that she hadn't inherited 'the strain'.

'So Edie and I aren't even cousins.'

'No.'

She looked away, into the past, remembering.

'She followed you around like a little puppy. She wouldn't go to school without you. It was unnatural, the way she adored you.'

'There was nothing wrong with it.'

And there wasn't. Even as cousins, there was nothing wrong with it.

'You were cousins; at least everyone thought you were. The children at school thought you were brother and sister.'

'So you sent us away to boarding school.'

She shook her head.

'I had to do something.'

'You separated us.'

Because we loved each other too much.

'You know Edie hated it.'

And so did I.

'You've always been harder on her, like you resented her or something.'

She shook her head.

'I love that child with all my heart, Charlie. I'd do anything to make her happy.'

He stood up.

'Sometimes that means letting go, Mother. You have to let her go. You have to let us both go.'

He was at the door when she spoke.

'You're going to take her away, aren't you?'

He nodded. Strangely, she didn't look surprised. It was as if she'd always known that this might happen.

Outside, in the car park, the significance of his mother had just told him suddenly hit him. Edie wasn't his cousin. They weren't related. The feelings he had felt, all his life, from as far back as he could remember, the feelings

294

he had crushed and ignored and suppressed and rejected, weren't wrong, weren't shameful. There was nothing wrong with his love for Edie.

That night, he drove down to Clonmel again. This time, he didn't turn right for Ardfinnan but continued on towards Powerstown. He stopped at the church. This was where he received his First Holy Communion and where he had been baptised and confirmed. It was where his parents got married. The religious milestones of his life, all in one place. It was also where his father was buried.

He picked up the bunch of daffodils and turned up the collar of his jacket to shield against the wind. Then he creaked open the gate. It had been years since he had been here. He wasn't sure when or why he had stopped coming. Probably the same reason he had stopped going to Mass. Laziness, mainly, too busy doing other stuff, like lying in bed.

A moment later, he stopped beside a limestone headstone. He bent down and placed the daffodils on the grave. Ashes to ashes. Earth to earth. He knelt down on the damp grass. The tears stung his eyes. In the distance, he could hear the soft shuffling of a grave being freshly dug. The peal of a church bell broke the night-time stillness. Today, somebody else's grief. He reached out and touched the headstone.

'I miss you, Dad.'

# 41

Edie gathered her hair into a ponytail and tied it tightly with an elastic band. Mother liked her hair back from her face. Her eyes darted to the clock on the wall. Ten past three. Mother should be here soon. Poor Mother. She'd wondered why she hadn't been to see her. Now, of course, she understood.

She smoothed her top again. Strange how nervous she felt. She crossed her legs. A moment later, she uncrossed them again. Mother always said that crossing your legs gave you varicose veins.

No doubt Mother would be annoyed. And she could hardly blame her. Not telling anyone about the course. Not to mention all that money. She took a deep breath and squeezed her hands, tighter and tighter until the knuckles shone white. It was her way of bracing herself against Mother - the constant reproaches, the free-flowing criticism. She'd plenty of practice. Then she felt a sudden twist of anger. She might have lied about the holiday but surely that was no big deal compared to lying about how your father died. Or who your father was.

She glanced out the window. The sky had darkened and heavy drops of rain were beginning to fall. Mother would get drenched. Suddenly the door opened and Edie jumped to her feet. Mother.

Her mother began to walk towards her and Edie felt all her anger float away. Her mother looked smaller, somehow, more faded, like a photograph left out in the sun.

'Edie!'

Her mother's arms were around her.

'I'm sorry, Mother. I wanted to do something, to make you proud of me.'

Her mother's cheeks were damp.

'But I am proud of you, Edie! I've always been proud of you.'

They stood for a moment in a silent embrace, then Edie stepped back.

'That day, the day he died, who found him?'

'I did.'

'He wasn't thinking straight, Edie. He wouldn't have done it otherwise.'

Edie felt a lump in her throat.

'I know.'

For a moment she couldn't speak.

'Where did he... where did it happen?'

Her mother closed her eyes.

'In the woodshed, under the old Scots pines.'

Edie nodded. She never liked that part of the garden; too many breezes, too many shadows. Now she understood why.

'He left a note. He said he loved you both very much, and that I was to take good care of his two little angels.'

Edie closed her eyes and swallowed. The tears could wait.

'My real father, what was he like?'

Her mother's eyes had a faraway look.

'He was a lovely, kind, gentle person, just like you, Edie. He wanted me to leave your father, to start a new life in America or Australia. We talked about getting an annulment, on account of your father not being well...'

297

Her voice trailed off. Edie looked away. In sickness and in health.

'Did he know about me?'

'No. I never got the chance to tell him.'

Edie closed her eyes. Ireland was a different place thirty years ago. It must have been terrible to lose someone you loved and not be able to grieve.

'After Robbie died, I knew I could never leave. There was no point. And it would have broken your father's heart if I'd taken you and Charlie away.'

Edie waited a moment.

'Like you took Charlie away from me?'

A brief silence.

'I'm sorry, Edie.'


After her mother had left, Edie went to her bedroom and closed the door. Then the tears came. She cried for the man she had always called her father, for his suffering and his pain, for the anguish that had finally killed him. She cried for her mother's sad and lonely life in a house and garden full of memories. And she cried for the father she never knew. But mostly, she cried for Charlie, with his curly hair and cheeky grin and his stupid jokes. Soon, Charlie would be gone. Thousands of miles away. Another country. Another continent. Another life.

# 42

Charlie stirred his coffee; round and round, watching the swirls grow fast and deep. Circles spiralling out of control, sucked into a vortex of indecision and uncertainty. This time last month, he knew exactly what he wanted. Now he wasn't sure about anything any more. He could hear Tommy clear his throat.

'So, Charlie, you going to say something at the launch tomorrow or are you going to keep your mouth shut like I told you?'

Charlie shrugged.

'Cardelia was a dirty drug.'

'Yes, but there's a time and place for everything and it's not tomorrow.'

'You know, I was certain that Diastora caused Mother's hepatitis.'

'And you were wrong, Charlie. You took it too personal.'

Charlie nodded. Tommy was right. His reaction to Diastora had been emotional and emotion played no part in professional distance and clinical detachment.

Tommy leaned closer.

'Think of your career, Charlie, all you've worked for. I know they're a shower of bastards, but there's too much at stake here.'

Charlie nodded. Tommy was right. OK, he might have proof about the Cardelia cover-up but it would be professional suicide to go down that road. If he blew tomorrow, it would be the end of his job in Johns Hopkins; it might be the end of his ever getting a consultant's job. Then he remembered Edie's words, about doing the right thing, about not letting the opportunity pass. He sighed. Decision time.

'I won't mention Cardelia.'

'Good man, Charlie. That's what I want to hear. Remember numero uno, it's the name of the game. Go home, get some rest, lad. It will all work out.'

'I hope so.'

Tommy touched his shoulder.

'Just remember, Charlie, this is it, the one you've been waiting for, the last hurdle.'

Charlie nodded.

'Of course, there's always other options. You could set up a screening clinic for the GAA, you know, echocardiograms, make sure they don't drop dead during a match.'

Charlie smiled.

'That's not a bad idea, Tommy. Mind you, they could still drop dead even after a normal ECG and echo.'

'Not your fault. Anyway, you'd be insured.'

Charlie laughed.

'Or what about doing General Practice, move back to Clonmel? I could move back too. It's time I quit this game, Charlie.'

Charlie looked away. It was never going to happen; neither of them was going to move back to Clonmel. They both knew that.

'It was you, wasn't it, Tommy? It was you who put the missing datasets on my computer, didn't you?'

Tommy shook his head.

'You told me yourself they were password protected. How in God's name could I get Clements' password, Charlie? But it wasn't from want of trying, I can tell you.'

So it wasn't Tommy. Or was it? He would never know for sure. Maybe it was best this way, the not knowing. Then it could be anyone he wanted it to be.

They sat in silence for a while. Then Charlie looked up.

'There's something else, Tommy.'

Tommy leaned closer.

'Shoot, boss. I'm listening.'

Charlie hesitated.

'Edie's father, he isn't... he isn't Dad.'

A slow nod.

'I thought that might be the case.'

Charlie shook his head.

'Edie's life has been a lie, she doesn't even know who she is.'

Tommy's eyes met his.

'Edie knows who she is and what she wants, Charlie. It's you who have to decide.'

Charlie blinked. Tommy knew. For a moment, neither of them spoke, then Tommy smiled.

'Hey, I almost forgot! Good news! Remember our little investment in WorldPharma?'

Charlie nodded.

'We're talking sixty percent up, should give us nearly three grand each if we sell now. Must be a Diastora high. Well, what do you think?'

Charlie smiled.

'Sell.'

Tommy rubbed his hands together.

'Exactly what I'd hoped you'd say. Looks like I might make Cheltenham after all this year.'

Then Tommy put his hand on Charlie's shoulder.

'Best of luck tomorrow, son. Remember, sine metu, have no fear.'

Charlie smiled.

'Sine metu.'


Later, back at the apartment, Charlie opened his blue document folder and spread the contents on the table in front of him. He picked up his passport and began to flick through the pages. After a moment, he stopped and smiled. His J1 visa. Memories of that summer came flooding back. They'd both worked as care assistants in a nursing home in Santa Cruz. It had been a blast, for sure. Parties and surfing and smoking joints on the beach at sunset. Afterwards he had been riddled with guilt; worried that it might have been the cannabis that had triggered Edie's illness. He was the one who passed her the joint.

He flicked through the pages again and stopped when he came to the page stamped with his new visa. Two years - it was a long time. But a cracking job, no doubt about it. Fifty percent clinical work, fifty percent research in a state-of-the-art cardiac lab. He'd always dreamed about working in the States. Medicine in America was right up there, cutting edge stuff, where you saw new treatments and techniques that were only being talked about in Europe. Things were happening in the States. Imagine being able to click your fingers and get an MRI done, or being able to check the lab results on your palm-held while you did the round. He knew all about the long hours, the short holidays, the onerous on-call rosters, having to eat, breathe and sleep medicine, having medicine in your pores and in your blood. He closed his eyes. It would be worth it. Two years in America and there was a very good chance he might be offered a consultant's post back home, especially now, with the new contract and all the new jobs. It was crazy to even think of throwing it all way.

Then he remembered Cardelia. And Mother's jaundice. And he thought about Edie. Most of all, he thought about Edie.

# 43

Charlie looked at the disk in his hand; it looked like any other disk: shiny, slim and smooth. With a cutting edge. He glanced around the room. Only a few empty seats. A photographer near the podium. A queue at the registration desk. He took a deep breath. He'd done dozens of presentations but somehow, today was different. Uncharted territory, so to speak. There was more at stake than hypertension or cardiac failure. What he said in the next thirty minutes could change his life.

Already he could feel his mouth begin to dry up and his palms begin to moisten. Maybe he should have taken a small dose of beta-blocker to mask his anxiety.

He looked down at the disk in his hand. Funny how something so small could change your life. A fine tremor wired his fingers. Could he do this? He took a deep breath. Yes, he could. OK, Archangel Michael, time to flap your wings and get down here. I need you, mate. He slipped in the disk. Time to get the show on the road.

He clicked on the first slide. It was a blood pressure cuff, nothing fancy. No clue as to what lay ahead. He glanced around the room again. All seats were taken now. Extra chairs were being brought in from the room next door. It was going to be a full house.

Suddenly, things started speeding up, like they do in the movies. Greg Harris looking at his watch, nodding, the doors closing, Marianne weaving her way towards him. They'd already agreed that her introduction would be brief.

A moment later, she was beside him, smiling, scanning the room, waiting until she had everyone's attention. She looked like a Eurovision presenter. Wonder if she was going to speak French. He took a deep breath. That's it, Charlie, cool down. Nobody's looking at you. All eyes are on Marianne.

'Today, ladies and gentlemen, is an important day in Irish medicine.'

The obligatory significant pause.

'We are all aware that the optimal control of hypertension is one of the most important factors in the prevention of cardiovascular disease. Today, our guest speaker, Dr Charlie Darmody, will take us through exciting new developments in the treatment of hypertension.'

Her hands moved together in an elegant little clap and her lips parted in a wide, stretched smile. Looked like she'd had her teeth whitened again.

He looked down at the crowd. The silence swallowed him. Take it easy, Charlie, pretend it's just the final meds; focus on one person. His eyes scanned the middle of the audience, looking for a friendly face. Already he recognized two faces from the medical trade press and a freelance journalist who wrote for everything from *Woman's Own* to the *Telegraph*. He could see Doctor Muiris Houston, the health correspondent with the *Irish Times,* sitting in the front row. He had a nice, smiley face. Charlie met his smile and clicked the first slide. *Hypertension – Medicine for a New Millennium.* Here we go. Now all he had to do was to deliver the following ten slides.

'Thank you, everybody, for coming here today.'

Mind you, the five-course gourmet lunch afterwards might have something to do with it. He could hear the clink of ice.

'The treatment of hypertension is one of the most important therapeutic areas in medicine.'

He paused.

'It is also one of the most lucrative.'

He could hear a sharp intake of breath. Probably Marianne. Then he felt a warm softness brush his cheek, like a summer breeze, and with it, a sudden confidence.

'In recent times, the pharmaceutical industry has been accused of being greedy, corrupt and self-serving. Every year, drugs are withdrawn that have not lived up to expectations and, in some cases, have caused serious side-effects, even death.'

Nervous coughing. Probably from the WorldPharma stable. Out of the corner of his eye, he could see Marianne, half-sitting, half-standing, a sort of nervous crouch. Good for the quads, Marianne, keep it up. Could help you on your next ski trip. He clicked the next slide. It was blank apart from some euro symbols.

'The pharmaceutical industry is the world's most profitable industry: the combined profits of the top ten drug companies in the Fortune 500 list are said to be greater than the profits of the other 490 companies on the list.'

A low mutter.

'The industry has been accused of protecting its interests by its stringent patency policies and the intellectual property protection covered in the laws on data exclusivity, which protect a drug's clinical trials data. Generic firms must have formal access to this information before they can get permission to start producing copies of original brand drugs.'

The silence was suffocating. Marianne's seat was empty.

'There have been many accusations against the pharmaceutical industry. Marcia Angell, in her book *The Truth about the Drug Companies* claims that the pharmaceutical industry concentrates on lucrative markets by designing 'me-too' drugs that we don't need, that it avoids head-to-head comparisons with existing medicines and, more recently, that the pharmaceutical industry promotes diseases in order to create new revenue streams. There have been repeated calls for an independent institute to regulate drug trials.'

She was standing right behind him. Quickly, he clicked the next slide.

'Angell accuses clinical trials of being 'rigged' and describes meetings like this as tradeshow hucksterism.'

He could feel her edge closer. Et tu, Brute. Let her come as close as she wanted. He wasn't finished. Even if she flipped the power, he could keep talking.

'Despite all this negative publicity, the pharmaceutical industry continues to be a major force in medical research. True, there have been problems; the recent withdrawal of Cardelia shows that we have to be vigilant in the post-marketing surveillance of any drug. But now and again, an innovative new drug comes along that changes the face of medicine and helps restore our confidence in the pharmaceutical industry. I believe that the new anti-hypertensive, Diastora, is one of these drugs.'

A sideways glance told him that Marianne was retreating, crisis over.

Fifteen minutes later, he clicked the last slide.

'Diastora is the latest addition to our anti-hypertensive armoury. Even though it has an excellent side-effect profile, we should always be on the alert for previously undemonstrated side effects and should notify the Irish Medicines Board. Unfortunately, herbal preparations and supplements do not have the same monitoring and regulation as prescription products, something that many of us feel urgently needs to be addressed.'

A mutter of agreement.

'In conclusion, Diastora represents a significant and important advance in the management of hypertension and is an excellent first choice treatment for all newly diagnosed hypertensive patients, including the elderly, patients with diabetes and patients with cardiac failure. My congratulations to WorldPharma on bringing us this excellent new drug.'

He paused to catch his breath.

'Thank you, ladies and gentlemen.'

He breathed a sigh of relief. It was over. Finally. He could hear clapping, loud and strong. He glanced over at the WorldPharma corner; just as he had expected, perennial grins still in situ. He felt a hand touch his elbow. Marianne, wide smile, eyes dancing.

'Nice one, Charlie, you had me worried there for a while. Great speech, wrong audience, honey. It's wasted on this crowd; they're only here for the food. I suppose I'd better do a little bit of damage limitation. Might even have to sleep with a few journalists to make sure they get the right copy.'

He smiled and stepped aside.

'Thank you, Dr Darmody, for an extremely interesting and enlightening presentation. It's not often we hear such honesty. In fact, that's one of the reasons we asked Dr Darmody here today. Anyone can stand up and say good things about Diastora, but very few can highlight the importance of a drug relevant to the background Dr Darmody has described. He is right when he says that Big Pharma has been accused of commercial bias. But there's no need for any games with Diastora. As Dr Darmody correctly pointed out, Diastora is a stand-alone, honest to goodness, does exactly what it says on the tin kind of drug. Dr Darmody also touched on some areas which, for a long time now, have been of major concern to WorldPharma.'

A protracted pause.

'One of them is the culture of a 'pill for every ill' that seems to pervade society today. I am delighted to take this opportunity to announce

WorldPharma's 'Giving Something Back' initiative. Next month, an expansive educational programme on cardiovascular health will be launched. 'Healthy hearts for kids' will be available to every school in the country. A dedicated team of community dieticians, exercise therapists, cardiovascular nurses and health promotion experts will deliver the programme to all primary schools and secondary schools throughout the country. A special module has also been developed for transition year. We hope that this programme, the first ever privately-sponsored public health initiative of its kind in this country, will show WorldPharma's commitment to preventing cardiovascular disease by healthy lifestyle.'

She looked at the WorldPharma MD and began to clap. Soon everyone was clapping. Charlie looked around; the journalists were writing furiously. After a moment, he began to clap too. Well done, Marianne. She'd probably spoken off the cuff; judging by the surprised looks on some of the WorldPharma faces. But, like she said herself, timing was everything. Then she was beside him.

'Congratulations, Marianne, that was excellent. I think they've forgotten what I said already.'

She smiled.

'That was the intention. I've given them the copy they want, Charlie, the positive stuff, the good news. Nobody wants to hear about avian flu when they're having roast chicken for dinner.'

He laughed.

'You'll be on the front page of all the medical journals.'

She smiled again and, once more, he realised how beautiful she was.

'It's only a job, Charlie. It's what I do. Same as you. You do your job and I do mine and we both do the best job we can.'

He nodded.

'Did WorldPharma know that you were going to announce this today?'

A familiar tinkly laugh.

'WorldPharma haven't even heard of it, honey. And frankly, Charlie, I don't give a shit. I've saved their bacon here today. They should run with this before someone else does. I've plenty of other pharma companies on my books that would only be too delighted to take this on board.'

Then she lowered her voice.

'Thanks, Charlie. You could have gone for the jugular but you didn't.'

'What do you mean?'

'Cardelia, those unpublished trials.'

He met her gaze.

'So it was you.'

She nodded.

'Everyone was sound asleep in that library. No wonder there's a health crisis.'

'Why?'

She shrugged.

'Maybe it's my way of saying sorry. I owe you, Charlie. Besides, it's what I do best, information laundering is what I think you called it. By the way, I'm leaving GoldMed. Just been offered a job with the Government, communications advisor to someone very important.'

'Congratulations, you deserve it. You're good, you know.'

She smiled and touched his arm.

'And you're good too, Charlie Darmody, you're a good doctor, and you'll be a great consultant. Don't let the shit get to you.'

He hesitated a moment then kissed her cheek.

'Goodbye, Marianne.'

# 44

Charlie looked around. The room was empty now, just him and his laptop. He took a deep breath. He'd done it; he'd made the call. Strange, really, how calm he felt; the anxiety that had clawed at him for the past few weeks was gone. Instead he felt a strange sense of what he could only describe as… peace. Peace. It was a word that he'd never quite understood until now. It was like a huge weight had been lifted from him. Maybe doing the right thing had its own rewards. Suddenly he felt a hand on his shoulder.

'Dr Clements!'

'Got here after all, Charlie. Slipped in just before you started.'

'How was your holiday?'

'Great. Fantastic snow, 'la poudre' as they say. You seem to have been on the slippery slopes yourself.'

His smile was quizzical, amused.

'I think we need to have a little chat, Charlie.'

Charlie nodded.

'When?'

'Now would be good, unless you're rushing off somewhere?'

'No.'

No, he certainly wasn't rushing off anywhere; not now, maybe never.

'Let's sit down.'

Charlie pulled out a chair. As usual, Clements' face gave nothing away. Deadpan and dangerous.

'Excellent presentation, Charlie, though for a while there, I thought you'd lost the plot, thought that you wanted to go to Outer Mongolia instead of Johns Hopkins.'

A narrow smile.

'A brave stance, I must say, taking on the pharmaceutical industry single-handed, you and John Le Carré. But, of course, it's fine for Le Carré, he's not a doctor.'

A short pause.

'Where did all this come from, Charlie, if you don't mind my asking?'

Charlie shrugged.

'Cardelia, I suppose. And I thought that Diastora might have caused my mother's hepatitis.'

Clements leaned towards him.

'But it didn't, did it? Look, Charlie, I know you've been under a lot of pressure lately with your family but you've got to keep the personal stuff separate from the job, OK?'

Charlie met his gaze. Keep the personal stuff separate from the job? This from the Casanova of St Anne's! Yet, there wasn't a pinch of irony in those steel grey eyes. Obviously Clements didn't know about him and Marianne. If he did, that thin smile wouldn't be long disappearing. But why bother? Let Clements find out the hard way, just like he had. Anyway, Marianne could do what she wanted. He didn't care. He'd never cared, really.

Just then, the door opened; Greg Harris, smiling as usual. But, of course, smiling meant nothing in the pharmaceutical industry. Charlie waited for the smile to fade but instead it seemed to be getting broader. And now Greg was holding out his hand.

'Well done, Charlie! Different kind of tack, but effective. You and the lovely Marianne make a good double-act.'

Yeah, if you only knew.

'I just wanted to give you this.'

He handed Charlie an envelope.

'It's just a small honorarium, a token of our appreciation.'

Charlie looked at the envelope, then slipped it into his pocket. He had a sudden urge to hide it; as if it was money earned illegally, drug money. Which, of course, was exactly what it was.

He placed a hand on Charlie's shoulder.

'When you've finished in Johns Hopkins, don't forget to call us. WorldPharma needs people like you on our team, Charlie, people with a strong sense of ethics, people with credibility. We'd love you to come on board. Europe, America, Asia, wherever you want.'

Charlie's mouth dropped open. WorldPharma was still going to fund him! And they were even offering him a job!

'I'm glad your mother is better, Charlie. John told me about the kava-kava. You know, I've been on about this kind of thing for years. The entire herbal market needs to be regulated. The industry has got to start lobbying for new legislation.'

Charlie nodded. Regulation of the herbal market was one thing but you can bet the real plan was to take it over. In Greg Harris' world, regulation and control were the same thing.

'I know things have been a bit hectic for you lately, Charlie. If you want to defer the States for a few weeks, I'll square it with our guys over there. It'll be all guns blazing once you get there.'

313

He held out his hand.

'Best of luck, Charlie. And remember, we're only doing our job. We're no better or worse than any other business.'

Charlie nodded. Greg was right. Was there any organization that wasn't corrupt? Or any country, for that matter? Was America, a nation that invaded countries for oil, less corrupt than Iraq? Was Shell less corrupt than WorldPharma? What about the funding of sports by the alcohol industry? Or the companies that added sugar to baby foods? Or the soya agribusiness that was destroying the rainforests? Or the cosy cartels of property developers and local government? Corruption, manipulation and misinformation were what life was all about. And nobody, anywhere, could change that.

'I'd best be off. Sure you don't want to join us in the dining room? The food's top class.'

Charlie smiled.

'No, thanks, Greg. I'm not hungry.'

'John?'

'I'll pass, too, Greg, thank you.'

The door closed and, for a moment, neither of them spoke.

Then Clements looked up.

'Looks like you played another blinder there, Charlie. Got it all off your chest and still managed to keep everyone happy. You should be in politics, you know.'

Charlie smiled.

'I've had a good teacher.'

'Greg's right, Charlie. The pharma industry is a business like any other business with profits as the bottom line. But it's probably a lot more ethical than many other big organizations.'

Charlie nodded. Only that morning he'd read an article about some well-known sports-wear manufacturer and Asian sweatshops. The pharma industry wasn't intrinsically bad, it just needed to be watched, the same way McDonalds and Coca Cola needed to be watched.

There was a short silence.

'So, Charlie, what's it going to be?'

'Pardon?'

'You're having second thoughts about going, aren't you?'

Charlie shrugged.

'Two years over there and you can name your job back here. You've got what it takes, Charlie, you've got the ability and the drive; you can go right to the top. And, like Greg said, defer it a week or two if you like. That brother of mine probably won't even notice. The lazy sod spends most of his time doing private angios down in Florida.'

Charlie smiled.

'A word of advice, though. Mind the women. Don't mess up like I did.'

There was an unfamiliar sadness in his voice.

'Is something wrong?'

Clements looked up. His lips were smiling but his eyes were dark.

'My wife says she's leaving for good this time. My son is gone off the rails, has dropped rugby, kicked out of Clongowes last week because of drugs, and I'm in deep shit over an offshore account my mother had the misfortune to leave me. Between my tax penalties and my wife cleaning me out, I'll be lucky to afford a one-bedroomed apartment in Newbridge.'

Charlie was silent for a moment.

'I'm sorry, John, I didn't realise.'

'Nobody realises anything until it's too late, Charlie. I look at you, I see youth, idealism, energy and ability; you  have everything, Charlie. Don't fuck it up. Don't fall in love with the wrong woman.'

He looked away, into the distance.

'I love her, you know. But she says it's over.'

Charlie swallowed. Marianne. Awkwardly, he reached out and touched Clements' shoulder. They had more in common than Clements realised.


At the door, Clements stopped and turned.

'You will go, won't you, Charlie?'

Charlie nodded. Yes, he was going. It might not be perfect, but it was the best there was. With knowledge came power. And it was up to him what he did with that power.

# 45

Saturdays were always quiet in the library; no whirr of the fax or click of the printers, nothing except the myriad of lights blinking behind the desk and the occasional sound of an ambulance siren in the distance. Charlie reached down and touched a textbook. He would miss this room; his refuge, this little oasis of tranquillity in the madness of the hospital that surrounded it. He placed his hand on the desk, skin against wood, and memories came flooding back, a cyberspace of memories. For three years, this had been his little spot in St Anne's. Everyone knew that sooner or later, along he'd come, his pocket full of chocolate and his bleep always bleeping. He blinked and began to gather up his books. Then the door opened.

'Mike, the very man, want my desk?'

A wide smile.

'Thanks, Charlie! And thanks again for all the tutorials.'

Charlie smiled.

'My pleasure.'

A few minutes later, he opened the door of his mother's room. Her glasses were perched low on her nose and the newspaper was spread across the bed, open at the death columns. It was Mother's own personal Sudoku, matching up the names and addresses for people she might know.

'Well, how did it go?'

'Fine.'

She folded the paper.

'How's Edie?'

'Good. They said she can go home today.'

He could see her left eye begin to twitch.

'It'll be nice for the two of you to have the weekend together. She's going to be very upset when you leave. I'm dreading it already.'

Charlie bit his lip. Mother was in denial mode again. It was as if their previous conversation had never happened.

'I'm not leaving her.'

Her eyes flashed.

'God above, Charlie, have sense! What are you saying, child? You can't just throw everything away because of Edie! She might be a little crazy at times but there's no need for you to stay! I can mind her, like I've always done.'

He sighed.

'Edie's not crazy. And I'm going to America.'

He fixed her gaze.

'I'm taking her with me.'

Her hand gripped his.

'You can't!'

'I'll take good care of her.'

'Please, Charlie, don't do this!'

He didn't reply. There was nothing to say. Mother knew how he felt. She had always known. From when they were little children, she had tried to

318

break the bond between them; a bond she considered unhealthy, incestuous. But he knew that his mother would never say those words. This subject would never be openly discussed, would never have a public airing. It wasn't Mother's way of dealing with things. She preferred to hedge around the truth, to shut things out, to lie. To pretend that it never happened. In time, she would push it out of her mind completely and convince herself that there was nothing wrong with her children living together. And she would never tell anyone, even when they commented how strange it was that neither Edie or Charlie ever married. No, she would cover it up, gloss it over, push it under the carpet. See no evil, hear no evil. Mother did deception very well. And denial. Nobody need know. Nobody need ever know. She would carry the secret to her grave.

But right now, this very minute, here, in this room, she knew. The truth sat between them, gaping and ugly, like an open wound. Her self-deceptions, her defences hadn't yet kicked in. He reached for her hand. She pulled it away. Her face was pale and fragmented, crumpled like a shattered mask. All the trophies, all the scholarships, all the medals suddenly meant nothing. He'd destroyed everything he'd ever done for her. He opened his mouth to say something, to explain, then stopped. Mother was right. Some things are best left unsaid.

Now it was time to tell Tommy. He took a deep breath and pushed through the doors of the canteen.

'Well if it isn't Michael Moore himself! I got the low-down from Dr Power, he said you were brilliant, got a few digs in at the multi-nationals, I hear!'

Charlie smiled and pulled out a chair.

'How's Edie? Is she going home?'

Charlie nodded.

There was a short silence. Then Tommy spoke.

'All that talk about general practice in Clonmel was just talk, right?'

Charlie nodded.

'That's what I thought.'

Charlie hesitated a moment, trying to find the right words.

'Edie's coming with me.'

A slow nod.

'Sure a few months away will do her the world of good.'

Charlie shook his head. Tommy was as bad as Mother.

'It's not just a few months, Tommy.'

Their eyes met.

'Stay over there? But she couldn't manage on her own, Charlie, you've said so yourself, especially in the States of all places.'

Charlie's words were slow and even.

'She won't be on her own. She'll be with me.'

After a while, Tommy spoke.

'So, it's like that, is it?'

Charlie looked at him.

'It's always been like that.'

There was a short silence.

'And what does Edie think?'

'I haven't asked her yet.'

Tommy looked up.

'Well ask her, son. Never let things like that wait.'

They sat in silence for a while.

'So, Tommy Porter, when are you coming over to see me?'

A slow smile.

'Soon, kid.'

'You still planning on moving back to Clonmel?'

'Maybe.'

Charlie swallowed. Tommy was never going to visit him in the States, same way Tommy was never going to leave Dublin. He could barely survive outside St Anne's, never mind move back down to Tipperary. All the talk about retiring and holidays and going to the States was all bullshit. They both knew that.

'You know, Tommy, all that time, it wasn't Tracy I was talking about.'

A nod.

'And I didn't mean a she.'

Charlie nodded. So Tommy was gay. He'd guessed as much. Strange how deep down inside, we always know the truth.

It was just after five when Charlie ran up the steps to the car park. There was a strange sensation in his chest. It was a need, strong and clear, to protect her, this woman who was his life, his love, his future. His everything. All his life, he'd tried to forget about her but it was no good.

Just being with her was enough. Maybe, just maybe, in time, their love would become something else. It was up to Edie. Until then, he would mind her, care for her, never let anyone hurt her. She needed him. And more than ever, he needed her.

# 46

Charlie took a long, deep breath, letting the air slowly fill his lungs, wide and deep. The air was fresh and sweet; a slice of spring, a hint of summer meadows, golden buttercups and barbecued ribs. He stood for a moment, savouring the colours, the scents and the sounds that surrounded him. This must be what Edie meant by living in the Now, by being in touch with the moment. It was as if he was suddenly acutely aware of everything around him, all his senses tuned in and turned up full volume - birdsong, the deep purple of the crocuses, the breeze in his hair. He smiled. It would be OK, everything was going to be OK.

A few minutes later, he shook his head and sighed. Not a parking space in sight. Typical HSE, building a new lab without planning for the extra traffic. À la carte planning, that's what it was, à la bloody carte. Had anyone given any thought to all the vans delivering bloods to the lab every day, or what about the patients coming for phlebotomy? Where did they think people were going to park? Up the trees?

He circled the car park a second time. Even his usual spot on the kerb was taken. Then he spotted a car just ahead of him, reversing out of a space. Thank you, missus!

Edie pulled back the blinds. Charlie should be here any minute now. She didn't mind waiting. She'd spent her entire life waiting. Then she felt a sudden wave of sadness. These were their last few days together. The thought of Charlie in America was like a knife through her heart. Two years, maybe three. It was a long time. He'd probably meet someone and never come back. It didn't bear thinking about.

Suddenly she heard a familiar sound; Charlie's rusty Primera with its dodgy silencer. She smiled and picked up her bag. Time to go.

Suddenly she remembered last night's dream. She was at home in the garden. There were acorns at her feet and a robin on a branch, singing to her. Primroses covered the ground in a carpet of liquid yellow. The birdsong was bright and beautiful, with a wonderful clarity; she could hear, she could feel, she could taste every note. The bell rang for dinner and then the angels came. Strangely, she knew each of them by name. Her own guardian angel, Betty (Charlie said you couldn't have an angel called Betty), Raphael the healer, Michael, the angel of light and goodness, Gabriel, God's messenger and Uriel, the angel of divine light. Even though none of them spoke, she knew what they had come to tell her. She was going on a journey. A happy journey.

Charlie locked the door and smiled. Knowing Edie, she'd be packed and waiting in the foyer. Suddenly he heard her voice, calling his name. He looked around and smiled. She was running towards him, her hair blowing wild and free.

Suddenly his heart began to quicken. There was a red van just ahead of her, reversing into her path. Surely she could see it? Oh God! He doesn't see her. He's not going to stop. He's not going to stop.

He was first to reach her. Strange, how even years later, he could still see the contents of her bag spilled on the ground beside her; her hairbrush, that

323

ridiculous neck pillow thing she'd worn at the airport and a king-size bar of Caramelo, probably bought for him that morning. He knelt down beside her on the wet tarmac. Her eyes were open. Big navy eyes full of fear.

'Don't move, Edie! I'll call an ambulance.'

A smile.

'I'm OK, it just missed me.'

Strange. He could have sworn she was directly behind it. He swallowed. He could have lost her. Right here in front of him, she could have been killed. But the angels had intervened. He had been given another chance. Any doubts he might have had were gone. Edie was coming with him.

Edie stood up and wiped her hands on her jeans. Poor Charlie! She must have given him a terrible fright. His face had that 'worried about Edie' look she knew so well. She could see the gap between his two front teeth and the little scar over his right eyebrow that he got in the county final. Trust her to get knocked down the minute she left the hospital! She could imagine what Mother would say. Typical Edie, eyes closed as usual, not watching where she was going. Maybe best say nothing about it.

Charlie's arm was around her shoulders now, guiding her. It was a nice feeling. Safe. Secure.

'C'mon, let's get you home.'

Just before they reached the car, he stopped and turned towards her.

'Edie, will you come with me?'

'Of course, dumbo, where did you think I was going?'

'I mean the States. I want you to come to the States. with me.'

For a moment, she said nothing.

'Do you mean it?'

'Of course I mean it.'

'What about Mother?'

'This isn't Mother's decision, Edie. You must do what you want to do, Edie.'

'I want to go with you.'

He guided a strand of hair behind her ear.

'You might be bored, I'll be working long hours.'

'I'm used to bored. Are you sure I won't be in the way?'

A dimpled smile.

'You're never in the way.'

She felt a warm burst of happiness. She was going to America with Charlie! All her life, she'd dreamed about this day and now it was here. They were going to be together again. After a while, she could get a job. Maybe even go back to college. Anything was possible. Anything.


Charlie wrapped his arms around her. He felt a deep, deep calm. Nothing could stop him now. A few years from now, he would be a cardiologist. He would do the best he could, he would try to make a difference. He would question every drug he used and the reason for using it. And he would speak up when he had to. And every day, every single day, he would thank the angels for not taking her today, for allowing her stay with him.

And, in time, Mother would forgive them, the children she had tried so hard to keep apart. Charlie and Edie Darmody. Her Fallen Angels.


******

# Acknowledgements

My thanks to Emma Bermingham from Arklow. The cover of the book is based on a wonderful pastel drawing that Emma created for *Fallen Angels.*

I would like to thank Tim Ilsley at Eireann Publications for proof-reading the manuscript and correcting my many mistakes. I would also like to thank Maura and Cora at Eireann Publications for their advice and expertise.

I would also like to thank the authors Vincent McDonnell and Karen Gillece for their support and encouragement.

Finally, I would like to thank my husband, Con, and my children, Helen, Joanne and David for allowing me the freedom to indulge my passion.

A special thanks to my daughter, Joanne, who read my book late into the night and who shares my love of reading